PRAISE FOR *MY DARL[ING BOY]*

"[Helen] Cooper offers a sinister story set in a close-knit English village involving broken friendships and murder." —*Library Journal*

"I was gripped by this beautifully written, intricately plotted tangle of secrets and lies. Bravo, Helen Cooper."

—Louise Jensen, author of *The Sister*

"Another masterfully constructed novel from the queen of psychological thrillers, Helen Cooper. *My Darling Boy* takes a cast of gloriously complex characters and throws them into a nightmare scenario to create a story that will keep you turning the pages until the very end."

—Sarah Bonner, author of *Her Perfect Twin*

"Helen Cooper is a masterful plotter. In *My Darling Boy*, she crafts an intricate thriller that explores grief, blame, and outsidership in a small village community. Taut, twisty, and utterly compulsive, it takes secrets, lies, and age-old betrayals and spins a gripping mystery."

—Kia Abdullah, author of *Perfectly Nice Neighbors*

PREVIOUS PRAISE FOR HELEN COOPER

THE COUPLE IN THE PHOTO

"A sharply constructed puzzle of a mystery, full of surprising twists and turns about marriage, friendship, motherhood, and how the truth really can be in the eye of the beholder."

—Kimberly McCreight, author of *Reconstructing Amelia*

"Readers will be sucked into this well-written, fast-paced, twisty tale."

—*LibraryReads*

"*The Couple in the Photo* had me hooked from the first page and I positively devoured this masterfully constructed tale of lies and deceit. An absolute must-read for all thriller fans."

—Sarah Bonner, author of *Her Perfect Twin*

"Difficult-to-put-down thriller . . . Brilliantly characterized, boldly plotted, and boasting an ending that readers will think they have figured out only to have everything turned around. The perfect vacation thriller."
—*Booklist* (starred review)

"[A] strong psychological thriller . . . Credible characters enhance the suspenseful plot. Cooper remains a writer to watch."
—*Publishers Weekly*

"In this captivating slow-burner, dark secrets lurk beneath a luxurious lakeside resort in Italy with mysterious connections to a handsome bartender in England. Helen Cooper deftly navigates between what seems like two completely separate narratives bundled in *The Other Guest*: One involves a murder hushed up by the victim's own family, and the other involves a blossoming romance. You'll be hooked on trying to solve this puzzle!"
—*Reader's Digest*

"A luxury Italian resort with a dark side. A cast of suspicious, secretive characters. *The Other Guest* is an eerie and atmospheric mystery that kept me guessing from start to finish." —Allie Reynolds, author of *Shiver*

"An exquisite setting masks layers of secrets. Beautifully written, powerfully conveyed, and swirling with mysteries you'll race to the last page to solve." —Megan Collins, author of *The Family Plot*

"Teased out against the slick and stylish backdrop of Lake Garda, *The Other Guest* is the perfect combination of glamour, intrigue, and sibling rivalry." —Polly Phillips, author of *The Reunion*

"A masterpiece of storytelling with twist after unguessable twist. I relished every delicious page." —Lucy Martin, author of *Stop at Nothing*

"Sinister and beautifully atmospheric, *The Other Guest* lures you with the promise of a luxury island before revealing its darker, claustrophobic side. I loved it." —L. V. Matthews, author of *The Twins*

"Fans of British mysteries will love this debut. . . . It is difficult to put down. This is one that readers may not figure out fully, if at all, in advance of the denouement, but the author ties all the secrets together in a most satisfying reveal."　　　　　　　　　—*Library Journal* (starred review)

"Perfect for fans of twisty plots that'll keep you guessing."
　　　　　　　　　　　　　　　　　　　　　　　　—*Country Living*

"A heart-pounding debut . . . Even avid suspense readers won't be able to predict all the twists."　　　　　　　　　　　—*Publishers Weekly*

"Cooper skillfully builds a house of cards, demolishes it, reshuffles the deck, and deals an even stronger hand, while keeping a few cards up her sleeve. An emotionally charged domestic-suspense debut, perfect for fans of Lucy Foley and Ruth Ware."　　　　　　　　—*Booklist*

"A gradual unearthing of long-held secrets wrapped in a smoothly plotted page-turner."
　　　　　　　　　　　　　　　　　　　　　　—Kimberly Belle,
　　　　　　　　author of *Stranger in the Lake* and *The Marriage Lie*

"Powerfully displays how we often think secrets are the best way to protect those we love, but they often cause more damage than good."
　　　　　　　　　　　　　　　　　　　—*San Francisco Book Review*

"Lock your doors, close your curtains, and sink into this claustrophobic tale of families, neighbors, and buried secrets. Tense and perfectly paced, this emotionally charged novel will keep you guessing right to the very end."　　　　　　　　—Emma Rous, author of *The Au Pair*

"The unrelenting tension of this well-crafted debut kept me whizzing through the book. Loved the tension, the secrets, and the satisfying, unexpected conclusion. Recommended!"
　　　　　　　　　　　　　—K. L. Slater, author of *The Apartment*

MY
DARLING
BOY

HELEN COOPER

G. P. PUTNAM'S SONS
NEW YORK

PUTNAM
— EST. 1838 —

G. P. PUTNAM'S SONS
Publishers Since 1838
An imprint of Penguin Random House LLC
penguinrandomhouse.com

Copyright © 2024 by Helen Cooper
Published by arrangement with Hodder & Stoughton Ltd.
First published in the United Kingdom in 2024.

Library of Congress Cataloging-in-Publication Data

Names: Cooper, Helen (Helen Mary), author.
Title: My darling boy / Helen Cooper.
Description: New York: G. P. Putnam's Sons, 2024.
Identifiers: LCCN 2024011322 (print) | LCCN 2024011323 (ebook) |
ISBN 9780593719930 (Trade paperback) | ISBN 9780593719947 (Ebook)
Subjects: LCGFT: Thrillers (Fiction). | Novels.
Classification: LCC PR6103.O686 M9 2024 (print) | LCC PR6103.O686 (ebook) |
DDC 823/.92—dc2323/eng/20240321
LC record available at https://lccn.loc.gov/2024011322
LC ebook record available at https://lccn.loc.gov/2024011323

Printed in the United States of America
1st Printing

Book design by Katy Riegel

For two darling boys,
Idris and Aryn

MY DARLING BOY

PROLOGUE

New Year's Eve 2021

The mothers are in the cellar of the pub when it happens.

Eight minutes until the new year, and the two friends are arguing. Standing between the barrels with their hands moving in the air. The one in the faded band T-shirt speaks quickly, shaking her head, thrusting back her curly hair as it falls into her face. The tall one in the green velvet dress presses her temples as if she's in pain. When her friend gives up pushing back her hair, she reaches out and tucks it behind her ears for her, with an angry, impatient intimacy.

The first thud reverberates over their heads. Louder than the rumble of pub noise; loud enough to make them pause and glance toward the closed cellar door. That's all it is, at first, just a pause. The woman in green frowns and touches the silver locket at her throat, her skin flushed from collarbone to chin.

When there's nothing more, they turn back to each other. Both talking at once, drawing closer together—skin still flushed, curls falling free again. Then a far bigger crash, an eruption of shouts, and they stop dead.

For a moment, they're still. Eyes locking. Chests moving up and down. Their argument is freeze-framed and dust particles hang in the air.

Then the cellar door flies open.

Alice! Chrissy! You need to come! You need to come now!

Instantly, they are running. Their sons' names are being shouted at them. Talk of an argument, an ambulance . . .

What? What is it? the mothers yell over each other. One trips on the stairs and the other pulls her upright. *Are they hurt? What's* happened?

In the dim chaos of the pub, a crowd blocks their way. They push into the gaps, clutching each other's hands, the crowd splitting wide open as people see them coming through. A hush falls. Heads turning, palms held over mouths. Spatters of red on the floor amid the trampled crumbs and spillages of the night.

The two women come to a halt in the space that has formed around them. One son is on the floor. The other stands over him. Somebody is sobbing in the crowd, saying they can't watch, they don't understand.

Is he breathing?

It all happened so fast.

The mothers each scream a different name as they break hands and run forward.

My darling boy . . .
Tell me you didn't . . .
What has he done?

Outside, the church bells start to ring in the new year and a blue flashing light streaks through the dark.

ONE

CHRISSY

Thursday, December 7, 2023

Chrissy clutches her phone and stares toward the tall metal gates. Where is he? What's taking so long? The whole place feels deserted and it strikes her that she's never been here in the morning before. The sky is winter white above the coils of barbed wire and the car park is only half-full.

She thinks of all the times she has waited in cars for him in the past. Picking him up from soccer matches, friends' houses, gigs in nearby towns. She used to crank her stereo up loud as she waited, Leo looking half-embarrassed and half-proud when he appeared. She was the only mum who listened to Nirvana live albums and Sabbath B-sides. The only one who owned a pub and sang guest vocals in her son's band.

Now she sits in silence, her stomach in shreds, waiting for him to come out of prison.

He really should've appeared by now.

Flicking on the radio, she whizzes through the stations in search of something he'll like. But all the songs seem fraught with pointed lyrics or painful memories, so she hits the off button and the silence returns. Maybe it's better, so they can talk on the way home. Leo has been subdued during her recent visits. She'd thought he'd be buoyed by the prospect of early parole, as it began to look more likely, but instead he seemed to withdraw, seemed to flinch at her tentative excitement. Now she realizes: He must've been terrified—must *be* terrified. She flings open her car door, unable to sit any longer.

Her curls blow across her face as she paces toward the prison. She can hardly believe he'll come walking out this time, that she'll be able to take him home with her. The *wrench* of those fortnightly good-byes. And the rush of guilt, always close behind, that Alice never got to say one to Robbie.

How will it be, though, once Leo is back with her in the village? Will they be ostracized even further? Will the whispers grow louder?

Will the notes continue to arrive?

Just shy of the gates, fresh panic stops her dead. She was so sure it was the right thing to do, bringing her boy home, refusing to be driven away. But now her heart pounds in every part of her . . . Is she making a terrible mistake?

"*Shit,*" she hisses, looking back at her phone as if it will tell her what to do.

All she has is a solitary email, but her head jerks back when she sees who it's from.

Alice, who never speaks to her anymore. Alice, who blocked her number a week after Robbie's death, when Chrissy said the stupid thing, the careless thing, and ruined their friendship forever.

Her stomach turns to liquid as she opens it and sees the words *Dear Christina*. Only her husband ever called her that. And Alice knows this all too well.

Dear Christina,

    I am writing to inform you that your son, Leo Dean, is strictly prohibited from entering Cromley's pub (previously the Raven) once it has reopened.

    Violence will not be tolerated under the new ownership. Strong action will be taken if he attempts to enter the premises.

    Although we cannot impose any restrictions beyond this, we also ask, on behalf of the village, that you consider the effect of your continued residency here.

    Sincerely,

    Alice Lowe and the Pub Committee

Chrissy exhales shakily, then reads it again, staggered by the formal wording, the sting of that final sentence.

It was manslaughter, she thinks, her eyes blurring with tears. *Involuntary manslaughter. He pleaded guilty. Haven't we been punished enough?*

If a parole board can decide Leo is no threat to his community, why can't people who've known him all his life *try* to do the same? People who saw the two boys grow up to be as inseparable as their mums. People who couldn't be certain, when questioned, whether it was a push or a punch that caused poor Robbie to fall.

And Leo has no plans to go bursting back into the pub. He looked stunned when Chrissy finally told him, only a couple of visits ago, that it was going to reopen. He knew she'd had to put it on the market, of course, after hanging on to the shell of it for longer than she could afford. But she'd put off admitting that half the village had joined together to "reclaim" the place.

"About . . . twenty of them put money in, I think," she finally explained three weeks ago, squirming in her plastic chair. "With a smaller committee doing most of the actual decision-making. Fixing it up"—she remembers pausing at the implication that it *needed* fixing, needed exorcizing—"and . . . reopening it."

Leo sat forward. "Why the fuck didn't you tell me, Mum?"

"I don't know . . ."

"*Who* owns it now, exactly?"

"Well . . ." She muttered a few names, including Georgie, the newcomer Leo has never even met; then she came, eventually, to the point: "It's being led by . . . Alice."

He stared at her across the table. They'd stopped mentioning Alice's and Robbie's names some time ago, without really acknowledging that they had. "*Alice?*"

Footsteps pull her back to the present. She looks up keenly, shoving the phone and its shitty email into her pocket. But it's an older man with a straggly silver beard, walking with a slight limp. Chrissy looks back at the prison. What if there's been a problem? A complication . . . a *delay* to Leo's release?

She knows it happens, but it never occurred to her, foolishly, that it might happen to them. Maybe she should go in and check. Leo asked her to wait here, though, said he wanted her to see him walk out.

That's it, she can't stand it anymore. She tosses back her hair and strides toward the prison entrance. Reaching the external reception booth, she peers through the holes in the glass screen at the uninterested man poring over crosswords that she has never, in two years, seen him finish.

"My son—my son's being released today," she says. "It should've happened already. Do you know if there's been a . . . a problem?"

He shunts the crossword aside. "Name?"

"My son's?" she says, then feels stupid. She tries to speak clearly as she tells him Leo's name, but her tongue sticks and she flubs her lines.

The man types something into his computer, narrows his eyes, then turns his back to pick up a phone. After a minute or so he swings around to face her, putting down the phone in the same motion.

"My colleagues inside the building are checking."

He returns to his crossword and Chrissy is left standing there, craving a cigarette, churning her keys in her pocket. There are some visitors arriving now. A woman with three children in tow and a baby bawling in her arms. Must be a special visit, extended family time; she remembers hearing about those. She has a precarious sense of wading against the current even though she's standing still. Preparing to leave with her loved one—*please don't tell me otherwise*—instead of going inside for regulated hugs and muted conversation. The longer she waits, though, the more her thoughts spiral. What if Leo's ill? What if he did something stupid, got in trouble just before his release? What if they're having second thoughts about him living in the village, even after all those discussions?

The phone in the booth rings. The guard picks it up without glancing at her, and she presses her face to the holes in the screen. He is nodding, frowning, not giving much away. She hears him mumble something like, *Thought so,* before he drops the receiver and looks up.

"Leo Dean was released an hour ago."

Chrissy stares at him. "What?"

"All paperwork was completed. He was free to go. And"—he gestures toward the main gates—"he went."

"But . . ." She feels her whole face start to twitch. "How did he . . . Did anyone collect him?"

He shrugs. "Sorry. Not our job to check that. Once the paperwork's—"

"I was almost here! Why didn't he wait? Where did he *go?*"

Something changes in the man's expression. "*Hopefully* to the agreed address or to his probation officer," he says, peering over his glasses. "As per the terms of his release."

Chrissy's stomach lurches. She steps back, clamping her mouth shut.

The guard continues to frown at her. "I don't know what to tell you, Ms. Dean. He's gone. If he knows what's good for him, he'll report to his PO ASAP."

"Yes . . ." Chrissy backs off, fumbling for her phone. "He will, of course he will."

Alice's email is still on the screen, an extra taunt. Chrissy closes it and brings up Leo's number, walking briskly away from the guard. She hasn't dialed her son's mobile in two years. Their last message exchange is too painful to dwell on and she stabs at the call icon. It goes straight to voicemail, as if his phone is still locked in a box, and she realizes, with a mental slap, that of course it wouldn't be charged.

Even so, she pleads with his voicemail. "Where are you, Leo? Are you okay? I'm here at the prison. I don't know what's happened. We agreed you'd wait if you got out early. And we've . . . I've . . ." Her voice catches, and she can't even finish her sentence: *I've been waiting for so long.*

Hanging up, she looks around desperately. Could he have made his own way back to the village or to his PO? But there aren't any buses; a taxi would cost too much. And why would he, when she'd promised she would meet him, cook him anything he wanted for dinner?

She drums out a text: Leo, please let me know you're okay xx

No blue ticks appear. It doesn't even flag up as delivered. As she turns on the spot, still hoping to glimpse him, one of the arriving visitors catches her gaze. Another woman with a brood of children, her weary eyes flicking to Chrissy's band T-shirt—*Leo's* in fact—beneath her battered leather jacket. Chrissy turns away, no longer feeling in a superior position. That woman knows where her loved one is, at least. For the first time in twenty-two months, Chrissy has no idea.

TWO

ALICE

Thursday, December 7, 2023

There is somebody in Alice's house.

She sits bolt upright in bed, listening to them moving around downstairs. All night she has dreamed of Leo's face at her windows, his silhouette in her doorway, and now it's the morning of his release and *there is someone in her house*.

She grabs her phone from the bedside table. Where is Beech? Why isn't he barking wildly at the intruder? She stretches out a foot and feels his warm, sleeping bulk at the end of her bed. He springs up at her touch, sticking close to her side as she gets up and edges to the door of her room.

Alice's heart is thundering. She gets her brother's number ready on her phone. She should call the police, really, but she still thinks of him *as* the police. Inching onto the landing, she listens hard. A deep male voice is speaking very softly. Beech's ears prick and then he is gone, bounding down the stairs, Alice's thumb hitting the Call icon in panic.

User busy. Fear spreads all the way through her. She takes dark comfort in imagining Beech pouncing on Leo, somehow knowing he's no longer a friend, tearing at his clothes, baring his teeth . . .

Then something clicks in her brain. The voice. Beech's lack of frantic barking, even now. She creeps to the top of the stairs and her legs almost fold. It's her brother. It's Peter. She leans on the banister, swearing under her breath, then walks unsteadily downstairs.

Through the half-open kitchen door, she sees him on his mobile, pacing back and forth, Beech dithering inquisitively around him.

"Okay," he is saying, quiet and serious. "Okay. Just . . . keep me posted."

"Peter?"

He swings around, hanging up the phone. "Al! Did I wake you?"

"I thought someone had broken in!"

"Shit. Sorry." He flushes a little. "I slept on the sofa after you went up last night. You seemed so upset, I thought I'd make sure you were okay."

Alice thinks back to their long evening in her living room, staring at the TV with an awful sense of waiting. She glances at the clock above her cookstove: 8:50 A.M. Has it happened? Is Leo free?

"Who were you talking to?" she asks.

"Uh . . ." He slips the phone into his pocket. "Just an old colleague. Wanted my advice on a case."

Alice raises an eyebrow. "They *do* know you're retired?"

He half-smiles. "Sometimes I'm not sure they do."

She sinks into a chair, clapping a palm to her chest. "I thought it was *him*." Adrenaline drains from her body, leaving her hollow and lightheaded. "God. I thought it was him."

Peter comes up behind her and touches her shoulders. "I'm really sorry."

She shakes her head, fighting tears.

"I'll make tea," he says, and she nods, because what else is there to do?

THEY DRINK THEIR tea in silence, Alice looking pointlessly at the clock, Peter glancing often at his phone. Then he stands up abruptly. "I've gotta go, Al."

"Have you?" She's been longing to be alone, but now she feels another flutter of panic.

"I've . . . got some things to do. But I'll come back later."

There's no point arguing or questioning. Peter's movements are mysterious at the best of times, but when he's upset, he can't seem to stay in one place for long.

"Don't forget you've got a session with Nadia this morning," he says, gesturing at the Dogs Trust calendar hanging on the wall. "Think it would be good for you to go?"

Alice sighs, picturing Nadia's room full of biscuit-colored cushions and boxes of luxury tissues. Therapy is the last thing she feels like. All her attempts to move forward, to deal with her grief . . . none of it has stopped this day from happening.

"Maybe call in at Ellen's afterward for a coffee?" he continues. "She mentioned you'd be welcome . . ."

He's trying to keep her busy. Annoyance flares but it doesn't last long; it never does with Peter. She glances at the photo pinned to her fridge—him and Robbie pulling stupid faces, never able to just *smile nicely,* please!—and she knows that none of the anger writhing under her skin is for her brother.

He hugs her tightly, pausing as if he wants to say more. She sees all her fear and anger mirrored back at her, though his face is almost completely still.

After he's gone, Alice grips the edges of her kitchen table, wanting to scream. Beech pads over and nudges his snout against her arm, so she wraps her arms around his neck and buries her face in his fur instead.

Lifting her head, she sees her phone lit up on the table in front of her. She picks it up in the anxious, almost suspicious way she checks all her messages these days. It's a text from Marianne. Her name on the screen, once so familiar, now feels like a curveball from the past.

Of course I'll come, she writes. Thank you for inviting me.

Alice frowns in confusion, then scrolls upward and remembers. Robbie's memorial. It's the day after tomorrow. A flush of shame comes over her as she realizes Leo's release has pushed it out of her head.

The link says RSVP to someone called Georgie. Is that right? Marianne adds. Who is she?

And then: Has Peter said how he feels about me being there?

Alice puts down the phone without replying. She has little idea what happened between Peter and Marianne. It wasn't just Alice who crumbled after Robbie's death: Within months of that horrific New Year's Eve, her brother retired abruptly from the police and then announced that he and Marianne were separating. *Have you ever thought maybe you should see someone?* Alice has challenged him more than once, when he's been nagging her to keep up with her therapy. *We're not talking about me,* is always his full-stop of a reply.

Alice doesn't know what to tell Marianne about Georgie, either. She was touched when Georgie first suggested the memorial, if a little surprised it had come from her, the only person in the village who never knew Robbie. Then when she offered to organize the entire thing, insisting Alice would have nothing to do except be there, she breathed out and thought, *Yes, let's do that, let's make this Christmas about Robbie, not Leo.* Now, though, it feels impossible. What if—her whole body clenches—what if Leo turns up? Will she need a bouncer at her son's memorial service? It's a ridiculous image, but this is everything she's feared: Leo stamping on Robbie's memory with every step he takes through the village.

The thought drives her into her study. She barely uses it anymore, since the university let her hide away on an indefinite sabbatical, but she sits at her desk and opens her laptop. The draft email to Chrissy waits in her outbox. Alice knows she should run it past the pub committee, but her blood is pumping now, her skin prickling as if Leo is breathing down her neck.

Impulsively, she adds a final sentence.

Although we cannot impose any restrictions beyond this, we also ask, on behalf of the village, that you consider the effect of your continued residency here.

She hits *send,* then presses her hands against her face. It isn't enough. Nothing is enough.

ALICE TAKES BEECH for a walk in Cromley Woods, trying to expel her tension with long, brisk strides over the frozen ground. Her route home takes her across the village square, past the row of shops and the giant Christmas tree. All her senses are heightened, looking and listening out for Chrissy or Leo. She stalls when she notices lights glowing from inside the pub. Somehow, she didn't expect Jack to be working on the renovations today, or any of the committee to be there.

She hesitates, then walks over to peer through the front windows. The place looks empty, despite the light bouncing off the dark wooden bar top, casting shadows on the freshly painted walls. She tries the door but it's locked, and she hasn't brought the right set of keys. A memory flies at her—*Robbie on the floor, Leo standing over him*—and she leaps back with an intake of breath. She told herself not to come here today. Calling to Beech, she turns and flees toward home.

BACK IN HER study, she steels herself and checks her email. She isn't expecting a reply from Chrissy, but she itches for *something,* a reaction, a sign that she's been heard. There is nothing. Her hands flex in frustration and she clicks on her web browser instead. When an open tab fills the screen, she rears back, sending the desk chair skidding.

Leo's face.

Mouth open, gums showing, singing into a mic as if he means to inhale it.

Alice claps a hand over her own mouth, her pulse soaring.

Why is his Facebook page open on her laptop? Had *she* left it that way? She's googled his name plenty of times in the last two years—wasn't she about to do just that?—but she doesn't remember looking at his Facebook recently; there didn't seem much point while he was locked up. Tentatively, she draws her chair forward. Perhaps Peter used her laptop. Maybe he had the same idea she'd had: If they can't follow Leo's every movement, at least they can try to keep tabs on him digitally.

There are no posts since 2021. Alice scrolls through his page, but the old photos are like flashes of hurt. Leo and Chrissy in feathered raven costumes at the pub's annual Halloween Spookfest. Leo and Robbie at their joint twenty-first birthday party, cutting a guitar-shaped cake with a huge knife as if they were getting married. All four of them, Alice, too, crammed into a selfie captioned *Cromley Mums 'n' Sons*. The pain twists behind her rib cage and she's about to turn away when something catches her eye.

What's on your mind, Leo?

The phrase sends a shudder through her. Then another, even stronger, as she realizes what it means: The page is inviting her to post as Leo. She is not just viewing his Facebook account. She is *logged in to* it.

She pulls back her hands in alarm. How has this happened? She doesn't know what to do, whether to close it down or to comb every inch of it. At arm's length, she checks again and she's definitely right. She can see it all, even his private messages. There might be things about Robbie in there, conversations between them, insights into that night. But she doesn't dare look too closely, afraid this is some kind of trick.

Instead, she calls Peter. The phone rings out and she hangs up, forced to stare back at the screen. When he doesn't pick up on her second or third try, she jumps to her feet.

Her brother will be able to explain this, she tells herself as she hurries out to her car. Driving away, she can't shake the image of Leo's face on her screen. Can't shake the idea of him in her house—just as she feared he was this morning—casually logging in to Facebook while she walked in the woods nearby.

THREE

CHRISSY

Thursday, December 7, 2023

Almost as soon as she gets back from the prison, Chrissy sees it.

She has spent the ride home on the phone to her sister, Tess, who has promised to call their mum—Chrissy cannot face it—and any other relatives Leo might, for whatever reason, have reached out to. Chrissy slams the car door and stands in front of her cottage, dreading walking inside to all the hopeful things she put in place for this moment. The bright blue DAB radio she positioned in the kitchen, aerial up and waiting, imagining them listening to Planet Rock together while steaks sizzled in the pan. The Tabasco sauce she bought because he always had it with everything, and the pint glasses she lined up on the shelf—scratched from their pub days—because he said he'd been craving Coke Zero in a tall glass with loads of ice.

She feels like a new mum who's had to leave her baby in

the hospital. As she drags herself up the drive, a flap of white paper catches her eye. It's taped to the frozen lid of her black wheelie bin. *Not today, surely not now.* Heat builds in her cheeks as she stamps across the gravel toward it. The words are written in the usual red marker pen, but as she rips it off the bin like a giant plaster, she sees that this message has a different pronoun.

Keep him away from our village.

Chrissy lets out a cry of anger, kicking the bottom of the bin and then spinning around as if to confront the long-gone culprit. This is a sick joke to come home to. A sick premonition, or worse.

She marches into her cottage, blind now to all the welcome-home paraphernalia. She goes to the drawer where all the other notes are kept, yanks it open, and holds this one alongside them.

She'd gotten used to them while they were just aimed at her. They had become a blur of unimaginative threats in red capitals—*NOBODY WANTS YOU HERE; HAVE YOU NO SHAME?*—and she could convince herself they didn't matter, could lump them in with the whispers in shops and the judgmental looks.

Except for the very first one, of course. The one she keeps folded up, out of sight—the anomaly in black pen. Her eye flits toward it in the shadows of the drawer, then she snaps her attention back to the latest addition, knowing she can't hide or ignore it. If they're starting in on Leo, it's different. Someone wished him gone and, inexplicably, he is.

She thinks of the email from Alice; the guard's expression changing from indifference to suspicion; the text with no blue ticks, as if it had gone into a void. And this note waiting for her, perhaps, all that time. Dropping it into the drawer, she fumbles in her jacket pocket for her mobile.

And then she deflates. Realization hits her stomach like a rock. She can't call the police. Leo has broken the very first condition of his parole by not being at this address. How can she risk sending him back to jail when he might just be taking some time to get his head together?

Please, please, let that be all it is.

As if in reply, her home phone starts to ring. Chrissy stands paralyzed, fearing it's the Probation Service, checking that Leo's here. He's gone out for a run, she could say. He's taking a hot bath; wouldn't you if you'd just gotten out of prison? She could make a thing of it, appeal to their human instincts. How long can she stall them, though, while she figures out where he's really gone?

Her voice is thick when she finally answers: "Hello?"

There is silence on the other end.

"Hello?" she says again. "Can you hear me? Who's there?"

She thinks she hears soft breathing down the line, but her own is so loud, her heartbeat thunderous. "Hello? *Hello?*"

A click, and the line goes dead. Chrissy hits the redial button, but a cheerfully robotic voice tells her the number was withheld. She stands next to the phone for a few more moments. The silence presses down, seeming unnatural, unkind, because this is the first day she isn't supposed to be here alone.

FOUR

GEORGIE

Thursday, December 7, 2023

So when are you coming back?"

Georgie sighs into her phone as she pushes through her front door. "We've been through this, Lo!"

"And you never answer."

"Because I don't know." In her narrow hall, she eases off her knee-high boots. There is a small hole in her sock and she twists it round out of sight, even though she is the only one here. "Perhaps never, if things . . . work out."

"What *things?* The raffle at the village fete? The folk-dancing championships?"

"Very funny, Lo." Georgie wanders into her kitchen and flicks on the kettle. She's glad her sister can't see the poky dimensions and twee décor of this cottage. She pictures Lola in her own kitchen in South London, its polished marble island the size of this whole room.

"Seriously, George—"

"I *like* it here, okay! And I'm doing great things with the local pub."

"You were doing great things in London. *Proper* things."

"People here need me. My marketing experience . . ." She catches sight of her reflection in the mirror as she heads into the living room with her coffee. There is extra color in her powdered cheeks, and she knows it's not the country air.

"But it was just all so sudden! And I miss you, Gee! Can't I come and visit?"

"When I'm settled," Georgie says too quickly.

"*How* are you not settled by now?"

"There's been a lot going on." She pauses, reflecting that this is an understatement, then continues in her breeziest voice: "I'm getting a spare room sorted—with facilities you'll find acceptable—and then I promise, Lo, I *promise* you can come."

"Or we could top-and-tail like old times."

Georgie allows herself a smile. "Can't say I recall ever actually doing that."

"No, neither do I, come to think of it. You'd take up too much room. Beanpole."

"You're not so tiny yourself . . ." Georgie almost blurts out something about Alice, who is even taller than them both, but she bites her tongue. The fewer details she gives her sister about the people here, the better. Unease stirs and she hurries the conversation to a close. "Anyway, I'll let you go . . ."

"Sure, sure . . . You've probably got cowpat to clean off your front step or something."

"Get over it, Lo. I live in the country now."

"But *why?*"

"Hanging up!" She almost does so in a huff but blows a conciliatory air-kiss down the phone at the last minute.

Her sister's *why?* echoes long after the call is over. Georgie closes her eyes and Alice comes back into her mind. Always so tightly coiled, so brittle and wary. Different from how Georgie imagined her before she came here, yet not so hard to reconcile with what she'd been told. Will Leo's release unravel her? Unravel everything? Will Georgie be able to grab at the fraying threads as it does?

A shiver darts through her and she strides over to make the fire in her wood burner. She's become pretty skilled by now, at arranging the newspaper and kindling, getting the logs to catch. There's something therapeutic about building the framework, watching the flames spark and spread.

Sitting back down, she tucks a blanket over her knees in a way that would make Lola snort with laughter and check it for a Burberry label. The days are lonely here, she has to admit. At least in London she could bury her demons inside liquid lunches and work. She picks up her phone and checks the RSVPs to Robbie's memorial. People are confused that she's organizing it, she can tell, and her own doubts keep swimming to the surface. But it'll be a chance to draw the whole village together, to be in the thick of things, inside yet outside. A chance she might not get again. She notes down a few new attendees and then strays over to Instagram, scrolling through her city friends' posts. Cocktails and client dinners; perfect families and new holiday homes. When she sees a photo of her old team celebrating *Targets smashed!* in her favorite sushi restaurant, she switches over to the Instagram page she set up for Cromley's pub.

It's a brand-new era, raves her latest post. We hope you'll love our FRESH new look! Georgie always tries to make the takeover seem like a cleansing in the eyes of the village, even though she knows that, in Alice's vision, it's more like an annihilation.

She's no idiot. No clueless London lightweight like some people in Cromley clearly think. She knows Alice isn't trying to "give the village back its heart," as the official line goes, but to break *Chrissy's* heart in the only way she knows how. Tearing down the Raven sign with its beady-eyed bird; erasing every trace of Chrissy or Leo or the time before.

But is there more to it even than that? And if Georgie can see through Alice, can Alice see straight through her?

Draining her coffee, she tabs over to Facebook, where all the pub's social media used to sit. Where she can lose herself for hours, some nights, poring over the old photos, the years of history. She homes in on the few pictures that remain from the night of the tragedy. New Year's Eve 2021. Alice in a green velvet dress, her black hair pinned, her lipstick dark. An intensity to her expression whenever she's caught by a camera unawares. Chrissy red-faced as she works to serve her punters, with a pucker of anxiety in her brow, as if some shadow of foreboding was already creeping in.

The two boys, Leo and Robbie, are glimpsed mostly in the background. Sometimes helping behind the bar; other times sitting together, strumming guitars, or mingling separately in the crowd. There is one photo Georgie always lingers over. They're standing at the dartboard, Robbie poised to aim, Leo watching him with a brooding expression that sends waves of complicated feeling through her every time. She zooms in on his dark eyes, the clench of his jaw, his features switching between familiar and strange.

Could he have the answers she has failed, so far, to find? Now that he's free, could he help unlock the next part of her plan; could he tell her—*would* he tell her—what she came here, to Cromley, to understand?

FIVE

ALICE

Thursday, December 7, 2023

Driving to Peter's house on the other side of the village, Alice thinks of Nadia waiting in her clinic room and feels a pang of guilt. The old Alice wouldn't have dreamed of missing an appointment or standing anybody up. She wouldn't have dreamed of leaving the house like this, with unwashed hair, no makeup, clothes she hasn't even checked in the mirror.

The old Alice wouldn't be gripping the steering wheel this hard, either. Letting her speed creep up and up.

She still has her eye out for Leo, imagining him emerging from buildings, lurking down lanes, leaping out in front of her car. Would she slam her foot down? Watch him fly across her hood?

It isn't as if she's never thought about it.

So why, when confronted with his private Facebook account, had she balked and run? She wants to yell at herself now, swing the car around, but she's on the fast road running parallel to the village and there's nowhere to U-turn. And what is she expecting to find among his messages and posts? He killed Robbie and *that's the end of it.* A punch or a push, it doesn't matter. A reason or not. Admitting there might be something to discover would make her as bad as Chrissy.

Alice often thinks back on that moment, in her kitchen, a week after the last New Year's Eve she would ever celebrate. She and Chrissy sitting numbly at the table, still hoping to be woken from their nightmare. Leo in custody. Robbie's belongings everywhere she looked. She wonders whether things might've been salvageable—maybe, just maybe—if the excruciating silence had simply remained. But Chrissy looked up from her undrunk tea and asked Alice if she knew what Robbie had said to Leo.

What he said? Alice was confused at first. Her thoughts were so slow at that time. Even lifting her head was an effort.

He must've . . . In Alice's memory, Chrissy looks defensive, almost defiant. She'd seen that look in her eyes before. *There must've been something . . .*

What she can't remember is whether Chrissy actually used the word *provoked.* She drives herself mad, some days, trying to recall her phrasing. But she knows it was implied. Knows Chrissy was trying to share out the blame, twisting the knife in her wound.

Get out. Get out of my house.

The tea spilling everywhere as she stood up and knocked the table with her shaking legs.

It was the last time they'd properly spoken. Even the pub sale, over a year later, went through solicitors and third parties as if they were strangers. Alice never saw Chrissy's face as the lease passed to her. Chrissy never got to ask her why on earth she wanted it.

Now Alice is shaking as hard as that day in her kitchen. There's no tea to spill but her car weaves in the middle of the icy road. She wrangles it under control and something snags at the edge of her sight. A familiar figure standing by the side of the road, half-camouflaged against a dark hedge.

She hits the brake, skidding to a stop. Peter's collar is caught skew-whiff inside his jacket, his left bootlace trailing, hat lolling out of one pocket. And he is swaying. Almost imperceptibly, but Alice can tell; she knows the signs. "*Shit,*" she hisses under her breath, unsnapping her seat belt. Perhaps she should've been more worried when he didn't answer his phone. But it's been so long since this last happened.

"Peter!" she calls, thrusting open her car door.

He turns, staggering. His eyes are bloodshot and unfocused. She hurries closer and smells the confirmation on his breath, sees regret tugging down the corners of his mouth.

"Oh, God," she says. "Have you been drinking since you left mine?"

His only answer is a long sigh. Alice takes his arm and helps him into her car. Fastening his seat belt, she notices a bright red scratch across the back of his hand, a smear of rusty-brown dirt on his jacket. She used to look for clues about what he'd got up to on these days and nights. But at some point she stopped agonizing. He would tell her once he'd sobered up, then go to a meeting, everything reverting to normal. But will this time be different? When the trigger, the obvious trigger, is living a stone's throw away?

She drives around the top of the village and down the track toward his house. Peter moans softly as they bump over the cattle bridge, lifting a hand to his temple. Alice lets them inside and flicks on the lights. There is a whiff of stale food. In the living room she sees a bowl of congealed noodles, several empty beer bottles rolling on their sides, a couple of greasy takeout wrappers. Peter collapses onto the sofa and she starts gathering up the mess. The kitchen is worse: crusty dishes in the sink and the smell of old onions wafting from the overflowing bin. How had she not realized he was living like this? He comes over to hers all the time, checking on her, but it's been a while since she's been here.

Racked with guilt, she fills the sink with ballooning suds and brings him some water. She inspects the graze on his hand, dipping her fingers into the glass of water to clean away some dirt.

He flinches but lets her keep washing it. "Sorry, sis," he slurs, and she draws a blanket over him.

It isn't the right time to ask him about Leo's Facebook. But the question gnaws at her.

"Pete," she says, leaning in close as he verges on sleep. "Did you use my laptop last night, or this morning?"

He squints at her groggily. "Uh? Maybe. Can't remember."

"Did you . . . Were you on Leo's Facebook? *In* it, in fact? The weirdest thing . . ."

He opens his glazed eyes more widely, looking up at her. "What?"

Then he waves a hand in front of his face and his eyes droop closed.

THE MESSAGE COMES through the next morning. A buzz pierces Alice's dreams and she wakes in a muddle on Peter's other sofa, pale light streaming through the windows. Peter is still sleeping. She grabs her phone, opening a WhatsApp from Georgie.

> Did you hear? Leo isn't back. He was nowhere
> to be seen, apparently, when Chrissy went to
> pick him up from prison. He's basically
> vanished.

Alice stares at the message, white noise building in her ears.

What do you mean, va— she types, but another message drops into the top of her screen.

There's something else as well, Georgie writes. Can you meet me at the pub? It's something you really need to see.

Alice's breath comes shallow and quick. She *felt* Leo's presence yesterday, from the moment she woke. Felt his nearness like a charge in the air. How can he have vanished?

She looks over at Peter, anxiety shifting and re-forming inside her.

I'll be there in five minutes, she replies to Georgie, then stands up and slips out of the room.

SIX

CHRISSY

Friday, December 8, 2023

Chrissy stirs as she spots the bleached-blonde hair and red furry jacket she's been looking out for. She hates that she has had to return here, to the gray building and the cage-like gates, but the sight of Izzy crossing the carpark lifts her.

She always used to admire how glamorously Izzy dressed to come here, as if her visits to her husband in prison were fortnightly dates. She reminds Chrissy a little of her younger self, when her dress sense was more outlandish—though more punky than glam—and she used to dye her curls the same Debbie Harry shade. She was just a barmaid at the Raven then, her life a blur of fun and friendship and saving up her tips for nights out with Alice. Ethan just a casual boyfriend, a teacher at the village school, older than her and not really suitable . . .

She shakes her head, banishing him. Now is not the time.

"Izzy!" she calls as the other woman struts toward the visitors' entrance in her platforms.

Izzy turns, and Chrissy is disproportionately moved to see her face light up in a wide, lipsticky smile.

"Babe!" Izzy throws her arms around her. "What the hell are you doing here? Your time in this shithole is done, my friend!"

Chrissy's burst of joy is punctured. She pulls back from Izzy. "I don't know where Leo is."

"What d'you mean?"

"I came to collect him but he'd already gone. And I haven't heard from him, I don't know where he went—"

"Oh, fuck . . ." Izzy draws her into an even tighter hug, smelling of hair spray and fruity perfume.

Chrissy untangles herself, not wanting to put too much of a dent in Izzy's visit. She knows what a nightmare it can be to book a slot, how quickly the time passes once you're in there. "Listen, Iz, can you ask Cliff some questions for me? I know it's your precious time with him, but—"

"'Course I fucking will!" She grips Chrissy's hand and Chrissy is choked again to realize she made a friend here, a real friend, after losing so many.

"Can you ask him whether Leo said anything? About having plans to go anywhere after he got out? Or if he seemed worried, or . . . *anything* at all . . ."

"'Course, 'course, babe. Cliff is bound to know. Those two got pretty close once they'd stopped arguing about snoring and farting!"

There's a moment's silence. Chrissy wonders if Izzy is having the same thought as she is: that she'd kill to be complaining about her loved one's snoring or farting these days. That every once-annoying habit now feels like a loss.

Izzy shakes herself. "Right, better get in there. I'll find out, I swear."

"I'll wait here for you," Chrissy says. "And thank you, Izzy. You're the first person I've been able to turn to."

"Solidarity, babe," Izzy says, squeezing Chrissy's shoulder and then sashaying away.

Chrissy returns to her car. Her stomach is churning but she still chews on some potato chips that taste of nothing. The bag is empty before she's even registered she's swallowing them, and self-disgust claims her as quickly as normal.

That started during her marriage, too. The bingeing. Then went away when Ethan did, only to come back, more compulsive than ever, after Leo was sent down. What kind of mum devoured junk food while her son was eating prison slop? Put on weight while he talked about bread rolls so stale they were practically a weapon? She hides the packet in her glove box, another shameful token, and checks her phone. Her sister has sent a string of messages asking if Leo's home yet, but there's nothing from anybody else, not even their mum. Chrissy buffers herself against the hurt. She's learned that the people closest to you can surprise you—often in the worst ways—when something terrible happens, something messy and confusing.

You always did attract trouble, Christina.

She blinks hard and opens Facebook instead. The village has its own group and none of its tech-inept administrators ever thought to block her. Most of the posts are about school closure days or missing cats, but today there is something else.

Georgie, the newbie, has posted an invitation to a memorial for Robbie in the village church this weekend. Why now? And why this *Georgie?* Chrissy clicks on the link to the event page but she can't access it. All she can see is the photo of Robbie at the top, and it brings another solid lump to her throat. The mess and resentment can't detract from the sheer tragedy of his death. And she misses him. Misses his obsessions with video games and comics that Leo considered himself a bit too cool for. Misses all four of them spending time together as if it was the most natural thing in the world.

Flicking back to the village page, she stalls over another recent post.

Is it true Leo isn't back after all?

It's by Ellen from the butcher's, who is also on the new pub committee. Chrissy clenches her teeth at the sight of Leo's name up there, tossed around by someone who once claimed to care about him, about her. How does she know he's not returned?

She opens the comments on the post.

I certainly haven't seen him, Rowena writes. Have they moved away after all?

Maybe they kept him in prison, adds Janice, another of Chrissy's former regulars, and Chrissy can almost hear her glee. She always seemed to disapprove of Leo—his cheeky swearing onstage, his occasional flares of temper—and acted as if she'd been somehow vindicated after what happened. *I'm glad Ethan didn't have to see him finally lose it,* Chrissy once overheard her saying as she walked past her chip shop. She'd wanted to scream at all the misapprehensions in that sentence, all the things stopping her from being able to correct them. The people who understood the least always seemed to talk the loudest.

Now Chrissy resists a fierce urge to reply, to tell them all: *He's a person. My son. And he's missing . . .* Instead, she takes note of whose voices are absent from the discussion. Georgie. Peter. Alice. Conspicuous in their silence.

But now here's Izzy, emerging from the prison gates with her bright hair and long legs, and Chrissy jumps out of the car and jogs toward her.

"Iz," she says, then catches herself before she can dive straight to her own agenda: "How's Cliff?"

Izzy finds a plucky smile. "He's okay."

"Did he . . . ?"

Izzy gestures to a nearby bench and they walk over and sit down. Chrissy perches right on the edge, legs jiggling, like Leo's always did when he was small, unable to sit still.

"Leo didn't mention anything about planning to take off anywhere," Izzy says. "He just said you were picking him up, taking him home."

Chrissy's eyes sting. "That was all I wanted."

"I know. I'm so sorry, babe."

"Did Cliff say anything else?"

"He said . . . that toward the end of his sentence, Leo seemed . . ."

"Seemed what?"

"Off. Not quite right. Cliff wasn't sure but—"

"I'd noticed that, too." Chrissy wishes she could stop interrupting. "I thought he was thinking about the future, wondering what it would be like."

Izzy nods. "It probably was that. Cliff didn't push him on it, apparently. But he said he definitely wasn't himself. Not sleeping, barely eating, sitting on his own at meals and association."

"Really?" Chrissy's mind tracks back, trying to remember if she'd sensed it was *that* bad. She recalls faint alarm bells, nothing more, and feels like the worst mother in the world.

"And there was one other thing . . ."

Chrissy sits forward.

"Nothing bad, exactly." Izzy pats Chrissy's hand with her long-nailed fingers. "Just that . . . you remember there was one week you couldn't make visiting, maybe a couple of months ago?"

"I had to work," Chrissy says breathlessly. She's been doing agency work since selling the pub, short stints in hospitality, whatever comes along. That one had been a well-paid, weeklong job in a hotel and she hadn't felt able to turn it down.

Is this all her fault, for prioritizing a job over her son?

"Cliff says Leo had a different visitor that week instead."

"My sister, maybe? She goes sometimes, especially when I can't."

"No." Izzy shakes her head. "Cliff knows who she is. This was someone Cliff hadn't seen before."

Chrissy holds her stomach, her mind racing.

"A woman," Izzy continues. "Apparently the guys all teased

Leo afterward but he wouldn't let on who it was. Older than him, kind of a fox by the sounds of it. But I'd take that with a pinch of salt; you know how long it's been since some of them—"

"What did she look like?" Chrissy interrupts again, possibilities swarming her brain.

"Tall," Izzy says. "Slim. Brown hair." She shrugs. "D'you know who it might've been?"

Chrissy's thoughts have tripped on the word *tall*. The word she's heard used as a shorthand description for Alice many times over the years. *Is your tall friend single by any chance? Are you still friendly with that tall girl from the village?*

The rest of Izzy's description sinks in more slowly, and with it comes an image of Alice sitting opposite Leo in the visitation room, other inmates turning their heads to get an eyeful. For some reason she is wearing the green velvet dress from the night of Robbie's death, her hair pinned up the same way, her lipstick dark and slightly smeared. She leans toward Leo, her hand sliding across the table . . .

Chrissy blinks and the scene dissolves. Izzy is watching her curiously, but she can't voice all the things that are tumbling through her mind. Why would Alice visit Leo in prison a few weeks before his release? And why would Leo not even mention it?

SEVEN

CHRISSY

New Year's Eve 2021

"Wow!" Chrissy stalled, clutching a box of dusty champagne glasses she'd dug out from underneath the bar, and gawped at Alice emerging from the upstairs flat. Her long legs descended the wooden stairs, her feet turning sideways so her heels didn't catch in the gaps in between. "You look fucking phenomenal!"

Alice beamed, smoothing her green velvet dress so the light rippled over it. "Why, thank you!"

Chrissy glanced down at her own outfit, an old *Dark Side of the Moon* T-shirt over beer-stained black jeans, the same thing she'd been wearing all day. Alice had been helping her get the pub ready for the big night ahead, but she'd made the effort to pop upstairs and get changed, whereas it hadn't even crossed Chrissy's mind. And *what* an effort Alice had made. Her teardrop earrings sparkled as she walked up to the bar.

"Your full-length mirror's much better than mine," she declared.

"Is it?" Chrissy had given zero thought, in her life, to what made one mirror better than another. She almost made a joke to that effect, but felt suddenly self-conscious, in a way she never usually did around Alice. "Who you trying to impress anyway?" she asked, more sharply than she'd meant. She was tired, she realized, putting down the box to wipe sweat from her face. It had been a long day, and she hadn't even opened yet.

"You know I love New Year's Eve," Alice said, touching the locket at her throat. "Fresh starts and all that."

Chrissy softened, giving her a smile. "You've always been better at those than me."

Alice reached over the bar to squeeze her hand. "I wouldn't say that." She drew back, and then she got that look on her face—*The Thinker,* Chrissy had dubbed it ever since they'd seen the Rodin statue on a girls' weekend in Paris. *Looks like you when you're about to get deep,* she'd teased Alice at the time, and the comparison had stuck. "Although . . ." Alice said now.

"Heeere we go," Chrissy said.

"A *proper* fresh start might not be a bad idea for you now." She held up her palms as Chrissy started to protest. "I don't mean give up the pub or move out of Cromley or anything like that. I know you wouldn't, and I would *not* want you to! I just mean . . ." She gestured upward again. "It can't be good for you, living up there?"

Chrissy turned away, opening the glass washer to a cloud of heat. She began emptying it noisily, hoping to drown out whatever Alice had to say, but the clinks and rattles were no match for her friend. Another one of their running jokes was that Alice's Lecture Hall Voice was almost as loud as Chrissy's Rowdy Pub Holler.

"I was thinking you could get a cottage in the village, and just come here for work. Have some separation. Get away from . . ." She paused, and now she *did* lower her voice, even though they were alone. "The memories," she finished as Chrissy gave up on the gin goblets and turned back to face her.

Alice looked so earnest, it disarmed and infuriated her all at once. They had been through everything together, but it was different for Alice; Ethan had never lived inside her head, under her skin; she probably didn't jump at shadows even now, thinking he was right behind her.

"Alice," she said, "you think it's going to make any *difference* where I live?"

"I just want—" Alice stopped as they heard the front door bang.

Chrissy recognized Leo's way of letting it ricochet against the wall—this was why there was an ever-growing hole—and motioned for Alice to drop the subject. By the time Leo appeared they were smiling in welcome, but Chrissy felt dread growling in her stomach, as if their conversation had cursed the whole night, the whole year ahead.

"Hey, Leo," Alice said brightly. "You all right? Robbie not with you?"

"Nope." He marched toward the stairs, his coat still on, hood up.

Chrissy watched him in concern. "Leo?" she called out,

but he was already gone, slamming the door to the flat behind him.

Chrissy and Alice looked at each other.

"Clearly *he's* going to be the life and soul tonight," Chrissy said, trying to make light of it. Alice smiled sympathetically, then picked up a pile of beer mats and began weaving around the room, placing them with a soft slap on each table. As she bent forward, Chrissy saw the swing of her locket and felt for the identical one around her own neck, under her T-shirt. Alice had given it to her as a present, on another New Year's Eve two years before. They each kept pictures of their sons inside, and wore them always, like a promise between them, a bond of trust.

The difference was, Alice kept hers on show. Chrissy preferred to tuck hers underneath her clothes, protecting it from harm she always said. The truth was, she didn't like people to notice it too much. Didn't like them to ask for the story behind her and Alice's matching silver hearts.

EIGHT

ALICE

Friday, December 8, 2023

The lights are on inside the pub when Alice arrives, just as they were yesterday, but this time the door is unlocked. She finds Georgie in the bar area, gazing around like someone viewing a house in a property TV program. She's dressed in her usual country chic uniform—quilted Barbour jacket, skinny jeans, high caramel-colored boots—and her hair is in a perfect plait. As Alice hangs back to watch, Georgie narrows her eyes and stares across the room. There's something intense about her expression, her lips moving very slightly. Perhaps she's imagining the place back open, taking an Instagram picture in her mind.

Alice feels a twinge of guilt. Georgie really seems to care about making the pub a success. She approached Alice so eagerly about getting involved, just as the sale was going through; she had a whole speech prepared about her marketing background and the money she could put in. *I know I only just moved here, but it's the kind of project I could* really *get passionate about.* Alice couldn't say no. Now she clears her throat and Georgie whirls around, color flooding into her cheeks.

"Oh, Alice!" she says. "Didn't hear you come in."

"You seemed in a bit of a trance, there."

"Yes . . ." Georgie's hands flutter. "I . . . was just thinking about the layout of the tables. Whether we could fit a few more in or whether it would be too cramped."

The tables already look squashed. In the old days they were mismatched and higgledy-piggledy, but there were open spaces where people would stand and mingle, laugh and dance. The new Ikea tables are in tight rows, like an exam hall.

"We should fit in as many as possible," Alice says.

Georgie looks at her for a steady moment. There is something else in her eyes now, almost a glint of calculation. Does she suspect, in fact, that all Alice wants is to rip the soul of this pub right out?

Then she breaks into a politician-like smile. "Absolutely agree," she says. "The more customers we can seat, the better."

There is another short silence. Alice isn't here to talk about tables. "So . . . Leo . . . ?"

Georgie's smile drops. "Rumor has it he's disappeared completely."

"How do you know?"

"Ellen said a few people had noticed he hadn't been seen. So she asked Jack to ask a guy he and Leo went to school with—Tom or Tim something?—because apparently he stayed in touch with Leo, wrote to him in prison a couple of times . . . and he said Chrissy had called to ask if he'd heard from Leo. Said she was really worried because he hadn't been there when she went to collect him."

"He just"—Alice blinks away an image of the gray prison building—"wasn't there?"

"Apparently."

"But he *was* released?"

"It seems so."

Alice closes her eyes, her thoughts spinning. Leo's Facebook picture blares in her mind: the frozen roar of his mouth around the mic.

"Is he . . . *missing* missing?" she asks, opening her eyes. "Are the police involved?"

Georgie pauses. "I'm not sure." She seems to scrutinize Alice's face. "Is there something I should know?"

Alice shakes herself. "No. I'm just . . . trying to understand."

But she wishes now that she had closed down his Facebook, not left it wide open on her laptop. Wishes she'd pressed Peter about his scrapes from yesterday morning, his dirty clothes.

She has nothing to hide, she reminds herself sharply, and neither does her brother. Maybe this is all part of the torture Leo seems determined to put them through.

"You said . . ." She turns back to Georgie. "You said there was something else?"

Now it's Georgie's turn to shift uneasily.

"What?" Alice says, her anxiety growing. "Is it something else to do with Leo?"

Georgie starts to walk across the room, beckoning for

Alice to follow. They slip between the regimented rows of tables and chairs. The dark wooden bar is the same as before, for the moment. Faint white rings stain its top like the ghosts of long-drunk pints, and a whiff of beer clings on, the smell of hundreds of nights out gone stale.

Don't look at the corner. Except Alice does. She can't help it: She stares at the spot just beyond the bar and thinks, as always, that she can still see the spatter of blood beneath the fresher layers of paint.

But there is something on the spot, something new. And Georgie is pointing straight at it.

Alice edges forward, her heart trying to jump out of her chest. It must be a trick of the light. A trick of her vision.

"I spotted it this morning when I popped in to measure up for the new blinds." Georgie looks anguished, touches Alice's arm. "It wasn't there before, was it?"

Alice is up close now, and she can clearly see the markings.

Initials in dark gray pencil.

R.L.

L.D.

Her legs go soft. Georgie puts out a hand to steady her, but Alice swings away and runs for the bathroom, reaching it just in time to shut herself in a cubicle and vomit. Tears stream down her face and she retches again, her throat raw, her hands gripping the sides of the toilet.

Georgie is rapping on the cubicle door. "Alice? Are you okay? I'm so sorry. I don't know who did this. If it's a prank, it's a despicable one. If it's not . . ." She exhales, seeming to run out of ideas.

Alice leans against the cold toilet seat and tries to breathe. Robbie's initials. Leo's. Is there *any* chance they could've been there all along? Perhaps Robbie and Leo scrawled them there, drunken graffiti artists tagging their favorite spot? But, no, she has *never* seen them before. And they're on top of the latest coat of paint.

She feels sick again, turns her head to aim into the toilet bowl, but her insides are hollow.

"Alice? Will you let me in?"

Alice hauls herself up, flushes the toilet, and opens the cubicle door. Georgie hovers, watching her, trying to put an arm around her, but Alice goes to splash water on her face.

"Who could've got in here?" she asks herself in the mirror. "Who has a key?"

Georgie's reflection looms up behind her. "Only the committee, I think? And not even everybody, actually . . . We share four keys between the six of us, right?"

Alice nods. She always keeps one, and so does Jack, but the others change hands between Georgie, Peter, Rowena, and Ellen, according to who needs access. "Did we change the locks when we first took over?" Her memory of that time is foggy. The pub project was born out of that fog, that hazy madness.

"Yes," says Georgie. "I'd only just joined then. But you were adamant—rightly so—that we should."

Alice walks back into the bar, across the room, Georgie following. The letters are so close to where Robbie fell. If they had a heart around them, they would look like lovers' initials carved into a tree. But Robbie and Leo weren't lovers;

they were best friends, like their mums, until they weren't, until he destroyed it all.

She glances at the ceiling, toward the boarded-up flat she tries to pretend no longer exists, and Georgie looks the same way.

"Is it secure?" Georgie asks. "Up there?"

"Yes," Alice says quickly.

"Shouldn't we—"

"It's all boarded up."

Georgie raises her eyebrows but falls silent. Alice covers her face, grappling with her thoughts. Is it *possible* Leo got into the pub, despite all their efforts to keep him out? Does he know this place too well: all its weaknesses, all the cracks where fears and secrets can slip in?

Perhaps he climbed in through the same window he smashed with a pool cue when he was fourteen. Angry, often, even then. The window Alice helped Chrissy patch up, not commenting on what had happened, not judging, just holding one end of the duct tape and telling a tearful Chrissy it made the pub look more rock 'n' roll.

Now her eyes dart wildly between the corner of the bar and the door to the flat.

"I have to go," she says, nauseous again. "I have to get out of here."

NINE

LEO

The day Frank Jordan first spoke to him was the day the fight broke out between Stevens and Hasan during association time.

Leo was playing cards with Cliff at the small, wobbly table, and Cliff was winning as usual. Leo's competitive instincts had withered to nothing in the last two years, but he liked the cards' rhythmic movements and Cliff's running commentary. He'd learned to tune out the surrounding racket of pool games. Nobody told you how loud prison was, *all* the time.

"You okay, mate?" Cliff asked, waving a hand in front of Leo's face.

Leo blinked back into the room. "Sorry. Yeah, yeah, I'm okay."

"Visit got under your skin?"

He nodded, shrugged, and Cliff dealt another hand, swearing as the table lurched. Leo wedged his knee under it, his mind drifting again. It wasn't what his mum said during her visits, but what she didn't say. All the topics she avoided, the questions he never asked. Afterward his brain would go into overdrive, darkly filling in the gaps.

Cliff showed him a winning card with a sheepish grin. "Lucky for you we've nothing to actually play for."

"I'd have nothing left by this point even if we did."

It was then that Stevens shoved back his chair on the other side of the room. "Thieving fucker!" he hollered, launching himself at Hasan.

"It's *mine!*" Hasan shouted back, pushing him away. Stevens staggered and Leo froze—always waiting for that thud, sometimes hearing it even when it didn't come—but Stevens stayed on his feet and went for Hasan again.

Everybody started moving. Most people scattered from the fight, some ran toward it, circled it, and then the guards swooped in, barking warnings, pulling the two guys apart.

Leo dived for the door out to the TV room. He was used to fights after almost two years in here, but some things he couldn't watch anymore, like the gleam of absolute blind anger in someone's eyes. Most of all, he hated the aftermath. Hated seeing who would be blamed or believed—whichever way it went, it always left him feeling sick to his stomach.

There were people in the next room watching the monthly film, taking little notice of the ruckus next door. A few looked up as he burst in, but most of them ignored him. The guards simply frowned, motioning for him to sit down. The room was hot and the flickering light of the TV made everybody's faces look strange.

As he searched for a corner to tuck himself into, Leo felt a pair of eyes on him from the dimmed back row. A hand in the air, seeming to beckon. A distinctive, bulky silhouette. Leo froze. Surely Frank Jordan wasn't gesturing for him to approach? They'd never even spoken, and Leo's instinct was to keep it that way.

Inching forward, he saw Frank motion, with one cocked finger, to the spare seat next to him. Leo longed to reverse out of the room now, back into the light and bustle of the main association space, fight or no fight. But Frank wasn't someone you refused. Warily, he slid in next to him. Frank's mates, on the other side, ran their eyes over Leo in the darkness.

Next to Frank, he felt tiny. The older man sat with his legs spread, a hand on each knee, one foot tapping even though no music was playing.

"Who's scrapping?" he asked.

His eyes were on the TV, so Leo wasn't completely certain he was talking to him.

"Uh—Stevens and Hasan," he said after a pause, realizing he must be.

"About?"

"I . . . I'm not sure. The usual, I think."

Most fights in this place were about *stuff*. About the few pathetic belongings they all had to their names. Who had nicked whose stuff, who had touched whose stuff without asking, who had the best stuff and how could other people get it?

Frank looked at him sidelong, then nodded toward the room he'd fled. "Not a fan of violence?"

Leo coughed and stared at the screen, but it was an interior shot now, a quieter moment, and the whole room turned dark and still.

They sat in silence for a while and Frank seemed to get genuinely engrossed. It was weird to see him doing something as normal as watching TV: the old-timer whom everybody feared, about whom there were so many rumors. He looked sort of childlike when he was concentrating: he tilted his head and widened his eyes, his mouth a tiny bit open. Leo realized the film was one of his mum's favorites. Homesickness went through him like an ache but left something cold and troubling behind it. Home was tainted now. Home was where he was the enemy.

"I think we have something in common," Frank said out of nowhere.

Leo turned his head. "Sorry?"

Frank studied him, his face suddenly close. He had milky eyes, deep grooves all around them, a distinctively misshapen nose. Nothing childlike about this angle. It was a hardlife kind of a face.

"Me and you," he said. "We've got something in common."

"What's that?" Leo asked, glancing nervously around.

"Or should I say some*where*," Frank said, with a slow, unsettling grin.

TEN

GEORGIE

Friday, December 8, 2023

I have to go," Alice says again, her voice strangled. "I can't . . . can't think straight."

Her eyes are huge and something has happened to her posture, as if her shoulders want to collapse but her spine won't let them. Georgie wonders if she should say something more, push a little harder. But maybe Alice has been pushed far enough for one day. Stepping back, Georgie lets her go.

Alice throws one last glance toward the corner and then rushes off, slamming the front door behind her. The whole pub shudders, plummeting into silence. Georgie leans on the bar and lets out a breath, still catching whiffs of vomit in the air.

Slowly, she turns and looks toward the door of the flat. *Boarded up* is something of an overstatement. There is just one large piece of wood nailed diagonally across the entrance—

and yet it's been enough to signal "out of bounds" all this time, even to her.

Why are they not using it for storage, or even renting it out? The business part of her brain starts running through all the possibilities, wondering why she's never raised these questions, but the core of her is pulled toward the flat with a sudden visceral need to see it.

She walks behind the bar and opens the cupboard where Jack's tools are stored. Scattered nails, blunt pencils, sticky pots of varnish. She pauses a moment, wondering what she needs—admittedly, this isn't her area of expertise—then she grabs a hammer and strides over to the flat door.

It's time to see it for herself. And it's easier, actually, than she expected. She hooks the claw of the hammer around a nail, imagining Lola watching her, wincing and bemused. After one last check over her shoulder she pulls hard, levering the nail out of the splintering wood. She does the same with the nail below it and the plank swings toward her. She prays the door behind it won't be locked. The handle is stiff but it opens, revealing the staircase, dark and dusty, rising toward another half-open door above.

Georgie hesitates, then slips quietly inside. The stairs creak beneath her boots and the wall feels gravelly, her left fingertips trailing along it. She's still gripping the hammer in her other hand. *This is where they lived.* Opening the upper door, she steps into an empty room: stale, musty, and cold as a fridge. She shivers as she looks around, unsure what she's expecting to find. If she didn't know better, she'd think nobody had lived up here in decades.

In the next room, she's surprised to see a green armchair, sitting like an abandoned island in the middle of the worn gray carpet. She brushes its fabric and pokes her hands down the sides of the cushions, recoiling at the tickle of old crumbs. Going to the window, she nudges back a curtain and peeks out at the pub garden and the rooftops beyond. The tall spire of the church, the little school sandwiched between its icy playground and empty soccer pitch. All places she knew, *felt* like she knew, before she even got here. She remembers the image of Cromley she once had in her mind: chocolate-box cottages, blooming gardens, lilac wisteria framing unlocked front doors.

The reality, as she gazes at it now, is so much bleaker. The village seems to hunker in the shadow of tragedy—unsurprising, of course, but still it shocked her how *visible* it was when she first came, how tangible. A draft chills her neck and she whips around, pulse flying.

Is this the room Ethan died in?

Right above the spot where Leo killed Robbie.

Leo who is now missing.

For a moment, these facts snatch her breath away. She averts her eyes from a dark stain on the carpet and hurries on through the flat, peering into the moldering bathroom and the two empty rooms at the very rear. One is smaller, with a sloped ceiling where the roof sweeps down: Leo's former bedroom, perhaps? There are remnants of Blu-Tack on the walls and she finds herself wondering what posters he had, what he was into before everything went wrong. Jittery now, she's about to leave when she notices a cardboard box in the corner of the larger bedroom.

Was this Chrissy and Ethan's room? She inches toward the box, coughing in a cloud of dust as she opens its flaps. Faces peer up at her. Flat, frozen smiles. Tentatively, she draws out one of the framed photos, puzzled as to why they were left behind, why nobody has cleared them since. Ethan and Chrissy stand stiffly in front of the pub, a young Leo wedged like a buffer between them. A banner in the background reads: TEN YEARS OF OWNERSHIP! COME CELEBRATE WITH US! But there's nothing celebratory about the picture. Tears spike Georgie's eyes and she lets her fingertips patter across the glass.

They never deserved you.

A thud from below makes her jolt. She stops dead, holding her breath, and hears a faint jangle of keys. *Shit.* Dropping the photo back into the box, she scrambles for a plausible excuse for being here. Considering possible uses for the space? Thought she heard rats? She hurries back to the armchair room and stands still, listening. A door creaks. There are footsteps. But they no longer sound as if they're directly underneath her.

Instinct draws her to the window, and she's right; there is someone in the pub garden. A broad-shouldered man wearing a woolen hat and a bulky coat. He pauses just inside the gate and looks around, unmistakably furtive. Georgie notices he's holding something against his chest. A small package, wrapped in a dark plastic bag. As he creeps further into the garden, she catches a glimpse of his profile in the morning light.

Peter Lowe.

He turns her way and she dives out of sight, knees hitting

the dusty floor. It's a few moments before she dares peer out again. He's leaning into the dumpster in the corner of the garden, the heels of his heavy-duty boots lifting off the ground. After a while he draws back, looks left and right, and walks quickly away. The package and the plastic bag are gone. He leaves through the gate and she hears him locking it behind him.

Clambering to her feet, Georgie dusts off her knees. What has she just seen? Her heart revs again and she sprints down the stairs and out the back door. It's even colder outside than it was in the flat. She breathes on her frozen fingers, striding toward the dumpster. The old pub sign rests, discarded, on the top, and the raven's eyes bore into her as she pushes it to one side. No sign of a plastic bag. She leans in further, clearing chunks of plaster and peelings of wallpaper until she sees it, right at the bottom, and strains until her fingertips grasp it.

The package is square, hard, with a ridge along one side, like a coil or a spring. Opening the bag, she draws out a plain black scrapbook, spiral-bound and fattened by whatever's inside. She glances around, then gingerly opens the book.

She almost drops it at the first double-page spread. Then the next, and the next, as confusion drives deep into her bones.

The scrapbook is full of cuttings about Leo Dean. Reviews of his gigs and an interview with him in a local music magazine. A flyer for a Halloween "Spookfest" at the Raven, featuring Leo in a black feathered cape and thick eyeliner. And several articles about his arrest, his conviction, his sentencing, his release . . .

Georgie shivers violently, drinking in the obsession that seems to fill each page. Familiar in a way she doesn't like to admit. She considers throwing the book back into the dumpster and abandoning it there, but she knows she won't. It could be another piece of the jigsaw, unexpected but important.

Never trust a Lowe, that man had said to her less than a month ago, that stranger outside the pub who mistook her at first for Alice. Georgie still has no idea who he was, what he meant. But his words come back to her often, strengthening her conviction that there's something very wrong with this village.

A bird squawks above her head, like a klaxon telling her she's running out of time. Clutching the scrapbook, she stumbles back inside. She retrieves the hammer from where she abandoned it on the floor of the flat and shuts the place up, nailing the plank back in place, disturbed dust settling in her wake.

ELEVEN

CHRISSY

Friday, December 8, 2023

Chrissy kicks her front door closed, stands in her hallway, and throws her car keys at the wall. She is seething with frustration, her head full of what Izzy told her, her teeth grinding in anger that the prison staff wouldn't allow her to see Leo's visitation record. *But I'm his mum,* she'd argued with them. They'd looked at her steadily, no intention of breaking protocol no matter how much she begged. *I'm trying to find him,* she'd almost blurted, before biting her tongue. They couldn't know.

Bending to retrieve her keys, she stalls when she spots a white windowed envelope on the mat between her feet. It's addressed to Leo. Marked *CONFIDENTIAL*. She picks it up and tears it open, hungry for clues.

Conditions breached . . . Please report immediately . . .

Sickness hits her stomach. Leo *has* missed his appointment with his probation officer. Her fear explodes like something unlocked and she drags her mobile out of her pocket. What had she been *thinking,* tiptoeing around, worrying about frowny prison guards? He could be in danger, could be—

"I need to report a missing person," she blurts into the phone, the envelope slipping out of her grip.

NOT LONG AFTER she's finished on her mobile, her home phone starts to ring. Did she give the police her landline number, amid all the other details she recited in a haze? She rushes to answer it, shoving back her hair as it flops into her face.

"Hello?"

Once again, there is silence on the other end.

"Hello?" Her voice sounds pleading now, then exasperated. "Leo? Leo, is that you?"

But whoever it is, they are gone.

CHRISSY RECOGNIZES THE two officers when they eventually arrive—the man with the bushy beard and the woman with braided hair—and even remembers their names, Ben and Kiri, just before they introduce themselves as PCs Lochland and Marley. She must've met them at one of the awards parties or other events Alice used to take her to in support of Peter. Or perhaps she'd served them in the Raven; he used to bring colleagues in there sometimes if they'd been on shift nearby.

She wonders what they're thinking as she leads them to the kitchen, repeating over and over that Leo wouldn't deliberately break the terms of his release. They must know what happened, why he's been in jail, but they go right back to the beginning with their questions.

"What crime was your son convicted of?" the woman, Kiri, asks.

Chrissy blinks. *He's missing but it's still* his *crime they're interested in?*

She despises the word she needs to say in reply, the violent, literal sound of it.

"Manslaughter," she murmurs, and watches Kiri note it down without reacting.

There is a word that's worse, of course. She remembers doubling over, tears on her cheeks, when she found out Leo would not be charged with murder. The relief was like a guilty secret, a tangle of hope and shame.

"It was an argument," she says now. "A-a punch or a push, it was never established. Robbie fell, hit his head . . ."

She's said it many times before, but it rarely makes a difference to how people look at her. Perhaps they think she's trying to trivialize it. Maybe she is? But what she said to Alice that day in her kitchen came out so wrong. She didn't mean that Robbie brought it on himself, got what was coming to him. Of *course* that wasn't what she meant.

After that, Chrissy didn't dare ask the question of anyone else who might've heard the boys arguing. Leo was the only other person she ever broached it with, but he would shut down, say it no longer mattered, his shoulders hunched and his fingers curled into half-fists.

"And he was intending to come back here?" the male officer, Ben, asks.

"Yes."

"Can you think of any reason he might skip parole? Go on the run?"

"He's not on the run!"

"In the case of a recently released prisoner—"

"He was let out two years early." Chrissy's voice rises. "He did everything that was asked of him inside. Education. Working. Behaving himself. Why the hell would he run away?"

Neither of them answers. Chrissy forces herself to breathe deeply, count to ten—losing her temper won't do her any favors. She has to get through to them: Leo needs *help*. She gets up from the kitchen table and walks over to open a drawer.

Her hands shake as she gathers up the notes, realizing just how many there have been. She smooths out the ones she screwed up in anger and pauses over the one right at the back—the very first, folded the tightest—wondering what the officers might make of it.

You have to show them everything, she chides herself. *For Leo.*

But she pushes that one deeper into the drawer, closes it, and brings the rest over to the table.

Kiri's eyebrows lift. "Are these . . . ?"

"I've been getting them every few weeks since I moved into this house."

"And you didn't report this?"

Chrissy ignores her faintly disapproving tone, sliding the most recent one forward. "This was left on my bin yesterday, on Leo's release day. It's the first one aimed at him, not just me. I didn't really *care* when it was me." She falters, thinking of the exception. "But Leo . . ." Her eyes cloud with tears and she gestures in exasperation. "Someone wanted him to stay away and now—"

"Do you know who they're from?"

Chrissy's hands sink to her lap. As her mouth starts to shape Alice's name, a lurch of sickness clamps her lips together. She takes jagged breaths through her nose, battling with herself. Why can't she say it? Is her loyalty so deeply ingrained?

Or is she afraid of what might happen if she accuses Alice outright? Afraid of how much she gave her, showed to her, back when it was unthinkable they would never not be friends. All those precious pieces of herself.

"The . . . the whole village turned against him—and me—after what happened. It pains me to say it, but . . . there are lots of people who might wish him harm. That's why I'm so worried. Why I need you to—" Her voice cracks and she holds a hand over her mouth.

Ben pulls out his phone and takes several photos of the notes. Kiri writes something down, murmurs about fingerprints. Chrissy sits forward and her words start tumbling out in panic. "Can you get a record from the prison of who visited Leo? I heard someone new visited him right near the end. And can you talk to some of the other inmates, find out if they know anything? I really think—"

"We'll do what we can," Ben interrupts, somewhat guardedly. "In the meantime, can we have a look around?"

"Around . . . the house?" The suggestion throws her right off. Nobody except her has even been upstairs in this cottage. "Um . . . well, yes. It just seems like . . . He hasn't even *been* here before. We lived above the pub, until . . . And I'm *very* certain he's not hiding under a bed . . ."

"You'd be surprised," Kiri says, with a slow blink that Chrissy can't interpret.

Ben goes to poke around the house and Chrissy sits with Kiri, listening to the sounds of him moving from room to room. This all feels wrong. Now that she's made the leap and told the police, she wants helicopters, search parties, CCTV. A trace on her landline, perhaps? She opens her mouth to ask, but Kiri gets to her feet and walks over to the collage of Chrissy-and-Leo photos pinned proudly to the wall.

They're both silent as the officer's eyes move over it. Chrissy feels herself growing protective of her amateur art project, which should have been another welcome-home surprise. She gazes at Leo, her boy who writes songs like nothing she's ever heard, who can make her laugh even when she's angry or exhausted with life.

"No photos of his dad?"

Chrissy stiffens. "What?"

Kiri turns with a new flare of interest in her eyes. "You . . . don't have any photos of his dad . . ." She gestures around the whole kitchen, as Chrissy's face turns hot.

It's true, she cherry-picked photos without Ethan. It seemed only natural as she was doing it—the collage was about her and Leo, reunited—but now she sees what it looks like, Ethan airbrushed out of their lives.

"Ethan, wasn't it?" Kiri says. "Head teacher up at the school, wasn't he?"

Chrissy stares at her. All pretense of not knowing each

other lifts like a curtain. Was she one of the officers who came to the flat *that* night, almost four years ago now? Who took a statement while Chrissy sat on the stairs rocking uncontrollably?

An image flashes into her head. How gray and shrunken Ethan looked—powerless, for once, hanging there—and how she gazed into his blank eyes, feeling nothing, not yet, before her vision blacked and she crumbled.

"Is that"—her voice breaks again—"relevant?"

The policewoman looks away without answering.

Chrissy kicks back her chair and stands up. The room pinwheels and she thinks she's going to fall straight over. "What happens next?" she demands, putting her hand on the tabletop. "Are you going to search for my son?"

"Of course." Kiri's eyes flicker back to the notes. "We're just the on-call officers, but a detective will be in touch."

"He's not just taken off," Chrissy says urgently, one last time. "Something's happened to him. I've been getting calls. Silent ones. Maybe he's . . ."

"We'll do everything we can," Kiri says, parroting her colleague's earlier promise. "In these circumstances, I'm sure they'll make this a priority."

But her words aren't comforting. They sound more like a threat. Chrissy hugs her elbows, dread binding itself around her.

"You've had a bad time of it," Kiri adds, almost matter-of-factly. "Losing your husband, then your son going to prison, and now . . ."

Chrissy gapes at her. Kiri looks calmly back, and Chrissy

can't tell if her tone is supposed to be sympathetic, or something else. And what the hell can she say in response? It's true, life has thrown everything at her. Leo is all she has left.

"Just find him," she croaks. Then picks up her cigarettes and walks out of the room.

TWELVE

ALICE

Friday, December 8, 2023

Peter is gone when Alice goes back to his house to check on him. She sees he's finished the washing-up she started, and emptied the bin, and she hopes it means he's back to some kind of normalcy. Where has he gone, though? She feels a pang of sadness as she looks at the dent he's left in the sofa, the fabric of the arm flattened where his long legs hung over the edge.

She crumples into the same spot, the initials from the pub wall dancing in front of her eyes. Other fragments crowd in: Robbie on the floor, Leo standing over him, Chrissy's hand slipping out of hers. Chrissy's face whenever Ethan . . . *Stop.* She opens her eyes, feeling as if she's emerging from a dark room into harsh, blinding light. Then she sees the note on the coffee table.

Sorry, sis, it reads, in Peter's recognizable scrawl. *Sorry for fucking up. Will call you. Love you. P x*

She is choked again. He never says *love you*. He would sometimes murmur it, gruffly, to Robbie, but always left it unspoken and implied with her. She doesn't know whether to be moved or worried. Picking up the note, she studies it as if she'll see something else between the lines, then folds it into her pocket and leaves.

AS ALICE DRIVES up to her house, still lost in thought, she snaps alert to see two officers in high-vis jackets at her door. She runs her tongue over her furry teeth and gets out of her car, walking tall.

"Hello?" She injects a question into her voice as she approaches them. The officers, a man and a woman who used to work with Peter, look slightly awkward, caught between smiles and poker faces. "Kiri . . . and Ben?" she remembers.

"Hi, Mrs. . . . *Miss* Lowe," Ben says.

"Never been a Mrs.!" Alice says, trying to cover her unease with a weird singsong voice. "I'd say Robbie's dad wasn't the marriage type but . . ."

He was so preoccupied with his wife and more important kids that he missed his firstborn's funeral, she thinks, but swallows it, keeping things light.

". . . but we were never that kind of couple," she finishes awkwardly instead. "And . . . you can just call me Alice. We're not strangers, are we?"

There is a stilted pause. Kiri clears her throat. "Can we come in?"

Alice sees them looking around as she shows them in, Beech buzzing curiously about. Her house is emptier than it once was: no tangled PlayStation wires, no size-eleven sneakers abandoned in doorways. Not even much of her own clutter anymore; no pens and half-filled notebooks waiting on every surface.

"Make yourselves comfy." Alice gestures them into the living room. "I'll just be a second . . ."

She doesn't wait to see their reaction, but hurries into her study. Pulling the door closed behind her, she wakes the laptop, jumping reflexively as Leo's face greets her. With a final hesitation, she logs out and closes the tab. There is a strange feeling of loss—a lost chance, perhaps, to peer into Leo's head—but what would it look like if the police saw him on her screen?

She takes a moment to compose herself, then fetches two glasses of water from the kitchen, as if that was what she left for in the first place.

"Sorry to disturb you, Alice," Kiri says as Alice returns and sits opposite them. "We just need to ask you a few questions about Leo Dean."

"Leo?" Alice says cautiously. "What about him?"

"We're aware that he . . ." Ben visibly squirms, looking over at his colleague.

"He killed my son," Alice finishes for him, pulling herself up straighter.

"Yes." He's blushing beneath that big beard. "And I'm sure you know he was recently released—"

"I know that, yes." She tries not to betray how she felt, still feels, about it. That his early release was another giant cut to her heart.

"His mother, Chrissy Dean, has informed us that he's disappeared."

Alice does her best to look taken aback. "Disappeared?"

"You didn't know?"

"Well, people had mentioned they hadn't seen him . . ."

"When did *you* last see him?"

"Um . . ." She pauses a second too long. "I guess it would've been his trial." She thinks of him in the defendant's box, head bowed. The surge of elation when he was sentenced, just to know he'd be locked up at all. But then the fury, and then the numbness: *Four years, which would probably, in reality, only be two?*

She remembers catching Chrissy's eye as she left court, feeling a shock of deep familiarity. Noticing—before she shut herself off from it—that Chrissy looked as bewildered and broken as her.

As if reading her mind, Kiri asks: "What about Chrissy, when did you last speak to her?"

Alice pauses again. Her kitchen table. The spilled tea. *Get out of my house.* Now, though, her mind fills up with dozens of other "last times." The last time they shared a bottle of wine and couldn't stop laughing at something ridiculous. The last time they watched their sons play a gig and squeezed each other's hands in mutual pride.

The last time they promised each other, *You can trust me.* Her hand goes to her throat, reaching for the locket as if for a phantom limb, but of course it isn't there.

"I can't remember," Alice says. "I wrote to her . . ."

This seizes their attention. "In what sense?"

She detects dangerous ground and rushes to explain. "I emailed her. On behalf of the pub committee. To say Leo wouldn't be allowed back in the pub. Obviously." She regrets adding the last word, regrets spitting it out so vehemently.

"And when was this?"

"Um . . ." Alice looks at the clock as if it's relevant. "Yesterday. The day of his release."

"I see." Ben takes over again, leaning forward. "We have to ask, Alice . . . where were you yesterday? The morning, in particular?"

"I was at home. I took Beech for a walk."

"Did you see anybody else?"

She shakes her head. "Not on my walk. Later on . . . I saw my brother. Peter. Who you know, of course."

She bats away the memory of him swaying by the side of the road. It isn't how she likes to think of him. She's normally the one leaning on him, not the other way around.

"Okay." Kiri writes for a disproportionately long time, and Alice reaches for Beech's soft ears. He rests his head in her lap and its weight is so comforting she wants to cry.

"One more thing." Ben's awkwardness is back. He shunts even further forward in his chair, and it takes Alice a moment to realize he's trying to show her a photo on his phone. "Do you recognize this?"

Alice's stomach jumps as she sees vivid red capitals.

KEEP HIM AWAY FROM OUR VILLAGE.

"No," she says, jerking back. "What . . . what is it?"

"A note sent anonymously to Chrissy Dean. One of several, in fact." He starts scrolling, showing her other pictures—

Why are you still here? Haven't you got the message yet?—and her vision becomes a streak of red.

"Oh . . . wow. That's . . ." She drops her gaze back to Beech, pretending to pick something out of his fur.

"Have you any idea who might have sent them?" Kiri asks, and Alice can feel that she's being carefully studied. She should look up, meet their eyes, but she hasn't the guts. Not even drawing herself up to her full height seems like the magic trick it usually is.

"Obviously, people are angry. But I don't know . . ."

"Alice, have you any idea where Leo Dean could be?"

Thoughts collide in her head. The high prison gates glinting in the sun. A hand with scarlet stains on the fingertips, bleeding into the skin. But she can't connect the images with herself, can't tell, in this moment, whether they're even real. She hooks her hands into Beech's collar and holds tight.

"I have no idea," she says. "Perhaps . . ." She swallows and moistens her dry lips. "Perhaps he realized coming back here was only going to cause more pain."

Kiri shifts in her seat. "Pain . . . for him? For you?"

Alice pulls Beech closer and he whimpers, his ears shooting back. "Pain for everyone."

THEY LEAVE A few minutes later, telling her that some detectives may be in touch. Alice stands in her hallway, her ears ringing as if they'd stood either side of her and yelled, rather than questioned her in those quietly awkward tones. She goes back over everything she said to them: Had she lied? Or dropped herself in it? She doesn't think so, but why won't her heart stop hammering?

She hears a knock at the door and nearly leaps out of her skin. She frowns, then opens it to see Ben standing there, alone, one finger scratching the side of his beard.

"Alice." He looks up. "Sorry. I left my notebook."

"Oh . . ." She lets him back in, half-wishing she'd spotted it before he returned, taken a peek at what he'd written about her.

She leads him into the living room but there's no sign of the notebook. He doesn't even seem to be searching for it.

"Are you sure you—?"

"Alice, just quickly . . ." His eyes dart toward the door. "Have you spoken to Pete?"

She blinks slowly. "Not today . . ."

"I think you should . . . maybe let him know . . ."

"About Leo?" She steps a little closer. Ben's face is lightly sweating. Beech trots forward and starts sniffing his hand.

Absentmindedly, Ben nudges the dog away. "No . . . well, yes . . . That this is happening. That I was here."

"You specifically?" Confusion makes her thoughts messy. She stares at his face, trying to read him.

He drags a hand over his mouth and all the way down to his collar. "Just . . . give him a heads-up. Maybe don't use my name if it's a text . . ." He shakes his head vigorously. "Look, I've gotta go. Just tell him there might be an investigation, okay?"

"But . . ." Alice shakes her head, too, wondering what she's missing.

Outside, a car engine revs up. Ben makes for the door.

"Ben . . . are you talking about . . . ?" But he is gone, pulling the front door closed behind him. She hurries to the window to watch him getting into the car next to Kiri, taking his notebook out of his jacket and waving it around as if to say, *Got it!*

Alice pulls her phone out of her pocket to text her brother. But she doesn't know what to say. What she's supposed to be saying.

There might be an investigation.

Why do those words seem bigger than just Leo skipping parole? Why do they send a shot of fear right to her core, to a place she thought she'd closed off long ago?

THIRTEEN

ALICE

New Year's Eve 2021

Robbie . . ." Alice broke off from wiping the beer pumps and turned to scrutinize her son. "Have you been crying, sweetheart?"

He avoided her gaze, hoisting a keg of mulled wine onto the bar top. She could see his profile, the telltale pinkness around his eyes. Why hadn't she noticed until now? Distracted by Leo's mood, she clearly hadn't paid enough attention to her own son when he'd arrived some fifteen minutes later.

"Is this where Chrissy wants it?" he asked, gesturing at the keg.

"Think so," Alice said distractedly. "Thanks for your help, love."

"Well, Leo seems to have checked out," he mumbled.

Alice glanced toward the stairs to the flat. Leo had been

up there for nearly an hour now. Chrissy had gone to talk to him and hadn't reappeared, either, as if the Raven had its own Bermuda Triangle. "At this rate, it'll be you and me running the show," she said, smiling at Robbie.

"Which will be bad news because you're *awful* at pouring pints."

"Hey!" She mimed cuffing him around the head, and used the chance to stand a little nearer, letting her hand drop onto his arm. His hoodie smelled sweet and musty, as if he'd taken a nap in it, or worn it one day too many. "Did you and Leo have an argument?"

He sighed. "Not really."

"What does that mean?"

"You know how touchy he can be."

"So you *did* have an argument?"

"*No.*" He backed away from her with a soft groan. "I just . . ." Anguish flashed in his eyes, and Alice felt a wave of sympathy: It wasn't easy for him, being best mates with Leo. His moods were so up and down, and Robbie was a sponge for them, always had been. "We were working on a song, and I made, like, a comment about one of his lyrics . . ."

"What lyric? What comment?"

"It doesn't matter." He threw up his hands. "It was . . . nothing. He writes some dark shit sometimes and he doesn't like it when I . . ." He paused, then shook his head. "He acts like he's the only one with problems."

"He *has* been through a lot, Robs."

Robbie heaved another sigh, and Alice knew it was the wrong thing to say. He got tired of being the "together" one, sometimes. Tired of everybody making allowances for Leo while having sky-high expectations of him. She followed as he stalked to the other end of the bar and flung open the fridge. He stared into it, cold spooling out, and she recognized the pulse in his cheek: He was fighting tears again.

"Sorry, Robs," she said softly. "Please tell me what's bothering you. It's not just Leo, is it?"

He stayed silent. She could see his cheek drawn inward now, as if he was biting the inside. Gently, she pried his hand off the fridge door and closed it, shutting off the stream of chilled air.

Robbie sniffed. "I called him," he finally confessed.

"Who?"

"Dad."

"Oh." Alice closed her eyes, cursing Mike for the millionth time.

Robbie turned and leaned his back against the fridge, all long limbs and sagging shoulders. "Thought I'd wish him a happy new year in advance. Since he didn't bother calling at Christmas. Thought I'd at least try . . ."

Alice already knew the end of this story. Bloody Mike. It was an infuriating catch-22 that she couldn't curse the guy completely, couldn't wish she'd never got talking to him in a PizzaExpress on a rainy research trip to Oxford. Because that unexpected night had given her Robbie. And it wasn't as if she wished they'd got together, become a family. Mike was never supposed to be anything more than a fling. She just wished he'd show *some* interest in his son, for Robbie's sake alone.

"He didn't want to know. Said they had a flight to catch,

Tenerife or something, and he wished he could chat but they were in a rush, blah blah blah . . ."

"Oh, Robbie." She put her hands on each of his cheeks, leaned her forehead into his. "I'm sorry."

"Why do I bother?"

"Because you're wonderful."

"He's never given a shit, not since the day I was born. So why do I keep thinking he might?"

"Because—"

A door swung open and footsteps sounded from the stairs. They turned as Chrissy appeared, her face pinched with worry, tugging her fingers through the giant tangles in her hair.

"Sorry about that," she said, mustering a thin smile. "Thanks so much for holding the fort, both of you." She checked her watch, which seemed to sink into her wrist where flushed skin had swelled around it. "Better open the doors in a minute."

"Everything okay?" Alice asked, gesturing upward.

Chrissy's smile twitched. "All good. He'll be down in a sec."

Alice glanced at Robbie and caught him rolling his eyes. He and Leo would patch things up quickly, though, she was sure. Once everyone was here, once the drinks and the music were flowing. It was his hurt over his dad's indifference—*lifelong* indifference—that worried her more. The older Robbie got, the more she realized how deep it ran.

"This season can be hard," she said to neither of them in particular. "Especially for people whose families are non—"

"All right, Mum," Robbie cut her off. "We're here to get

drunk, not write a paper." But he was smirking now, his eyes dry. She went over and hugged him, pressing her face into his musty top.

"Mum . . ." he said, the note of a question in his voice.

"Yes?"

He paused. His chin rested on her head and she felt his jaw moving slightly against her skull.

"What?" she said, looking up toward him.

He looked back at her, his face serious, then shook his head and stepped away. "Nothing," he said before walking off, murmuring something about needing the toilet.

Alice smoothed her ruffled hair, frowning after him. As she turned, trying to remember what she'd been doing before, she jumped to see Chrissy watching her intently. Something in her expression made the coolness return to her skin, as if the fridge had swung back open.

"Can we just knock it on the head tonight, Alice?" Chrissy said, her voice strangely clipped.

Alice blinked. "What?"

"All the references to the past. Our 'problems.' Please, can you just stop bringing it up?"

"I didn't mean—"

"And that goes for Robbie, too, okay? I don't know what you've said to him but he's been making comments to Leo . . ."

"I haven't said anything!"

Chrissy fell silent, staring into space.

"Chris," Alice said, "I didn't mean to be insensitive. But to not talk about it at all—"

"Let's just stick to what we agreed, okay?"

Alice bit her lip, confused, stung, but not wanting an argument, not tonight. Chrissy strode away and Alice heard the slide of bolts, followed by a cheer as the first New Year's Eve drinkers tumbled in.

She straightened her dress and clasped her locket, picturing the dimpled baby Robbie inside. Her favorite night of the year, and everything felt off-kilter. Beyond the growing sea of heads, she caught sight of Leo coming down the stairs, at last, looking smart in a white shirt and vintage jeans, but with shadows under his eyes like deep black holes. Alice tried to smile at him, but a shiver rippled through her. Punters surged toward the bar, seeming to leer now rather than laugh, and the waft of outside air painted goosebumps all over her skin.

FOURTEEN

LEO

Friday, August 25, 2023

The credits rolled before Leo could answer Frank. They had something in common, he'd said? Or some*where*? The TV was abruptly turned off and the guards started urging them out of the room. "Cells! Time for lockup!"

Leo dithered, unsure whether to separate himself from Frank or stick with him to find out what he'd meant.

"You're from Cromley way, right, Dean?" Frank clapped a hand to his shoulder as they were jostled toward the landings.

Leo glanced at him. The hand was heavy, forcing him to walk with a stoop to one side. "I . . . yeah."

"Same neck of the woods," Frank said, pointing at his wide chest.

"Oh?" Somehow, sticking to minimal syllables felt safest. Leo had no idea how Frank knew about him, but it probably wasn't hard to find out about other inmates, he supposed, especially if you were someone like Frank.

"I'm from further north, but still the Dales," Frank said. "Been to Cromley once or twice, back in the day. Funny little place."

Leo raised his eyebrows. His feelings about Cromley were a mess these days, but in the past he'd never thought of it as anything but a normal village. As home.

Funny little place.

There was something compelling, though, about hearing it called that. As if Cromley might be the problem, not him, not what he did.

"Yup," he said, regardless, and Frank laughed.

"Don't give much away, do you?"

"Nope?" Even Leo was half-grinning now, relaxing a fraction. Maybe Frank was just being friendly. Maybe he just wanted to talk about where he came from, after however long he'd been inside. He'd been transferred here from a cat-B prison about five years ago, Leo had been told. How long he'd been in the higher-security place—or for what crime—nobody here quite seemed to know.

"Who are your people there?" Frank asked.

Leo tensed again. Places were one thing. Talking about people didn't feel so safe. And who *were* his people, now, apart from his mum? He remembered glancing at the public gallery during his trial, seeing rows of familiar Cromley faces. Feeling the hatred coming off them, stronger and stronger, and from the witness stand, too, as they brought their fragments of that night.

A push or a punch? I-I wouldn't like to say . . .

He always had a temper, but something came over him that night, scared us all . . .

"Not that I'd know them," Frank said, snapping him back. "But small world and all. You got family?" His face was suddenly closer to Leo's, like in the TV room, and Leo found himself subtly checking where the nearest guard was.

"Jordan!" bellowed Perez, gesturing for Frank to follow him to his cell.

Frank's nostrils flared. For a moment Leo thought he was going to argue—there always seemed that possibility with him, always an undercurrent—but Frank just tipped an imaginary hat at Leo and strode away, overtaking the guard without acknowledgment.

Leo sped up along the other landing, relief mingling with his usual gloom at the prospect of the long, locked-up night ahead. He glanced back and saw that Frank was also looking at him over his shoulder.

"Sleep tight, neighbor," Frank called, turning a few heads. "We'll . . . talk some more, yeah?"

Leo flushed and dipped his chin, hurrying to catch up with Cliff in the ever-noisy flow. The back of his brain was ticking now. Rewinding to when he'd first got here, when Cliff had warned him about Frank as part of a general things-you-should-know chat. Don't eat the cheese (*I don't know what it is, but it* isn't *cheese*) and don't piss off Frank Jordan. Amid the sheer relief of realizing his cellmate was a good guy, Leo had thought, fleetingly, that Frank looked a tiny bit familiar. That maybe he'd seen a broken nose like that somewhere before.

FIFTEEN

GEORGIE

Saturday, December 9, 2023

Hurrying toward Cromley church, Georgie checks her watch. She is late. It's the big day, the memorial she's worked so hard to arrange, and she's late and it's her own fault.

She just *had* to go to him this morning. Despite the distance, the lack of time, she needed to talk, off-load, admit her nerves about today.

Most important, she had to tell him that Leo was missing. Her voice cracked unexpectedly over the words. His disappearance is muddying everything; his face haunts her thoughts more and more.

But she didn't feel much better for getting it all off her chest. It seemed more desolate than ever, up in the Dales, and her bones grew cold from standing in the biting wind, talking and talking—checking, as always, to make sure she hadn't been followed.

Now her phone vibrates in her pocket. Lola. Again. Georgie cuts off the call and lengthens her stride: She can see, through the tall, thin windows, that some people are already inside the church. She strides past; she needs to pop into the pub first, to finish setting up for the post-memorial drinks. She pictures everybody in there for the first time since New Year's Eve 2021 and shivers with anticipation. Is it the right move? Is any of this going to help her get under Cromley's skin?

On the far side, she stops in her tracks. Chrissy is standing there, leather jacket zipped up to her chin, staring fixedly at the church.

Georgie is thrown. She's hardly seen Chrissy since she moved to the village. She tries not to show too much interest in her, not outwardly, but she's had a couple of slipups recently, curiosity getting the better of her. And now she is meters from her with nobody else around.

Steeling herself, Georgie walks closer. Chrissy's head turns her way, a flicker crossing her face. They appraise each other and Georgie's heart begins to thump.

Chrissy's hair is even more chaotic up close. Thick coils of it spring in counterintuitive directions, making Georgie's feel too flat, too salon-smooth. She looks older than she does from a distance, or in the Facebook pictures, but there's a spark in her tired eyes, a defiant set to her mouth. Georgie draws herself up taller, as she's seen Alice do. She doesn't normally feel the need, but Chrissy's presence, even as a much shorter woman, makes her want to add a couple of inches.

"Chrissy," she says warily. "Is everything okay?"

"No," Chrissy says. "No, everything is not okay."

Georgie nods slowly. She can smell the old leather of Chrissy's jacket in the cold air. "I heard about Leo." She keeps her voice even. "I'm sorry." She half-means it, her thoughts briefly drifting, but then she looks back at Chrissy and her edges re-sharpen.

Chrissy stares at her, hands twitching at her sides.

"What do you know about it?"

"Only . . . what I've heard . . ."

Chrissy's face darkens. "If you know something, now's the time to say."

"No, no, I don't know anything. I'm new here. And I know there are bad feelings in the village—"

"I will find him," Chrissy cuts in, her voice fierce but trembling ever so slightly. "Whatever's happened to him, I'm going to find out and bring him *home*."

She points at the icy ground, almost territorially. Her nostrils flare and her green eyes blaze, and Georgie wants to look away but somehow she can't. She never expected to see such fire in her. Such . . . *life*, even after all the deaths. Then something seems to catch Chrissy's attention, her gaze drawn to Georgie's hands. Georgie winds them together, conscious of the dirt under her nails from this morning's trip.

She thrusts them into her pockets and Chrissy frowns and seems to shake herself, pointing toward the church. "Someone in there knows where Leo is."

"But today is—"

"It's a public church. I could walk straight in, if I wanted. I could ask all the questions I need to."

Georgie starts to feel nervous, picturing Chrissy storming her carefully curated day. Could it work for her? The stir it would cause? The truths it might force to the surface? But things could whirl out of her control, and she hates to feel out of control.

In her moment of indecision, Chrissy steps past her, heading determinedly for the church.

"Wait . . ." Georgie snaps alert. Suddenly this feels like a battle of wills, which some deep-seated part of her needs to win. Ahead, she sees another group of people approaching the church from the opposite side. There's Rowena—in a mournful shade of her usual purple—and Janice with her husband and granddaughter. And, just behind them, a woman Georgie only recognizes from old Facebook pictures. Peter's ex-wife, Marianne. She's taller than she looked in the photos, and her hair is darker, almost black. In fact, from this distance, it's as if Peter married a near-copy of his sister.

"Chrissy," she says, following breathlessly, but it's too late, Rowena and Janice and Marianne have spotted the uninvited guest. They're turning, gaping, and Georgie doesn't want to be blamed for the ambush, can't give the villagers any more reasons not to trust her.

She sprints forward, pulling ahead of Chrissy. "It's okay," she says to the small crowd, who have stalled in front of the church. "It's okay—I'm dealing with it."

"You can't let her in there," Rowena says, looking stricken. "Not today."

"I won't." Georgie puts herself between Chrissy and the church doors, spreading her arms like a goalkeeper.

But Chrissy has stopped and is staring at the group, eyes still blazing. "I just want to know where my son is."

They shuffle worriedly. Janice grips her granddaughter's hand.

"We have no idea," Rowena says. "Why would we?"

Chrissy shakes her head, a flush in her cheeks. "One of you knows something. One of you out here, or in there . . ."

Georgie plants her feet in the entranceway, feeling faintly ridiculous. From inside, behind her, she hears organ music and subdued chatter; nobody else seems to have noticed the disturbance. Then suddenly Chrissy dives at her, shouldering her aside. Georgie stumbles and tries to grab her, but somebody else jumps forward, pulling Chrissy back by her elbow.

It's Marianne. "Chrissy, what the *fuck?* Don't do this! It isn't the time!"

"Stay out of it, Marianne." Chrissy pushes her away, and Marianne's face goes slack with anger.

It's fascinating, Georgie has to admit. She almost wants to let the stirred pot boil. But she's playing the hero now, the others looking at her pleadingly. "Let's all just stay calm," she says, scrambling back to her position in the doorway. *"Please."*

"The police are in there," Rowena says. "Shall I go and . . . ?"

"Police?" Georgie is distracted. "At the memorial?"

"Ellen texted me to say they're sitting in the back row. Just . . . watching everyone."

At this, Chrissy steps abruptly back. She draws her arms into her chest, looking around, blinking and breathing hard.

"I . . . I'm . . ." She takes another step back, shaking her head as if she doesn't quite know what happened.

Georgie stares at her. *Don't you fancy a run-in with the police, Chrissy Dean?* She squares her shoulders, looking her in the eye. "Shall we fetch them?" she asks. "Or are you going to leave people to pay their respects in peace?"

Chrissy's gaze darts back to Georgie's hand, as if the phrase *pay your respects* has reminded her. But Chrissy can't possibly know the dirt is from a grave. *His* grave. Georgie thinks of the cold earth tumbling over her skin as she planted snowdrops all around his headstone. *I'm doing my best for you,* she'd rambled as she patted down the soil. *I'm in among them all, as much as I can be, watching and listening. But everything is crazy lately. Leo . . . Leo is . . .*

Then something else occurs to Georgie, in this strange moment, and her heart drops into her stomach. Could it be her ring catching Chrissy's attention? It's such an integral part of Georgie's hand that she's barely conscious of it anymore, but if she took it off, she'd feel like she'd lost a finger. Has she been foolish to keep wearing it? Does Chrissy recognize it, somehow?

Chrissy's eyes travel up to Georgie's face, locking with hers. Georgie itches to tug down her sleeve but doesn't want to draw further attention. Is this it? The moment her cover's going to be blown? Then she hears footsteps, sees Chrissy's attention slip, and turns, gratefully, to see a man in a suit emerging from the church.

"I'm Detective Colella." He casts a look at Rowena and the others, who have become a huddle again, apart from Marianne standing watchfully apart. His eyes flicker over Georgie, landing back on Chrissy. "Can we speak with you, Ms. Dean?"

A woman in a lighter gray suit emerges behind him. She

doesn't introduce herself, but it's clear, somehow, that she's a detective, too.

Chrissy looks from one to the other. "I was just . . . I only want to . . ."

"We have some updates for you," Colella says, and Chrissy's expression transforms.

"About Leo?" Her voice is full of strained hope. Georgie tries to keep her own face neutral, but something strains inside her, too.

"We were going to call at your house after the memorial," Colella says. "But since you're here . . ." He narrows his eyes. "Perhaps we could go there now?"

Chrissy nods. "Yes. Yes, we can do that."

They walk away, leaving a dazed silence behind them, everyone straightening their clothes, composing themselves. Georgie exhales and fusses with her hair, trying to stop her thoughts from chasing Chrissy and the detectives, longing to know what they've found. She has to get it together. Get back to her plan. Smile, observe, notice. Ask questions, *subtle* questions, when opportunities arise. She can't mess this up. She's doing it for him, for everything that should've been.

She looks at Marianne, whose expression is still rigid with anger. "Right!" Georgie finds the smile she's been practicing in the mirror: sad but warm, respectful but engaged. It falters but she pins it firmly in place. "Let's get back to what today is supposed to be all about. Shall we?"

SIXTEEN

CHRISSY

Saturday, December 9, 2023

Chrissy scoops up the empty sweet wrappers that litter her sofa cushions—flustered, fumbling—and motions for the detectives to sit down. She's no longer comforting herself by bingeing on chips, but sucking hard-boiled sweets is the only thing that keeps her anxious nausea at bay.

She glances from one detective to the other: the dark-haired, clean-shaven DC Colella and the woman—DC Wright—with a sharp silver bob and penciled-on brows. She's shaken from her encounter with Georgie, her own outburst at the church. *Let them have good news for me. Please, please, please.*

"Is it Leo?" she blurts. "Is there something?"

"We're the detectives who've been assigned to his case," says DC Colella. "We haven't tracked him down yet, but we have some things we'd like to talk through with you. We're all very anxious to resolve this."

Chrissy tugs at a tangle in her hair. *Resolve this.* Not *make sure he's okay.* There's a difference that seems bigger and harsher the longer she dwells on it.

"Leo's phone and bank card have not been used since his release," he tells her.

"Is that . . . ?" She chokes on her own question: *Is that good or bad?*

She knows it's bad.

"But we have some CCTV footage," Wright says briskly, and Chrissy jolts in her seat.

How do they know about the camera in her hedge? It's been hidden there for less than twelve hours and she's told nobody about it.

"It shows Leo leaving the prison at eight thirty A.M. on the day of his release," Detective Wright says.

Of course. Not *her* CCTV. Chrissy shakes herself, refocusing on what they're telling her. Leo left almost an hour before she arrived to collect him. She should've got there at dawn, camped out all night. Her guilt starts spiraling, but she hauls herself back once again.

Detective Colella is opening a laptop on the coffee table. "Can we show you the footage, Ms. Dean?"

Chrissy clenches her stomach. She wants to ask what she's about to see but her mouth has frozen and the laptop has been swiveled toward her, footage starting to play. The familiar prison gates, the grim-looking building behind them, the white sky and low gray clouds.

Then, Leo. Her heart soars at the sight of him. He's stepping out tentatively, walking into the world as if he doesn't quite believe nobody will stop him. Chrissy aches as she watches him clutching his few belongings in a clear plastic bag, like a schoolkid on exam day. How she wishes she could climb into the computer, wrap him up tightly in her arms.

She sees him pause. Something has caught his attention off to the right—or some*one*, perhaps, exasperatingly out of shot. Chrissy shifts the laptop as if it will make the camera pan around. Leo is absolutely still, looking that way, his face unreadable in the grainy image. He snaps his gaze back and continues walking, glancing warily—almost furtively—around him. Then he stops again. Turns back to the right. He pulls up his hood and starts moving in that direction, half-jogging, disappearing out of shot.

Chrissy lets out a cry of protest, turning to the detectives. "Is there another camera? Another angle? Can we see where he's gone?"

"I'm afraid not," Detective Colella says. "He isn't picked up on camera again. But . . ." He takes the laptop back and moves his finger on the mouse pad, clicking several times. "We *are* interested in this."

He turns it to face Chrissy. She is still recovering from seeing Leo, breathing choppily, wanting him back. Now she's looking at an image of a quiet, unremarkable street.

"This is just around the corner from the prison," Wright says. "Twenty minutes before Leo was released."

Chrissy sits forward, hardly daring to blink. A battered white car pulls up and idles for a moment. The driver is indistinct but appears to be a man wearing a dark baseball cap and a scarf. One of the detectives leans over Chrissy and zooms in. The image granulates even further, but the driver is clearly on the phone, one large, gloved hand gesticulating in the air.

After he hangs up, he half-opens the door of the car, then pauses, his gaze seeming to snag on the camera. For a second he stares directly at it. Still his face is fuzzy, his eyes the only focal point between his hat and scarf. He slams the door and the car roars off.

Chrissy sits back. "What . . . what has that got to do with Leo?"

"Maybe nothing," Wright says. "But we ran the registration through our systems—we've been checking vehicles captured by CCTV in the area around that time—and discovered that it's a stolen car."

"Is there anything to indicate Leo might've gone off in it?"

"Not as yet. It was caught on a speed camera an hour later, heading north. But since then, nothing. We'll be alerted anytime its registration triggers a camera. It could be a false lead, but . . ."

"You don't recognize the car, do you?" Detective Wright jumps in.

Chrissy frowns, shaking her head. "Where was it stolen from?"

"A residential address in Derby, two weeks ago. Has Leo ever been involved in vehicle theft, to your knowledge?"

"No!" Chrissy straightens up. "Of course not!"

She can't process it all, can't fit it in with anything else she thinks she knows. Detective Wright is standing up now, Colella closing the laptop, zipping it back into its shiny leather case. They're leaving and she is floundering, playing catch-up. As they make for the door she shakes herself alert.

"His visitation records," she blurts. "Did you get those from the prison?"

Colella pauses with one foot out of the living room. "We've requested them. We'll contact you as soon as we know anything further."

"While we're here," Wright says. "Do you have anything that might have Leo's DNA on it?"

"What?"

"A hairbrush, toothbrush? It's . . . procedure. Just in case . . ." Wright clears her throat. "We may need to identify . . ."

Chrissy's lungs shrink in her chest. *This can't be happening. None of it.* And she doesn't have anything to offer them, because Leo has never lived here, has been using prison toothbrushes and combs, leaving his DNA all over a cell instead of his spotless, untouched bedroom.

"No, no, I don't . . ." It is this, on top of everything else, that chokes her up completely. Not even a single strand of Leo's hair is in her home.

The detectives exchange an inscrutable glance and then leave her be, promising to get back in touch. Chrissy watches them go, left with more questions than answers. Was someone other than her waiting for Leo near the prison that day?

She closes her eyes as it all rushes over her. White cars and red marker pen and the gray sky behind the gray prison gates. After a few moments she walks to the window, letting in a blast of fresh, cold air. Her gaze falls on the frosty hedge in front of her cottage and she thinks of the camera hiding inside. She ordered it yesterday, after realizing the police weren't entirely in her corner, that she might have to take matters into her own hands. *And after you made the decision not to show them all of the notes,* she reminds herself with a twist of guilt. Express delivery, and the camera had arrived late last night, in a conspicuously large box for such a small thing. Maybe she should've done it a year ago. Swallowed her fear and pride and found out who hated her enough to hand-deliver threats to her house.

She grabs her phone, opening the associated app. She didn't hear anything overnight, but the compulsion to check is irresistible.

She scrolls through an hour or so of dark nothing, just the icy moonlit lane and the occasional bird or bat flitting across the lens. It makes her think of the wildlife camera Ethan bought her for her birthday one year. He'd said it was to capture birds and foxes in the garden of the pub, said little Leo would love it, too. But she wonders now whether he wanted to keep tabs on her comings and goings, and a shiver drops down her spine.

Then her breath catches and she is back in the present. There *is* someone on the screen: 12:23 A.M. and there's a figure advancing up the lane. Head down, hood up, ends of a scarf flapping in the wind. Not wearing the same clothes as the person the detectives showed her, but with the same sense of being bundled up, frustratingly unrecognizable.

There *is* something familiar about them, though, as they get closer. Their walk, their stature. They stop right in front of her house, staring up at it. Just like in the prison CCTV, the eyes are the only distinct part of their face.

But this time, she recognizes them. She looked into them less than an hour ago.

Georgie.

What the hell was she doing outside Chrissy's cottage after midnight?

Georgie stands there as the clock in the bottom corner shows the passing of one minute, two minutes, almost three. Then she turns and walks back the way she came, her hood blown back to reveal her long dark hair.

Chrissy puts down the phone, her heart racing. Was she right, then? About Georgie's ring? It was just a thin gold ring, but there was a delicate leaf pattern etched into the metal, only noticeable if you really stared. A coincidence, she'd thought earlier, even though she couldn't *stop* staring. But Georgie had acted so strangely. And she'd been outside her house in the early hours of this morning.

Could it really be the same ring Chrissy had seen, once, on Ethan's computer screen? The night he'd called her a nosy, suspicious bitch for asking, as mildly as she could, who he was shopping for?

She closes her eyes, picturing the ring, remembering that evening. And all the times he would disappear overnight, never explaining, but furious if she wasn't at home waiting for him when he returned. She suspected there were other women, of course. But she knew better than to ask, trained herself to stop caring.

If Georgie was one of them, what is she doing in Cromley, nearly four years after his death?

Her thoughts propel her into the kitchen, to the drawer where the note she held back from the police still lurks inside. She studies the handwriting—black pen, this one, not red—and the wording, the message: so much more pointed, personal, than all the others. So much more knowing.

Next to it is a small velvet pouch, covered in dust. She opens its tightly knotted drawstring, unfurls the locket on its silver chain. Flipping the heart open, she kisses Leo's pudgy, perfect face, then she brings the note and the locket over to the table and studies them side by side. A threat and a promise. From the same person? About the same binding, inescapable thing? Or does somebody else have a window into her past? Somebody she wouldn't have given a second thought to until today?

A bang sends the question flying out of her head. She jumps up in shock and feels a gust of cold wind and then there is someone here, someone in her house, advancing toward her with a balaclava over their face and something raised in their hand. Chrissy freezes. Scissors. It's a pair of scissors. She sees the glint of the metal, the black fingers of a glove, and a scream dies in her throat as the sharp point of the blades rushes toward her.

SEVENTEEN

ALICE

Saturday, December 9, 2023

Alice is suffocating, as if the church is filling up with water rather than people. She can see Marianne near the entrance and wants to push her way through to her, but she keeps getting stopped by people offering condolences that seem displaced in time. As soon as they move away, they're back to whispering about Leo, passing around rumors in hushed tones.

Have the police spoken to you?

Do they think he's done a runner?

What if he's up to something?

I don't trust him. And who knows what prison might've—

She keeps making her way toward her ex-sister-in-law, growing more and more desperate. Peter seems to have disappeared; it's becoming his party trick, and it does nothing to help her anxiety when she can't lay eyes on him. She spots Jack skulking at the edges of the room, looking as if he doesn't know what he should be doing, either. He always seems happiest when painting or drilling or sawing, lost in his own world. Alice thinks about going over to talk to him about the initials on the wall of the pub. But she sees Georgie striding in through the main doors—she's been coming and going since she arrived, a swirl of strange energy—and heading purposefully toward her.

"Alice, are you okay?" Georgie asks. "We're nearly ready to start. What do you . . ." She gestures around the church. "What do you . . . think?"

Alice is caught off guard. What does she think? The church has been swept and cleaned and filled with strong-smelling lilies. There is an enlarged photo of Robbie at the front that Georgie must've pulled off social media because Alice doesn't remember giving it to her. It's a picture he hated. Or is she mixing it up with another one, his prom photo after that bad haircut? She presses her temples, feeling suddenly drowned in pollen.

"It all looks . . . nice." It's all she can muster, but Georgie puts a hand to her own chest.

"I'm so glad," she says. "I never knew Robbie, but I feel like I did—I've heard so much about him . . ."

Alice stares at her baldly. The light through the stained-glass windows shines in Georgie's expensively cut hair and turns her cream trench coat into a rainbow.

"Why are you doing all this, Georgie?" The question slips out before she can stop it. "All this, today . . . ?"

Georgie's cheeks redden and she looks briefly offended. Then Alice sees her demeanor change, like a swap to a different mask, and she smiles gently. "I care, Alice. I know you might not believe that, but I do. I care about you, about this village. It's my home now. And I think . . . I might be being presumptuous . . . but I consider you a friend. A friend who's going through something unimaginable. Who needs people on her side right now."

The words are all the right ones but something about them rings hollow. Maybe it's just the way she's feeling. Nothing and nobody seems straightforward.

"I'd better . . ." Georgie gestures vaguely, and Alice nods, letting it go. Georgie gives her arm an encouraging squeeze and then bustles away, pulling a box of candles out of her enormous handbag.

Alice releases a long, long sigh. She wants to go home. Wants to lie on the sofa with Beech and smell his doggy breath and stroke his fur while he snores.

But she turns to her right and there, at last, is Marianne.

"Alice," she says.

Peter's ex-wife looks much the same—smartly dressed, tall in her heeled ankle boots—except there is *something* intangibly different, some sign or reminder that she is removed from Alice now, and from this place. A different perfume, her mascara smudged as if she's been rubbing at her eyes.

"It's good to see you," Alice says, feeling wobbly.

Marianne hesitates—they both do—and then they hug, clumsily at first, easing into a firmer embrace. They haven't seen each other since Alice scattered Robbie's ashes in the most beautiful part of the Dales, at the top of the tall viaduct he had a fascination with as a kid. Peter drove her out there, but Marianne joined them unexpectedly, even though the two of them had separated by then. Alice was so surprised and moved to see Marianne that her tears erupted even before she'd flung Robbie's ashes into the wind.

"It's . . . strange being back," Marianne says as they draw apart.

Alice nods. "Everything is strange."

"And Peter . . ." Marianne looks around with a sigh. "Peter seems to be avoiding me."

"Where *is* he?" Alice looks again, too. People are starting to take their seats, at Georgie's instruction, and the church is becoming a map of the village cliques, more evident in their little groups than Alice has ever seen. An image shoots through her mind of Peter lying in a ditch, bottle in hand. She should've known he wouldn't be able to handle today. He hates anything that turns his private sorrow public.

"I don't know," Marianne says. "I don't think he's quite forgiven me."

"For what?" Alice frowns, turning back to her. "I thought . . ." She pauses. "I didn't think any of it was your fault? I mean . . . he hasn't told me much about why you split up. But I got the impression he just . . . stopped trying? After . . ." She glances toward the photo of her son at the front of the church, painfully huge, and then she is choked again, knowing she could easily be describing herself. She remembers how close Peter and Marianne once were—never showy about it, rarely soppy, but always in harmony, it seemed, always considerate of each other. Peter used to slip out to the pub when Marianne's favorite TV shows were on, but Marianne would join him afterward and he'd look so happy to see her—*every* time—that Alice's unsentimental heart would melt.

"I don't mean the breakup," Marianne says. "We . . . argued a couple of days ago. I think maybe he's still upset."

Alice is thrown. "I didn't know you were still in touch."

"He didn't tell you?"

"No . . ."

"We've been trying to talk things through. Not very successfully." Marianne presses her hands on either side of her neck. She's wearing two chunky silver rings but not her wedding one. "He's a confusing man, your brother. I'm still trying to understand him, even after all these years."

"Tell me about it," Alice says faintly. Her mind is wheeling back over the last few days, trying to remember if Peter mentioned anything. "He's been . . . We've both been under a lot of strain. Since Leo got out."

Marianne's face visibly tenses. "Yes." She drags a finger across her left eyelid, smudging her mascara even further. "That's obviously been . . . difficult."

"When was it you argued?" Alice asks.

"Um . . . Thursday, I think?"

The day Peter fell off the wagon. Did they argue while he was drunk, or did he get drunk because they argued? Before Alice can ask, Marianne grabs her hand.

"Alice, Chrissy was here," she says, almost crushing her fingers.

"What? When?"

"Just now. She was trying to get in here. Shouting about Leo."

Alice feels a white-hot surge of rage. "That bitch," she breathes, shocking herself with the force of her tone. "Today? How dare she . . ."

"She was *out of order*." Now it's Marianne's tone—normally so mild—that startles her. Each word is a precise cut. It makes Alice feel better, less alone, yet a chill goes through her that she doesn't quite understand.

She looks toward the door, rolling her shoulders in agitation. Will Chrissy try again? What if she does? Her eyes pan the church and she sees Georgie going from person to person, collecting pieces of paper and slipping them into a black leather folder. *Now* what is she doing? Alice is momentarily distracted, then her eye is caught by something else: Kiri and Ben in the back row, staring straight at her. Ben averts his gaze more quickly than Kiri, looking down at his hands.

"I sometimes think we never really knew Chrissy," Marianne says, tugging Alice's attention back. "She was always . . ." Her eyes have hardened. "There was always something. Like she was hiding stuff, not being honest, even back when we were all friends."

Alice wants to agree, to vent some more, but her throat narrows and she can't seem to say a thing.

A crackle of microphone feedback interrupts them, and Georgie's voice booms through the speakers in the high ceiling of the church.

"Take your seats, please, everyone! Our tributes to darling Robbie are about to begin."

Alice's heart starts to pound. *Darling Robbie.* Georgie didn't even know him. But she is beckoning her, pointing to a pew right at the front. Everybody gawps as Alice begins to make her way slowly toward it. She's walking down the aisle, but there's no music this time, no coffin, just silence and suspense and the extra weight of knowing that Chrissy could burst in, or even Leo, choosing this moment to reappear from wherever he might be.

A few people stand up as she passes them, as if it's a wedding and she's the unsmiling bride. Kiri's head turns, watching her all the way. And now she's even more self-conscious about the flat thud of her footsteps, the expression on her face, the people she makes eye contact with as she tries to reach the end of an apparently endless aisle.

What if, when it comes to her moment to say a few words about Robbie, other things pour unstoppably out of her mouth? All the secrets, the history, the lies that even the village gossips would never suspect.

What if she chose this day—this strange, skewed day—to blow all their minds?

EIGHTEEN

CHRISSY

New Year's Eve 2021

Marianne was as dressed up as Alice that night. From behind the bar, Chrissy looked over at the pair of them, sitting near the jukebox, laughing and pouring from a bottle of wine that anybody and everybody seemed to be sharing. Marianne normally dressed as if she'd just come from the office, even though she worked from home, designing websites, but tonight she wore a fitted black dress with a shimmer of gold jewelry and high-heeled rose-gold boots. Peter kept touching her leg, smiling dotingly at her, and some of the other men were sneaking admiring glances at her, too, and at Alice, everyone's skin a little flushed from the booze.

Chrissy felt a pang of envy as she mopped beer off the bar, splashing yet more drops down her T-shirt. Not just because she was stuck here, distanced from the fun, but because of the flirtatious energy that seemed to swirl so naturally around the others, skimming them with the lightest touch. If she so much as winked at a punter, she'd still hear Ethan's voice in her head calling her a slut and a prick-tease. If she ever felt a stirring of desire, even for a guy on the TV with nice eyes or sexy tattoos, she'd tell herself, *No, that's not for you, not after everything.*

She sighed and looked around the rest of the pub, doing her usual checks that all was okay. There were more flushed faces, bright eyes, loud voices, tides of laughter. Ellen sitting on Dave's knee while he jiggled her up and down and she spilled her sherry and shrieked at him to pack it in. Poppy and Jack playing darts dangerously close to where Sara and her wife were dancing and trying to turn up the volume on the jukebox, even though that wasn't possible. Rowena buzzing around selling tickets to an amateur production of *Jesus Christ Superstar.* And everyone reminiscing, it seemed, with the wistfulness that New Year's Eves often brought, exchanging old pub stories and becoming misty-eyed and reflective.

Chrissy's heart sank when she saw Leo sitting on his own in the darkest corner, flicking a beer mat into the air and trying to catch it between finger and thumb. It was a game he and Robbie usually played together, but there was no sign of Robbie, and Leo looked joyless, even when he pulled off what they'd normally dub an "epic catch." The repetitive motion, the cartwheel of the mat in the air, the mechanical flick of his wrist. She couldn't help thinking of the coping rituals Leo had retreated into after Ethan's death. Throwing that wretched tennis ball at his bedroom wall again and again. The constant, maddening thud. It was Alice who'd talked to him eventually, persuaded him to stop: Chrissy had just accepted it as part of their new life, part of the haunted claustro-phobia Ethan had left behind.

They should've talked more, after it happened. She should've been a better mum. But she couldn't, she just couldn't.

Now her gaze flitted back to Alice's group and she was startled to find Marianne staring over at her. Chrissy blinked, and Marianne looked away without smiling. *Weird*, Chrissy thought, reaching for her glass and taking a glug of IPA. Feeling eyes on her again, she glanced up, but Marianne was talking to Peter now, whispering into his ear. It was Peter's eye that Chrissy caught this time. Paranoia bloomed and she tried to stamp it down before it could grow; tried to tell herself, as she had before, that it was all in her mind. Nobody knew her secrets. Nobody knew the truth.

Except for one person. She saw Alice fiddling with her locket and touched hers under her T-shirt, too.

To match mine, Alice had said when she'd first pressed it into Chrissy's palm, making a heart-shaped dimple in her skin. *A reminder that I'll always be here for you. That we'll always have each other. And nobody will ever hurt you again.*

Robbie emerged from the garden and Alice looked up, as did Leo from his table across the room. Alice motioned for Robbie to join—or perhaps rejoin—her group, and Chrissy felt a flicker of anger: Why had she left Leo to drink alone? She knew, really, that Alice would have tried to coax him over, that it was probably Leo who had chosen to isolate himself, but her earlier irritation clung on. Alice's pushiness about the flat. And what Leo had said upstairs: *Robbie keeps bringing up my dad—or dads in general, at least—and I wish he'd fucking stop with it.*

To her surprise, though, she saw Robbie hesitating, looking between his mum's lively crowd and Leo's solitary table, as if torn. Where had he been sitting before he'd gone outside? Chrissy wasn't sure; she'd had a rush on at the bar. Peter shuffled to make a space for Robbie next to him, which Chrissy thought would be the clincher: Robbie loved nothing more than having a pint with his uncle. But his mouth turned down, ever so slightly, and he went to sit with Leo.

It should've made Chrissy happy. Robbie started doing the beer-mat-flicking thing alongside Leo, almost a reflex, but they didn't cheer and heckle each other like usual. It was like two tennis balls thumping wretchedly against a wall. Robbie kept glancing over at his mum and Marianne and Peter, as if he regretted his choice. Or as if, perhaps, his choice had been less about wanting to sit with Leo and more about not wanting to sit with them. Peter looked confused, a little crestfallen, and Alice glanced Chrissy's way.

"What is going on tonight?" Chrissy murmured under her breath, then masked it with a smile as Ellen came up to the bar asking for another sherry.

She checked the clock as she poured it. Less than an hour to go. Chrissy fought an urge to hide under the bar, raise her head only when everyone had gone and it felt safe to look the new year in the eye, ask it what it had in store.

NINETEEN

GEORGIE

Saturday, December 9, 2023

Georgie sits in a pew toward the back of the church, rows of heads in front of her, as people stand up one by one to pay tribute to Robbie. She twists her ring around her finger and draws a diagram in her mind of everybody who is here, those who aren't here, how they connect to one another. Rowena is ostentatiously passing tissues around. Poppy blows her nose into one; Ellen clutches Dave's hand; Jack runs his thumb over the smooth curve of the pew arm.

At the center of her diagram are Leo, Chrissy, Alice, Robbie, Peter.

Ethan.

It all comes back to the six of them, she is sure, and the toxic tangle of their relationships. But the more she watches and mentally adds to her diagram, the more questions crowd in. She remembers the way Marianne and Chrissy snarled at each other before the memorial. She notes that Peter isn't here, that Robbie's dad doesn't seem to be in the picture at all. And she thinks, again, of the stranger who spoke to her outside the Raven that time—*Are you Alice Lowe?* he'd said, and then, when she'd told him she wasn't: *Never trust a Lowe.*

His words were so similar to what Ethan used to say about Alice, back when she was just a faceless name to Georgie. That he didn't trust her. That she was jealous of him for taking Chrissy's attention away from her, even the meager amount Chrissy deigned to give him. Ethan never talked much about his life in the village, but Georgie held on to the names he did mention; she circled back to them after his death, again and again, wondering what it was she hadn't seen.

Now Rowena is at the front talking about Robbie's sweet, sweet nature, and Georgie opens the black folder in her lap as quietly as she can, sliding out the papers inside. She asked everyone who RSVPed to either bring along their favorite photo of Robbie or write down their fondest memory. She shunts through them all, scouring for insights into Cromley's past. There are a few photos she hasn't seen before. She drinks them in with the same feeling as always: a sense of peeping into the parts of Ethan's life she never had access to while he was alive. And Ethan *is* in some of them: running a raffle stall at a school fete, while a young Robbie shows off his prize in the foreground; sitting in the corner of the Raven while Robbie plays guitar in the middle of the shot, turning to look at something, his face in profile, a little blurred from movement. Leo has clearly been trimmed out of some of these. But his dad has been left in, as if any pain about his death has been subsumed by the tragedy and scandal of Robbie's.

Not for Georgie, though. There is a connection; she feels it. There is a truth that needs ripping out from the center of it all.

She swallows and turns her attention to the memories of Robbie people have written down. White sheets of paper, folded in half like voting slips. She unfolds them one at a time and reads about funny things Robbie apparently said, his infamously bad driving, the sponsored gaming marathon he did for charity. Some older memories from when he was little: *such a cute baby, such a bright little boy.*

There is only one that makes her pause. Robbie's old primary school teacher—Layla, is it?—has brought a piece that Robbie wrote when he was young, under the assignment "Somebody You Admire." "My Uncle Peter," it's called. The wobbly handwriting and drawing of a stickman in a policeman's hat should be endearing, moving, but as she reads the words, all she thinks about is Peter hiding the scrapbook of Leo-related cuttings deep inside the dumpster.

My uncle peter is a policeman. He helps peeple and peeple like him and ask him for things. Everybody nose him. He catches bad guys like the man who made things go on fire. He is very brave.

Georgie looks at the drawing again. There is something next to the grinning stick figure, a scribble of orange crayon, like a flame. *The man who made things go on fire?* Then she sees a flicker out of the corner of her eye, a blaze of orange, and she jolts upright until she realizes Rowena is lighting a candle for Robbie, its flame leaping high at the front of the church.

Everyone claps and Georgie blinks out of her reverie. But as the clapping dies away, there's a disturbance on the other side of the aisle: urgent voices and people springing to their feet in a flurry of unexpected activity. It's the police—the constables in uniform and the detectives in suits who returned just as the tributes were starting. They are pushing past people to get out of their pew. Their radios are buzzing and everyone is turning, like a wave, trying to steal a look. In the arched doorway of the main part of the church, they have a whispered conference. Georgie hears one of them say, "Injured?" and then two of them leave—the female PC and the female detective—while the other two remain, hovering awkwardly.

Silence falls. Georgie sees a fluorescent uniform and a dark suit flash past the window. The atmosphere in the church is ruffled. Somehow the candle that Rowena lit has blown out, and everyone frowns at each other in confusion.

Georgie shoves the papers and photos back into the folder. Alice is standing up, her head turning between the window and the remaining two officers standing at the back. Who is supposed to be speaking next? Georgie can't remember; she let herself get too absorbed. Alice is moving toward the lectern. She isn't due to speak till right at the end but she has a determined look in her eye and nobody, of course, will stop her.

TWENTY

ALICE

Saturday, December 9, 2023

Alice grips the sides of the lectern and looks out over the rows of familiar, expectant faces. She feels that burn in her belly again, that pulse right through her core. There is total silence. She catches Ben's eye at the back of the room, the dark-haired male detective standing next to him, before focusing on a random spot of sunlight in the center of the aisle.

Time for the truth, says a voice in her head. But even as she opens her mouth, she isn't sure which of her truths she wants to tell. Which she *can* tell.

"I appreciate you all being here," she says, and pauses, wondering if even *this* is true. Realizing, actually, that it is. Gossips and cliques aside, her neighbors have all turned out for her son today. They're looking up at her with soft, sad faces and they're her people, whether they drive her mad sometimes or not.

She takes a deep breath. "But the awful truth is . . . I don't feel Robbie's presence here today." At this she catches Georgie's eye, sees displeasure flash across her face. "All I feel . . . all I can think about . . . is Leo Dean."

A ripple goes through the crowd, though surely they can't be surprised. She notices Marianne bowing her head and pressing the bridge of her nose. Sees the detective straightening up, Ben shifting his weight, and she falters, wondering if she's making a mistake being this honest, this public, especially with Peter acting strangely and Ben giving cryptic warnings about investigations. They should know, though, how she feels. That she won't apologize for it. This has nothing to do with Peter. Besides, he isn't here, is he? *He isn't here.* She realizes she's more angry about this than she even knew.

"We were all so worried about Leo coming back to Cromley," she continues, swallowing. "I know *I* was. I was horrified, furious, *sick* with it, as soon as the Probation Service told me he'd be allowed back. I'd tried so hard to hold on to the things I used to love about this village—that Robbie used to love—and to take control of the things that got destroyed that night. The night that he . . ." Her voice breaks and she flattens her palms on the lectern, leaning against it. "So to think of Leo Dean back here, free to go wherever he wanted, do whatever he wanted . . . it was devastating. *Terrifying.*"

Through her tears she sees some people nodding, some people looking down at their laps, some fidgeting as if unsure how to respond. She presses on. She needs to say it all out loud and then she needs to get the hell out of here.

"But this . . . this limbo . . . It's even worse. Where is he? What's his plan? Strange things have been happening . . . appearing . . . Like messages, or . . ." She trails off, taking in her audience again. Marianne has lifted her head and is watching her intently. Georgie is on the edge of her seat, wide-eyed, as if poised to intervene. The detective writes something discreetly in his notebook.

"All I'm saying is . . ." *What are you saying, Alice? What are you doing?* Her confidence starts to die but she seeks out the people who are still nodding supportively, feeling another squeeze of gratitude amid all the bitterness. "I want to re-member Robbie. Talk about him. Of *course* I do. But I can't do that while . . ." She turns her head toward the window just as the light shifts across the square, and suddenly, like some-thing looming out from behind a cloud, she sees it. Beady eyes. Black wings. Like an apparition floating in midair.

She freezes completely, staring out at it. There is some shuffling in the crowd as people lean forward to try to see what's diverted her. Alice opens her mouth, but nothing more comes out. She steps down from the lectern and runs out of the church.

AS SHE STRIDES across the square toward the pub, she glances back and sees that almost everybody is following her. The cliques move together and the people who no longer live in the village are on the edges, all murmuring worriedly. The police are there, too, the flash of Ben's jacket somewhere to-ward the rear.

"Alice?" she hears Georgie calling. "Alice! What's wrong?"

Alice comes to a stop in front of the pub and feels the energy of the crowd surging up behind her.

She raises her hand. "What the . . . ?"

Georgie finally clocks what she's pointing at. She lets out a small, surprised noise.

"Why is the sign back up?" Alice breathes.

She'd sawed it off herself, as soon as the pub became hers: her first small defiant act after taking control. But now the raven is back in place. It even looks as if it's had a fresh paint job: Its eyes seem sharper, its wings a deeper black; the pub's former name blares in yellow letters underneath. The bird stares down at Alice, as if to say, *You can't change anything, really. You can't fight back. You can try, but you won't succeed.*

"Did you put it back up?" she demands of Georgie.

"No." Georgie sounds bewildered. "No, I don't . . ."

"Jack?" Alice seeks him out in the crowd. "Ellen?"

Heads shake. Other people move in closer, trying to understand. Alice imagines the painted raven flapping its wings to rise out of the dumpster and fly to its previous perch. But a more realistic scenario elbows that aside: Chrissy, or even Leo, creeping around the garden of the pub, pulling it out of the trash, hanging it back up like a reassertion, or a threat.

Rage floods into every part of her. She turns and peers through the crowd to where Ben and the detective are hovering.

"Excuse me!" she says breathlessly, and begins to push her way toward them, not caring anymore what they might think or ask or infer. She hears Marianne's voice, and Georgie's, urging her to slow down, take a moment, but she blocks them all out, seeing only the initials in the wall, the brightened eyes of that horrible bird, the red blaze of her own anger.

She won't let Robbie's memory be trolled. The pub is her battleground now, and she'll fight for her son, who can no longer fight back himself. She won't let the blows keep coming, over and over again.

TWENTY-ONE

LEO

Wednesday, September 20, 2023

"Leo?" Cliff looked up from his book as Leo wandered, dazed, into their cell. "Leo, man, you okay?"

Leo didn't know. He really didn't. He sank onto the bottom bunk and closed his eyes. Behind his lids he saw Cromley as if from above, as if he were a bird soaring over it, looking for somewhere to land. A raven, maybe: the raven from the pub sign that he'd dreamed about constantly when he'd first got here. He hovered at the windows of his old flat, saw his dad sitting in his green armchair—always exclusively his—and his mum in the bedroom, keeping out of his way. Downstairs, there was Robbie, with a beer mat pinched between his finger and thumb, and a strange, dark look in his eyes.

"Where you been?" Cliff asked. "What's going on?"

A guard rapped his knuckles against their open cell door.

"Time to go! Nicholls—you've got education! Dean—you're on gardening!"

Leo opened his eyes. Cliff was gazing at him curiously. But he couldn't say the words yet. He was starting to wonder if he'd imagined the entire meeting he'd just had.

IT WAS FREE-FLOW out of the wing for work and training. Leo walked beside Cliff in silence, other inmates bumping his shoulder as they strode past talking in loud voices about nothing much. There was never anything new to say, not really, yet everybody talked and talked and it echoed all around.

"Bloody hell," Cliff said as they stepped outside into searing heat. It was always impossible to gauge the weather from inside, but the sun was beating down, bouncing off all the concrete, and the inmates who were being stopped for random searches were complaining about standing in it for too long.

"Don't envy you being in the garden today," Cliff added, but Leo was glad he'd be planting and watering, not sitting in a class trying to act as if his head was in it.

As they passed the first lot of workshop blocks, he spotted Frank Jordan. He was with his usual crowd but he turned to nod at Leo, made a gesture that seemed to mean, *Fuck it's hot.* Leo flapped his collar and puffed out his cheeks in agreement. He and Frank had spoken a few times since that first day in the TV room. Frank was friendly now that they'd made a connection, surprisingly funny, occasionally even fatherly. But, also, still profoundly intimidating. He'd stepped in once, when someone had accused Leo of cutting in front of him in the lunch queue. All it had taken was one look from Frank to make the other guy back down, and Leo had felt a new sense of power, of protection, as everybody in the cafeteria had seemed to take note.

He walked on with Cliff, but Frank appeared at his side. The three of them seemed to take up too much room, like a wide load blocking a motorway. Frank looked pointedly at Cliff, and Cliff glanced at Leo, who gave a tiny shrug. A few more awkward seconds and Cliff took the hint, turning off toward his classroom with a probing backward glance.

"How are you, Cromley?" Frank asked.

He'd taken to calling him that. Leo wasn't sure how he felt about it. Only his mum ever said the name of the village to him these days, and not often. He'd started dreaming of the place again, since Frank had brought it up: not specifically the Raven anymore, but the hunkering hills and the surrounding woods and the lanes that curved off into darkness. Last night it had been the viaduct, north of the village, where he and Robbie used to throw stones when they were young and *get* stoned when they were older. The dream came back to him and he felt the lurch of peering right over the edge.

"I'm . . . okay," he told Frank.

"Saw you meeting with your POM earlier," Frank said.

How did he know and see everything? Leo thought of the letter his prison offender manager had pushed across the desk toward him—*Leo Ethan Dean* in bold; his mum's address; one of those scribbly signatures that didn't resemble letters or words. His POM watching expectantly for his reaction, for the right reaction.

It had happened. He hadn't imagined it.

"All okay?" Frank asked with an edge to his voice.

Leo nodded. Frank was a fast walker, faster than Cliff, and he felt a little breathless. Maybe that was part of Frank's technique. Leo's blood was pumping and it was waking up his thoughts and he wanted to talk now, wanted to tell someone.

"I think I'm . . ." The words still caught. "I think I'm getting out."

Frank stopped walking. "For real?"

Leo stopped, too, and looked at his shoes, the sun fierce on the crown of his head. "For real."

There was a loaded pause. Anxiety swilled in Leo's gut. What if Frank resented him for this? The pause stretched on as beads of sweat crept down the sides of his face. Then Frank broke into a grin and pulled him into a bone-crushing hug.

"Cromley, that's fucking great!"

Leo felt the first small rush of happiness. *I'm getting out. Getting my life back.*

But what kind of life?

"You know your conditions yet?" Frank asked, letting him go. "You going home? Back to village life?" He did a piss-taking little dance as he said the words *village life,* but the glint in his eyes was still friendly.

"I . . . I don't know." The cloud of doubt encroached further. "The board said I can. But . . . people despise me there." It was the first time he'd admitted this out loud. It prodded at the dark, ugly spaces inside him.

People despise me there.

He used to call Alice "auntie," yet at his trial she'd looked at him as if she wished he was dead. Whereas Peter couldn't look at him at all. Peter whom he used to go to for help and advice instead of his own father.

And now his mum was being victimized, ostracized, by people who could've chosen to support her. She never talked about it outright, but he read between the lines of the things she said at visiting, and it made him furious. Made him *want* to go back there and face the haters and pretend he had no shame.

Sometimes he fantasized about going even further than that, and goosebumps would crawl across his skin. They all thought the worst of him, so why not give them the worst?

Other times, he had so *much* shame he could barely lift his head from his rock-hard prison pillow.

As if reading his mind, Frank grabbed hold of Leo's chin and nudged it upward. "You gonna let that stop you?" he said. "You gonna be pushed around by some small-minded country cunts?"

Leo blinked in shock. "I . . ."

"Listen." Frank took him by the shoulders, checking left and right for watching guards. "I don't know what you did and I'm not gonna ask. I've done some bad shit myself. But I had my reasons, and I bet you did, too. Once you've done your time, that's it. Don't let anyone keep on punishing you."

Leo squirmed in his grip, closing his eyes. *But they will keep on punishing me, and I'll be doing it, too.*

"You get what I'm saying?" Frank said, his fingers digging in.

Leo opened his eyes. Frank's expression was intense, as if he really wanted Leo to take his words on board. And Leo nodded, because he was still scared of Frank, even though he was starting to like him, and because he wanted to please him, somehow, wanted to be able to say *fuck you* to the world like Frank could.

Frank let go and clapped him on the back, his expression all the way back to warm in an instant.

"Congrats, man," he said, sounding almost emotional. "You're young, you've got your whole life ahead of you. Don't let anyone fuck with that, okay? Don't let some shitty village act like it's better than you."

Leo adjusted his clothes, panting slightly. He looked up at the barbed-wire fence rising behind the library, and the distant shape of the hills beyond, which had started to feel like a painting during his time here, a film set. Now, though, those hills seemed to shimmer with something more real. He tried to hold on to the sense of power that Frank's giant presence seemed to bring. Maybe he was right. Maybe the only way to go back was fighting.

TWENTY-TWO

GEORGIE

Saturday, December 9, 2023

"Please come inside the pub!" Georgie springs into action, shouting to the agitated crowd. "Refreshments will be served!"

There are a few glances her way, but most people are still twittering about what's going on with Alice and the police and the pub sign.

So is it called the Raven again now?

Never liked that bloody bird.

Oh, really? I was kind of fond of it. Always been there, hasn't it?

Kind of inappropriate now, though . . .

Georgie watches them for a few moments, then tries once more to move things on. "FREE DRINKS INSIDE!" she yells, like a market stall owner hollering about their produce. She can imagine her sister watching her with an arched eyebrow, but it seems to have the desired effect: People turn toward her, torn between freebies and gossip. She walks purposefully to the door of the pub, saying, "Welcome, welcome," as if the place is hers and hers alone. And she flings one last glance toward the raven, meeting its black eyes before she disappears inside.

Following her into the bar area, the crowd slowly falls quiet. For most of them, it's their first glimpse inside the pub since the night Robbie died. People ogle the new tables and chairs, stare at the stripped and varnished floor. Georgie senses them drawing ghosts in the air, conjuring up the last things they saw here. The initials in the wall are now hidden by the fire extinguishers, but eyes dart inevitably to that corner.

Georgie draws the black folder from her handbag and takes out the photos and written memories of Robbie she collected before the memorial. She weaves around the room distributing them on tables. The villagers gravitate toward them, murmuring sadly, pulling up seats. Georgie watches once again, noting who becomes more quickly at ease, who still seems spooked. She feels a little unsettled herself, she realizes, by the events that have forced them into the pub earlier than planned. Slipping behind the bar, she starts pouring glasses of wine and juice, making cups of coffee and tea. Some of the locals gawp at her, and she wonders if they're seeing Chrissy, feeling the strangeness of Georgie in her place. If only they knew just how strange. She knows she should take off her ring, so conspicuous as she pours and stirs, but she can't bear to; it would feel like a betrayal.

I miss you, Ethan. I miss you so much and I still can't make sense of any of it.

Every drink she prepares, she imagines what he'd think.

His compliments were everything. His disapproval, on the rare occasions she experienced it, was always the end of the world. She remembers the first time they met, in London, when Georgie was hosting a cocktail-making session for some of her clients in the same hotel he was staying in for a teachers' conference. How he complimented her French martini, said he'd been thinking about introducing cocktails at the pub he owned, but his wife was dead set against it. *She's not the martini type,* he added, as if sharing a cheeky confidence. His smile was like a pool of golden light for Georgie to bask in. And the comparison between her and Chrissy was set up right from the start.

How could a man with such an appetite for life now be dead? A man who'd wanted a life *with* her? Georgie had been with him the week before his suicide. They were supposed to be together *that night,* their usual hotel, the highlight of both their weeks. What happened in between? What changed? She thinks of Chrissy, earlier, desperately thrashing around for answers about Leo. Georgie had felt everything from anger to fleeting empathy, but mostly she had burned to shout back at her: *Tell me why the love of my life is dead.*

"Let me help you, Georgie!" Rowena barges past her and begins to slosh milk into coffees at random.

"Honestly, Rowena, I'm fine. I've got this. Those two actually need to stay black—" Too late, the milk has gone in. "Why don't you sit down, relax?"

"No, we're in this together! I know I didn't necessarily approve of doing this today, this little *sneak preview* . . ." She glances around the half-finished pub. "But we're here now, and we're a team."

"Right." Georgie's smile strains. "Well, these red wines are for—" But Rowena has picked up two coffees and taken them over to a table where people have already ordered wine.

"Where's Alice?"

Georgie jumps, startled, and turns to see Peter standing at the end of the bar looking frazzled.

"Peter." She is tongue-tied for a second. Impossible not to think of the dumpster, the scrapbook. "Alice is . . ." There's another twinge as she remembers her pushing toward the police, shouting about the sign. And earlier, questioning Georgie's motives, her interest in Robbie and the memorial. "She's . . . just talking to the police, actually. I'm sure she'll be back soon. Can I get you a drink?"

"The police?" A deep frown line appears between his eyes. "Why?"

"Well . . . I don't know whether you noticed . . . but somebody put the pub sign back up. It was probably just a mistake, but Alice found it very disturbing. Which is completely understandable! I'm worried about her; she seems—"

"Why has she gone to the police about it?" Peter cuts her off. "She shouldn't be . . ." He presses at the frown line as if he can push it back in.

Georgie watches him carefully. Why does he seem so nervy about the police, given that he was a high-ranking officer himself, not so long ago?

Probably for the same reason he hid a book in a dumpster. A book full of photos of a missing person.

She considers mentioning something pointed, hinting that she saw him, but before she can decide what to say, he fires out another question.

"Is it Kiri and Ben who Alice is talking to?"

"I don't know—"

"Where are they?"

"They were out on the square—"

"She should've called me," he half-growls, pulling out his phone. He passes a hand across his jaw, then strides out of the pub.

Georgie stares after him. When she turns away she catches Marianne's eye. She is sitting alone at a table near the window, hands clasped in her lap, and has clearly seen Georgie and Peter's exchange. Georgie pins on a smile and goes over to top up her glass.

"What did he say to you?" Marianne surprises her with a question as direct as Peter's.

"Peter?" Georgie's wine bottle hovers. "He asked where Alice was."

"Has he gone to find her?"

"I think so."

Marianne stares at the wine as Georgie finally pours. "Always sorting out other people's situations," she mutters.

Georgie raises her eyebrows. "Does that come from having been in the police himself?"

"I don't know." Now Marianne's gaze roams the pub, sharp yet distant. "Avoiding his own stuff, I often think. And, God, there's plenty . . ." She stops and shakes her head, as if remembering she's having a conversation, and not just with herself.

Georgie waits, hoping she'll say more. There is an advantage to appearing impartial. A trick to a well-timed silence.

But Marianne sighs and shakes her head again. "Sorry. Today's been . . . a lot."

"I'm sure Alice is really grateful you came."

"Alice is . . ." Marianne glances at the window out onto the square. It looks like an ice rink from here, shining in the weak sunlight. "I don't really know where Alice's head is at, either, to be honest. Shit, it's all such a mess." She closes her eyes, touches her forehead. "Maybe I shouldn't have come."

Georgie leaves another pause. Marianne's eyes move back to the table, drawn by the photo Georgie placed there earlier. It's one of the pictures with Ethan in the background, the school fete one. Georgie doesn't know how well Marianne knew Ethan. Doesn't recall him ever mentioning her name. But she must've been around when he was, and when he died. She must've seen and heard things.

"Poor Robbie," Georgie murmurs, hovering her fingers over his smile in the foreground of the photo. His skinny arms wrapped around the giant teddy bear he's won. She leaves a careful pause before she lets her fingertips drift to the edge, to where Ethan is rearranging the remaining prizes in his stall. "That's Leo's dad, isn't it?"

Marianne flinches. "What?"

"Ethan, right?" Georgie keeps her tone soft, even though saying his name out loud feels like opening up her chest to expose a tattoo of it on her heart.

"I . . ." Marianne's hands close around her glass. "Yes. Ethan."

"He . . . passed away, too, didn't he?"

Georgie hears a slight change in the rhythm of Marianne's breath. "He took his own life."

A stillness comes over the table and Georgie stays in it for a moment, making sure she can keep up the pretense of ignorance, of distance. "I did hear that," she says in a voice that isn't quite her own. "How awful. Chrissy must've been devastated. And Leo. And all of you." After each mention of a different person, she leaves a small beat, watching Marianne. Marianne sits back in her chair and Georgie can feel her disengaging, almost deliberately, tactically so.

"Of course," Marianne says, looking away from the photo.

"Chrissy's been through so much," Georgie says. "I guess that explains some of her . . . behavior."

Another flicker in Marianne's face.

"I just mean, like earlier, outside the church . . ." Frustration rises and Georgie is suddenly desperate to ask some direct questions after months of just laying groundwork, watching, pretending. "Were they a happy family?" she blurts.

Marianne's shoulders stiffen and she turns to examine Georgie, as if seeing her properly for the first time. "I don't really know what you're asking me," she says. "Or . . . why?"

"Sorry, I didn't mean to—"

"I don't know you." Marianne speaks coldly now. "I came here for Robbie, and Alice, and"—a slight hesitation—"Peter. I don't know what your involvement is, but . . . I'd rather just sit on my own for a bit." She turns her head away, lifting her wine. "Rather not take any more trips down memory lane."

For a moment, Georgie doesn't move. Defiance locks her in place, standing over Marianne. *Talk to me. Answer me. Tell me what you know.* Then she catches sight of Rowena looking over, others, too, and she snaps back into character.

"Of course!" She lifts her palms as if to say, *My mistake.* "No problem. Sorry. Please, let me know if you need anything else. On the house, of course . . ."

She backs all the way off but can't stop staring as Marianne pushes the photo away from herself, screwing up her face as if the wine—or the conversation—has left a sour taste in her mouth.

TWENTY-THREE

CHRISSY

Saturday, December 9, 2023

Chrissy sits hunched in an armchair, still shaking, her fingers gripping the newly shorn ends of the left side of her hair. Activity buzzes all around her, surreal and distorted. She hears noises in stuttered bursts, as if she's wearing headphones and lifting them up at random, jarring intervals.

Her living room has become a makeshift investigation room for the police. They have set up camp in here with laptops, radios, mobiles, and a map, and the two of them—Kiri and Detective Wright—are talking urgently, taking phone calls, occasionally glancing up to check that Chrissy is okay.

Is she okay? The surreal feeling coats everything, even her memory of the person bursting into her kitchen, the balaclava, the scissors raised. Her fear at the time was like a memory in itself. Muscle memory. She froze at first, like she used to when Ethan turned to her in a sudden flare of rage, before her hands shot out to protect herself. But the scissors didn't come for her face or her throat. They hovered over her head, shining under her bright kitchen lights, and then swooped down, the snip-crunch of them slicing through a thick strand of her curls.

And then the intruder was gone. A shock of her blonde hair in their gloved hand. Chrissy reeling, gasping for breath, touching the side of her head in disbelief.

The police arrived soon after she called, a mix-and-match of the two pairs she had encountered before now. *He cut your hair? And then he left? Did he say anything? Did you recognize him?*

She kept shaking her head. The action felt familiar, too— the helplessness of it. After Ethan's death, and after Robbie's, she had shaken her head to so many questions, shocked and mute and unable to provide answers. This time, she was at least able to lead them outside and show them the camera wedged inside her frosty hedge. Should she have told them about it earlier? They raised their eyebrows in surprise but she'd gone past caring.

The footage showed a darkly dressed figure, seemingly male, average height and build. He hadn't come up the lane from the center of the village; he must've come from the direction of the woods. The police played it again and again, looking for distinguishing features, asking her if there was anything familiar about him. But he was just a blur of black clothing, his face already covered, scissors hidden, movements quick and purposeful.

They think it's Leo, she realized as they fixated on the "anything familiar" question. *They think my son would skip parole and then come and attack me in my house.* They haven't said it, but she still feels the undercurrent of it as they hunker over their laptop, papers spread around them, occasionally lowering their voices to talk to each other.

Something else had happened, almost the same time as she'd called them about her intruder. That afternoon, just as Robbie's memorial would've been starting, the white car from the CCTV footage near the prison triggered a speed camera a mile outside the village. Then another one further north. Detective Wright and Kiri are trying to pinpoint its current location on the map, receiving updates from someone back at Derby police station, and communicating with an unmarked police car that has been sent out to try to find it. Chrissy's heart beats a little harder as Wright leans forward and puts another red pin in the map, like a neat drop of blood.

What if that trail of red pins leads us all the way to Leo?

The thought is too big to handle. Too much hope, too much fear. What if it brings her attacker back instead? What if he's got Leo; what if he's done much worse to him than cutting a strand of hair?

"It seems to be traveling fast," DC Wright says. "Pretty reckless considering the car is stolen."

"Have our guys got eyes on it yet?" Kiri asks.

"No. They're still too far away. We need to keep tracking the plates with ANPR as best we can."

Chrissy exhales nervously, and Kiri turns to look at her.

"How are you holding up, Ms. Dean?"

Chrissy shakes her head yet again. "I think I need some air."

As she picks up her cigarettes, Kiri stands up, too.

"I'll come with you." She glances at Detective Wright, who nods. "I'll do another sweep of the outside of the house."

It is still bitterly cold outside, and the frigid air rushes into the gap where her hair has been cut. Chrissy darts fearful glances at the woods, glad Kiri is with her, even though it feels as if she's under surveillance. What about tonight, when they leave, and she has to stay here alone? She starts drawing up a frantic list of everything she can use to barricade the door, everything she can turn into a defensive weapon. Kiri examines the muddy track that leads toward the woods, but any footprints are lost in the brown sludgy ice.

"Do you have older footage from the camera?" she asks, straightening up and squinting into the winter sun. "Has there been anything else unusual since you put it there?"

Chrissy pauses, thinking of Georgie staring up at her house. Of the ring on her finger, the way she asked about Leo, blocked her from entering the church.

"Well . . . actually . . . the night before . . ." Still there is that unease, that instinctive reticence. But she pulls out her phone, opens the app, and shows Kiri the footage.

Kiri watches with a frown. "Is that Georgie? The one who organized the memorial?"

Chrissy nods. "She's new to the village. But she seems to have got pretty friendly with Alice." Something taps at the back of her head as she says it. Georgie and Alice. The notes, the threats, the silent calls. Could they be working together? The idea is painful in a strange, specific way. Alice lashing out alone is one thing. But alongside someone who wasn't there for any of it, who doesn't know all that has happened, all that's at stake . . .

"Any connection between her and Leo?" Kiri asks.

"They've never met."

But she may have known my husband.

Her stomach curdles and she keeps the thought to herself.

"Any reason she might come here? Wanting to speak to you, perhaps?" Kiri watches the footage once more. "It's almost as if she changes her mind."

Chrissy lifts her shoulders. "I don't know."

Kiri looks around again, her cheeks pink in the cold air. Chrissy has a distant memory of seeing her tipsy on prosecco at a Derbyshire Police awards night, years ago. Chrissy, Peter, and Alice had got pretty tipsy that evening, too. None of them could've predicted the situation they'd be in now. Does Kiri know the half of it? Does she have her own theories about what's happened to Leo?

"We're hoping to get a forensics team over here," Kiri says, handing Chrissy back her phone. "Resources are tight, though, and this weather makes it hard . . ."

She wanders around the side of the house, and Chrissy follows, watching her examine every crevice. Chrissy stares through the window into her empty kitchen. It feels small and distant, like looking into her entire shrunken world from the outside. She's been slowly putting away the things she bought for Leo's return—the Tabasco sauce, the little blue radio—but now she wants to run inside and get them all out again, in case he happens to look through this window, debating whether to go in. Imagine if he came back of his own accord and disappeared again because he thought she was better off without him.

We're better off without him.

The phrase bounces out of her memories—out of a different time, a different situation—and she bats it breathlessly away. Then her eye falls on the kitchen table and her heart stops because the note is still there, the one she didn't disclose, the one she was looking at just before the man in the balaclava ran in. She had forgotten to put it away again before the police came. They've settled in the living room, thankfully, but she needs to get it out of sight.

"Chrissy." Kiri straightens up from her inspection of the ground, her eyes suddenly sharper.

"Yes?" Chrissy turns, flustered. "Have you found something?"

"No . . . I need to ask you about something else . . . A text I just got from my colleagues still in the village . . ."

Chrissy's muscles tense up even further.

"Have you still got a key to the pub?"

An image of the Raven pops into her mind, as it often does, unbidden. Snapshots of her life behind the bar and in the flat above it. "No," she says. "Of course not."

"You haven't been in there recently?" Kiri asks. "Or in the garden?"

"God, no. Why?"

"You may be questioned more formally about this."

"About *what* exactly?"

But Kiri's radio buzzes, and she presses a button to speak into it: "Yes?"

"They've managed to catch up with the car," says the voice of DC Wright. "They're following at a safe distance."

"Right," Kiri says. "I'm coming in."

Chrissy's head is still in the previous conversation, trying to understand it, until she hears her name.

"Can you ask Ms. Dean to come in, too? We've also had Leo's visitation records back from the prison."

Chrissy's heart booms. "What do they say?" she says into the radio, craning forward, but DC Wright has already gone.

Kiri touches her arm, friendly again. "Let's go inside." She gestures at the house, which is feeling less and less like Chrissy's own by the minute. The feeling only intensifies as Kiri walks ahead, through her side door, and Chrissy trails behind like a befuddled visitor, jumping at shadows.

TWENTY-FOUR

LEO

Tuesday, October 31, 2023

The walk back from the visiting room that day seemed far longer than it ever had. And yet, when it was over, he couldn't even remember doing it. He was back in his cell as if he'd teleported there, leaning on the empty bunk bed with a thudding heart. Where was Cliff? Had he said something about putting his name down for the gym? Leo didn't know if he was glad to be alone or desperate for company. He was convinced that if he let go of the bedpost he would sink right down to the floor.

"Fuck," he murmured to himself, amid flashes of panic. "Fuck."

He hadn't expected her today. Hadn't expected her any day, despite approving her out-of-the-blue request to be added to his list. He'd been confused, thought twice about approving it—especially so near the end of his time—but he hadn't imagined she'd actually come. Seeing her sitting there, hands clasped on the table, he'd almost turned around and walked out. Because it couldn't be good, could it? Why she was there, surely it would only mess with his head.

If he'd known just how much, maybe he *would've* walked away.

He replayed the conversation in his mind, trying to tell himself it wasn't such a big deal. It didn't mean what he was making it mean, didn't capsize everything. But the truth was like a hammer inside his brain, hitting again and again.

I didn't come here to do this, she'd said. *But now that I'm here, looking at you . . .*

Disgust in her eyes, or pity, or something else?

And now it was all awake and writhing inside him, everything he'd processed while he'd been inside, everything he'd come to terms with about himself and what he'd done. Because he'd processed it all wrong. He let out a moan and banged his forehead against the hard bedframe.

"Leo?"

Groggily, he raised his head, expecting to see Cliff. But in the doorway to his cell, there was Frank. His eyes ran over Leo's half-folded-up body, his fingers white-knuckled around the bedpost.

"What's happened, Cromley?" He stepped inside the cell. "It's not your parole, is it? Those fuckers haven't changed their minds?"

Leo shook his head. He almost wished they would now.

"Then tell me." Frank grabbed his shoulder, gave him a little shake. "Don't hold out on me, Cromley. What's wrong?"

Leo looked at him and began to cry. Somewhere in his rational mind there was a distant awareness that he shouldn't break down in front of Frank, shouldn't make himself vulnerable, expose too much. But he was desperate, bursting with it, and when Frank held out his arms he slumped into them.

"I got it wrong," Leo said. "I was wrong. I *am* wrong."

Frank was solid and calm, smelled like roll-up cigarettes, didn't care what shitty things Leo had done in his life. So Leo started to talk. All of it. The whole fucking mess of it. It came out in a confusing order and he had to keep looping back and explaining who people were, but it was out there, purged, confessed. Another thing he couldn't take back.

TWENTY-FIVE

ALICE

Saturday, December 9, 2023

It isn't *just* about the sign, though." Alice can see she's losing the police. She can't seem to get across the significance of what's happened, what it means, how it makes her feel. Putting up a pub sign seems like reverse vandalism, she realizes as the detective looks at her dubiously.

"Has something else happened?" he asks. DC Colella, he said his name was. He has short, spiky brown hair and a suntan that looks out of place in this village in the middle of winter.

Alice pulls herself up tall again. They're back in the church—the nearest empty building now that everyone has moved over to the pub—with the photo of Robbie watching over them. She keeps glancing at it. Sometimes it gives her courage; sometimes it only brings her fears back to the surface.

"Something appeared in the pub wall," she says, her voice

echoing in the big near-empty space, which still smells strongly of lilies. "Initials . . . Robbie's and Leo's. They . . . they weren't there before."

The two men frown at each other. Ben has barely looked at Alice since they came in here. He constantly dodges her gaze, as if avoiding eye contact will stop her from mentioning their conversation at her house.

"Initials?" DC Colella asks. "I'm not sure I—"

"My son's and the person who killed him!" Alice can hardly keep herself from shouting. Why don't they get it? Why doesn't anybody? "And I don't think it's a coincidence that all this is happening now that Leo is out of prison."

"Leo Dean is missing," Colella says pointedly.

"I *know* that."

"So it's unlikely he had anything to do with any initials in the wall or a pub sign being fixed."

"It wasn't *fixed!*" She presses her hands against her cheeks. "It had been taken down for a reason. It had been thrown *away*. Nobody wanted to see that raven ever *again* . . ." She takes a deep breath, lowering her hands. "What I mean is, whoever did it knew what they were doing. It was a taunt. And so were the initials—"

"Do you know where Leo Dean is?"

"No!" She feels the conversation slipping through her fingers. "Of course I don't. But his mum . . ."

"Chrissy Dean," he says, turning a page of his notebook. "Tell us about your relationship with her."

Alice sits back against the pew. The church is cold, growing seemingly colder, and she shivers and holds her own elbows. "Maybe she did this," she says. "She was here earlier, before the memorial, trying to get in. Maybe she's the troll. And maybe *she* knows where her son is."

The detective raises his eyebrows. Ben's radio buzzes and he jumps a little, murmurs into it, then flicks a switch on the top and slides it back into his belt.

"Chrissy Dean has been receiving abusive messages herself," DC Colella says.

Alice looks away. She knew this would come up again, yet she's squirming.

"The email you sent her, on 'behalf' of the pub committee, was pretty unequivocal."

Her eyes snap back to him. "I was only informing her what we'd decided. It was essential to bar him from the pub. Anyone would think so."

She's shocked when he pulls out his phone and starts reading her words: "'. . . Your son, Leo Dean, is strictly prohibited from entering Cromley's pub . . . Violence will not be tolerated . . . Strong action will be taken . . . We also ask, on behalf of the village, that you consider the effect of your continued residency . . .'"

He leaves a pause long enough for Alice to shrink down in the pew. Did Chrissy give them the email, or did they pull it off the server? She feels as if her privacy's been violated, even though she put those words in writing, signed them with her own name.

"Pretty similar in theme to the more threatening notes that were left at her house," Colella remarks.

"It's totally different," Alice insists, panic grabbing at her throat.

"You and Chrissy are having a kind of feud—is that fair to say?"

Feud. It sounds both over-dramatic and over-trivialized. Shakespearian and playground-level. It doesn't encapsulate the depth of the damage, the hurt; the length and complexity of the history.

"Her son killed mine," Alice breathes. "And she could've left me—all of us—to grieve in peace, but she didn't. She stayed around, and then she chose to bring him back here, and now these things are happening—"

"But he *isn't* back here."

"I know," Alice says yet again, grinding her teeth. "But her intention—*their* intention—"

"Did you ever visit Leo Dean in prison?"

Alice stills. An image crystallizes in her head: the tall metal gates, the comforting coils of barbed wire. She sees herself sitting in her car, windscreen steamed up, a storm of nerves and doubt in her belly.

"I . . . I was going to," she says softly. "I even put myself on the list, a while ago . . . and was pretty surprised when Leo approved it. But I couldn't go through with it. I don't know why I wanted to in the first place."

A sour taste has come into her mouth. She never went past the gates. Maybe she didn't trust herself.

"Did you have a good relationship with Leo and his mother *before* what happened?"

It's hard to explain the feeling she has when people ask this. It's like being reminded of loving someone—blindly and completely—before they betrayed you. Like having made a misjudgment that shapes your whole life and wearing its scars on your skin for everybody to see.

"We were close. Chrissy and I . . . Leo and Robbie . . ." Her words slow as if her mechanisms are breaking down. "And Leo and I . . ." Her stomach tenses over this final admission. Nadia once tried to suggest, in a therapy session, that Alice was not just mourning Robbie; she was grieving for Leo, too. But Alice couldn't follow her down that road.

"And your brother, Peter . . ."

Alice's head jerks up. Out of the corner of her eye, she sees Ben's do the same, as if they're two puppets on the same string.

"Was he close to them, too?" Colella asks.

"He was close to Robbie. He was his uncle." She says this as though it's obvious, while knowing it doesn't begin to describe how much Robbie idolized Peter, how much Peter doted on him.

"How did Peter feel about Chrissy and Leo . . . how *does* he feel about them?"

"He . . ." Alice has the almost physical sensation of walking into a trap, and she slows her words down again, as though this might stop it from happening. "He . . . was friendly with both of them, before." She decides not to say it any more insistently than that. Leo once looked up to Peter almost as much as Robbie did, but there doesn't seem any point getting into it. "And now . . . well, he feels the same as me. Same as all of us here."

"He has problems with alcohol—is that correct?"

"Who told you that?" Alice asks sharply, wondering if it was Chrissy. She notices Ben scratching awkwardly at his beard. Maybe Peter's problem is common knowledge among the people he used to work with. The idea makes her feel protective; their respect was everything to him, at one time.

"We're just trying to get a picture of the village and what's been happening," DC Colella says, swerving the question.

"He's had problems in the past." Alice flicks her eyes toward Robbie's photo, feeling guilty talking about his beloved uncle in any negative terms. "But he's in recovery."

Ben's phone rings then, and he looks almost relieved to be able to stand up and move away to answer it. Alice watches as he turns to face a wall, speaking in a low voice.

The detective stays focused on her. "We're going to be conducting some more formal interviews with people from the village. Would you be willing to make an official statement?"

"Well, yes, I suppose so. I just don't know whether I—"

"And have your fingerprints taken?"

"My *fingerprints?*"

She looks down, instinctively, at her hands. How long have they been shaking? Can the detective see it, too?

"Will that be a problem?"

"No, I—"

They're interrupted by Ben hurrying back over. For a moment, Alice thinks he's intervened deliberately, until she sees the genuine urgency in his face. "Detective . . . sorry, but . . . something else has come up."

"What is it?" Colella asks, standing up from the pew.

Ben shows him a page of his notebook. Colella glances at Alice and then gestures for Ben to move away again, walking close beside him and speaking into his ear. Alice watches them whispering in a huddle, DC Colella pulling out his own mobile. Their twitchy movements, the new alertness in their eyes.

She turns her hands palm up and looks at her fingertips. Not red-stained, of course, but she imagines them black-stained after having her prints taken and bites her lip until it hurts.

Just one note. That was all she wrote, all she sent. A moment of pure anger, her finger hovering over the destruct button of Chrissy's life, aiming for where she knew she could hurt her. A sense of power, of leverage, that still consoles her sometimes now, like a weapon in storage.

One note that, as far as she could tell, was not among the ones the police had photos of. So where is it? And who has been sending the others?

TWENTY-SIX

CHRISSY

Saturday, December 9, 2023

What's happening?" Chrissy asks as she and Kiri walk back into her living room. She wants to reassert herself, claw back some control, but she hears the catch in her voice. DC Wright is sitting on her sofa, leaning close to a laptop screen, a radio in her hand.

Wright stands up, not taking her eyes off the laptop until the last possible moment, when she picks up a tablet from the coffee table and walks over to Chrissy.

"Our unmarked car has caught up with the stolen vehicle. They're following it north at the moment. Destination still unclear. In the meantime . . ." She tucks her silver hair behind her ear and taps the screen of the tablet several times. "This is a list of everyone who visited Leo in prison . . ." She holds it out toward Chrissy. "Can you tell us if anything strikes you as unusual?"

For a second, Chrissy can't take in a single name; the list is just a series of fuzzy dots. She blinks and the dots become letters, but the list is still overwhelming: two years' worth of regular visits. She sees her own name over and over, until it becomes alien, like a word used too many times. Interspersed is her sister's. She visited Leo more often than Chrissy gave her credit for, and the realization makes her eyes fill. She blinks again and scrolls to the end, looking for the anomaly, the name that doesn't belong.

Finally, she sees it.

"Marianne," she says out loud, unable to contain her surprise. "Marianne . . . visited Leo?"

It makes no sense. Or does it? Chrissy's head whirls, her heart beating painfully.

DC Wright is gazing at her. "Who is Marianne?"

"She's . . . Peter's ex-wife."

"As in, Alice's brother?"

"Yes."

"And"—Wright throws a glance toward Kiri, who has taken her place on the sofa, monitoring the laptop—"you didn't know she'd been visiting him?"

"No. Not at all. It was . . . just the once by the looks of it . . ." Chrissy scrolls back frantically, double-checking. "Yes, just the once, about six weeks before the end of his sentence . . ." Izzy's words echo in her head, about Leo being on edge, not sleeping toward the end.

A chill washes through her. She can feel DC Wright still watching her, but she can't speak anymore; her mind has gone into overdrive.

"Why would she have visited?" Wright asks.

"I . . . I don't know."

She needs to say more, ask more, but she's got that feeling again, that if she starts to speak she might be sick instead.

Wright turns back toward Kiri and the laptop. "What's the latest on the car?" she asks, raising her voice. "Are they still on its tail?"

"Yes," Kiri says. "And it's still driving north. Through countryside, currently close to the border between Derbyshire and Yorkshire."

DC Wright swivels back to Chrissy. "Are there any places of significance to Leo around there?"

Chrissy is still in a daze. "Sorry?"

"The stolen car . . ." Wright raises her voice even further, over-enunciating. "It's near the border between Derbyshire and Yorkshire. Is there anywhere in that area that might be relevant?"

Her words register at last, and Chrissy turns even colder. She moves her eyes from Marianne's name on the list, drags them slowly up to meet Wright's. "Well, it depends . . . exactly where you . . ." She walks around so she can see the laptop screen, feeling as if she's moving through water.

"We still don't know if the car is important," Kiri points out hesitantly.

"Either way, it's a stolen vehicle," Wright says, sounding impatient. "And it's driving suspiciously fast. And it was near this village only a few hours ago. We need to—"

"His dad's buried close to there," Chrissy blurts, pointing at the laptop. As they both turn toward her, she tries to steady her breath.

"Whereabouts?" Wright asks.

"Shirebrook."

"The car is just south of there."

Chrissy's pulse is galloping. Why would a stolen vehicle be at the prison on the day of Leo's release, then near the village on the day of Robbie's memorial, and now driving, it seems, toward her ex-husband's grave?

There is silence for a while, as if they are all hypnotized by the progress of the blue dot on the screen. Chrissy can hear her own breathing, her own heart. Can feel DC Wright shifting beside her and see Kiri glancing over. Nobody has asked the question she expected them to. Nobody seems to think it strange, at least not yet, that Ethan is buried so far away.

Chrissy has fended off this question before, always using the excuse that his grandfather was from Shirebrook. The truth is, she didn't want his grave in the village churchyard. She didn't want to give him the satisfaction of being buried in the place where he did his phony worship and his pillar-of-the-community act; didn't want to walk past it every day and remember. It was bad enough hearing all the tributes to him at the time, all the speculation that an impending inspection by the Office for Standards in Education had put him under so much pressure he'd taken his own life. There was outrage in the village that the strains of the job had robbed them of their local hero. But there was kindness toward Chrissy, too, and so she'd wanted to stay there, with Leo, free of him.

Why she continued to stay, after the kindness disappeared, she has never been sure. Willfulness? Fear?

She studies the screen more closely. The blue dot is traveling quickly along a winding road. North, north, north, following a route Chrissy hasn't taken for years. But she can picture it. The craggy hillsides and the blustery churchyard.

She saw him lowered into the earth there but hasn't been back since.

"They've turned off," DC Colella says, pointing. "Look, they're not heading for Shirebrook anymore."

Chrissy holds her stomach. She feels as if she's in the car, feels the lurch of the nauseating bends. It makes her remember how travel-sick Leo used to get. She's not a good passenger, either—Ethan used to drive deliberately fast, laughing at her queasiness—but soothing Leo was her distraction, his little head against her chest.

If he's in that car, he'll be gray now. He'll be begging them to pull over.

The thought of him trapped and sick makes her feel wretched.

"Where are they going?" Wright asks, but it isn't clear who she's talking to.

Kiri zooms the picture outward. "More toward Bakewell now."

"Anything of significance there?" Wright turns to Chrissy. Chrissy shakes her head.

There is silence for a few more moments, and Chrissy digs her nails into her own palms.

Where is it going? Could Leo really be in there?

She jumps as a radio buzzes to life right beside her. It's DC Wright's. The detective stirs, looking almost annoyed to have to move her attention from the blue dot.

"This is car 1164 with eyes on the target," says a disembodied voice from the radio, and Wright switches from annoyance to attentiveness.

"What can you see?"

"The car is still traveling at speed. It's just turned off down a much smaller road, basically a dirt track, so we're having to stay back so as not to arouse suspicion. There's someone in the front passenger seat as well as the driver. Both appear to be Caucasian males, from the little we can see. Wearing hats, partial face coverings, too."

"What about the area—anything of note around you?"

"Barely anything, just fields. But there is a large barn up ahead."

"Do you think the car's heading there?"

"Given the turnoff, it seems likely." There is a pause, then the voice in the radio says: "We've requested a helicopter, and some backup. It's hard to be sure from here, but . . ." The voice gets louder, and slightly higher. "There's possible smoke."

Chrissy grips the back of the sofa.

"Smoke?" she says, with no idea whether the person on the other end can hear her.

"Confirm what you mean by 'possible smoke,'" DC Wright urges.

There's another pause, and a crackle as if the signal is faltering.

Then, finally: "It looks like the barn might be on fire."

TWENTY-SEVEN

ALICE

Saturday, December 9, 2023

Alice sits in the church for a while once the police have left. They were cagey about the news that had come through on the radio, vague about where they were rushing off to, but something is happening. Everything is spiraling.

Here in the church, though, there is silence.

There are a dozen things she should be doing but she is paralyzed, her backside numb on the pew, her eyes fixed on the photo of Robbie. What would he make of all this? If he could see everything that has happened since his death, everything that's fallen apart, would he tell her to forgive Chrissy? Forgive Leo?

She's glad, in a way, that he can't see what the village has become. What *she's* become. She was better when he was around. Being his mum *made* her better.

But isn't that why she's fighting so hard? For him? For his goodness? How can she forgive the person who ripped him away from her? The people who are dancing, even now, on his grave?

She stands up, summoning energy from deep inside. She has to get back out there, work out what she's going to do. And anger is the only driving force she has.

Wiping her cheeks, she blows a kiss toward Robbie, then turns her back on him. It's remarkably painful and she falters, thinking about taking him with her. Just as she decides to leave him be—he looks peaceful, now that the crowds have gone—the church door bangs and she hears footsteps in the entranceway.

For just a second, she's convinced it's Leo. Here for whatever confrontation he might've been planning. An instant later, though, she recognizes the gait. Peter comes into the main part of the church.

"Al! Where have you been?"

"I could ask you the same question."

Neither of them answers, as if they've stumbled into deadlock, and then they both speak at once.

"I'm sorry, Al, I just couldn't face . . ."

"I've been talking to the police," Alice says.

Peter jumps on this. "What about?"

"The weird stuff that's been happening. The vile stuff. Pete, someone is . . ." Her throat constricts. "Someone's sending messages. Robbie's and Leo's initials appeared in the pub wall and then the pub sign was back up and it—"

"Wait, what? Initials?"

She struggles through an explanation for the second time today, while his expression grows more and more perturbed.

"What did the police say?" he asks eventually. "Who was it you spoke to?"

"Detective Colella asked most of the questions. But Ben was there, too."

Something flares in his face. "What were they asking about?"

"A lot of stuff. Our relationship with Chrissy and Leo—"

"*Our?*" His eyes are flinty-sharp. These are the times he looks least like Robbie, when his anxiety makes him curt and edgy. The times, bizarrely, when he reminds her of Leo.

"Yes, you and me. And they . . ." She hadn't planned to tell him this part, but she's still that uncomfortable mix of angry with him and worried about him. "They asked about your drinking."

"What did you tell them?" He sounds almost aggressive and she recoils. He seems to notice and makes an effort to soften his tone. "Sorry, sis, I'm wound up today. I just—" He sighs. "What specifically were they asking?"

"Whether you had a problem with alcohol."

"And what did you say?"

"That . . ." What exactly *did* she say? She struggles to recall, her stomach flipping with the possibility that she might've dropped him in it, somehow. "That you were recovering. Recovered."

"You didn't mention . . . the other day?"

Alice shakes her head, then appraises her brother. Her anchor, her rock, and also, at times, a complete enigma.

"I didn't know you and Marianne were back in touch," she says.

He flinches. "It's just the odd message," he says, looking away.

"She said you argued recently. The day you were drinking, in fact."

He still won't look at her. "It was just a stupid thing."

"What was it about?"

"I can't even remember. We were just going over old ground. She gets frustrated with me. Can't blame her."

"Can't blame her," Alice agrees, but fondly, sadly, touching his arm. "Pete . . . You can talk to me, you know. If there's anything . . . If you . . ." She trails off because she can already see his face closing again. "You've not been drinking today, have you?" she finally asks, though it isn't the question she was really searching for.

He frowns and shakes his head. "Just driving," he says. "I just went for a drive."

She lets it drop, though the unease clings on. Before they leave the church, they go to the front to light a candle for Robbie. It's Peter's idea, but when he gets close he becomes flustered and distressed, searching through his pockets for something to light it with.

"Here, don't worry, there are some matches . . ." Alice spots a box that Georgie must have put there for this purpose.

Peter still seems distracted, so she strikes a match and lights a candle, staring into the flame as it blooms. Glancing at Peter, she sees the flame refocus him, and he stares at it, too, reflected light dancing in his eyes.

"He really looked up to you," she tells him, squeezing his hand with an almost unbearable rush of affection.

Peter's shoulders start to shake. She moves in closer and he wraps his arms around her, crushing her cheek into his chest.

"I wish I'd been a better uncle," he says, and she hears the echo of her own pain in his voice.

"You were the best," she tells him. "He talked about you all the time. You were like a father—"

"Don't say that."

She peers up at him. "Why not?"

"I don't deserve that kind of . . . I just don't deserve it. I wasn't his dad."

"But you meant the *world* to him," Alice protests. "Remember how he used to boast about his uncle the policeman? And how possessive he used to get? Like when—" She pulls herself up short. She was going to evoke the time Robbie got upset because Peter was helping Leo with his homework instead of him. *He needs more help than you, sweetheart,* Alice had placated him, but Robbie kept looking over, waiting for Peter's attention to be free. She doesn't want to use an example that involves Leo, though. Why does every train of thought lead back to him?

"I wish I'd been there when they fought," she says instead. "Wish I'd been able to stop it . . ."

"Me, too," Peter says, still holding her. "I wish so many things, Al."

"We can't change anything." She is dampening his crumpled shirt. "We can only . . . only make sure . . ." Her words die because she's so confused now about what she's trying to make sure of. That others will hurt as much as her? That no-body will trample Robbie's memory? That the right kind of justice will be done?

All of the above, perhaps. Moments of confusion and guilt don't mean she's willing to let any of it go.

"Al . . ." Peter releases her, stepping back. She doesn't think she's seen him cry—not properly—since they stood outside the pub watching the ambulance take Robbie's body away. Even at the funeral, he was quiet and ashen but he didn't break down. And when they scattered Robbie's ashes, side by side above the tall arches of the overgrown viaduct, the wind was so strong it blew any tears off their faces.

"Yes?" she says, a coil of worry returning to her gut. "Talk to me, Pete."

The candlelight flickers across his unhealthy-looking skin.

"What is it?" she urges, but it's a press too far: She sees him draw back into himself.

"Nothing," he says, shaking his head. "Nothing, it's just . . . It's been a day. And I'm sorry I haven't been here. That's . . . basically what I wanted to say."

Alice is doubtful but knows further cajoling will only have the opposite effect. She wipes her face and rubs her thumb under her eyes. Though she hasn't worn makeup in a long time, she still wipes away imaginary mascara stains, like drawing a line under the crying.

"Let's go see what's happening," she says.

Peter nods, his eyes back on the flame. He leans forward, as though he intends to snuff it out, then snaps up at the last moment, turning to follow her out of the church.

OUTSIDE IN THE square, they both look toward the pub. The Raven sign sways in the wind and Alice can hear it creaking, she thinks, even from this distance away.

"I can't face going in for Georgie's drinks," Peter murmurs, and Alice nods in agreement, even as she feels the usual push-pull of the place, both calling and repelling.

Peter's phone buzzes and he fishes it out of his pocket. Alice keeps staring at the pub with a sense that it's staring back. It's strange to see all its windows lit, shadows of movement within.

"Something's happening," Peter says.

"In the pub?" She uses her hand as a visor against the low sun.

"No . . . I just got a text from Ben. He's been keeping me in the loop. We used to be good mates, so—"

"I know you did," Alice interrupts with an edge to her voice. Yet another conversation with Peter she needs to have. But she pushes it aside for now. "What is it?" she asks, leaning over, trying to see his phone.

"I'm not quite . . ." Peter moves the phone slightly away from her. "They're following a car. Something about a barn . . ." He turns a little paler. A glint of alarm in his eyes. Then a phone call starts to flash on his screen, from a mobile number he doesn't have in his contacts. Alice waits for him to answer but he swipes to dismiss the call instead.

"Wasn't that Ben?" she asks.

"No," he says abruptly. "I don't know who that was."

"It might've been important."

He waves a hand. "Looked like a sales call."

Alice frowns, unconvinced. She feels as if she recognized the number, but she only saw it for a second or two. "What's Ben saying? Anything more?"

Peter is silent, studying his phone. It keeps lighting up as new messages come through. She sees the name *Ben* at the top of his inbox; but also, in a separate thread . . . she's *sure* that's the number that called him just now. She leans in again, but Peter opens up the conversation with Ben.

"There's a car that's of interest to the Leo investigation," he tells her. "They've tracked it as far as a barn."

"What barn?"

"I-I don't know. But . . ." He stalls, his eyebrows knitting, and finishes his sentence with a breathlessness to his voice: "Apparently the barn's on fire."

"On fire? Is it . . . Is anyone inside it?"

Is Leo in there?

"They . . ." His eyes dart from side to side as he reads. "The fire brigade are there . . . They think there *is* someone inside. Unconfirmed . . ."

"Where is this happening?"

"I don't know." He types rapidly, then waits. Alice looks over at the pub again and sees imaginary flames bursting through its roof. She used to fantasize sometimes about setting it on fire—before she decided to rally her neighbors to help her buy it instead. There are times now when she wishes she'd had more guts, less conscience; wishes she'd carried out her more violent ideas.

A barn on fire might be nothing. But she wonders how she

would feel if Leo were to be killed. Not just in the dark imaginings she'd never share with anybody else, but in reality.

"North Derbyshire," Peter says. "Weirdly near the churchyard, apparently . . ."

"Which churchyard?"

"Shirebrook."

Of course. She closes her eyes and sees Ethan's face. The charming smiles she came to realize were entirely false. The transformation whenever Chrissy upset him or made some minor mistake at the pub. His open, lifeless eyes the day Chrissy called her—not making any sense, not knowing what to do—and Alice went rushing to the pub.

"There's something strange about all this," Peter says.

"Yes," Alice agrees, with an even tighter twist in her stomach.

"I'm going to go over there. See if I can speak to the detectives."

"Over where?" she asks. "The police station?"

He is silent again. Alice begins to realize what he's going to say. Why he's hesitating.

"They're at Chrissy's," he says eventually.

She inhales. "You're going to Chrissy's?"

"Well, I . . ." He looks almost apologetic. "I probably won't go in. I'll just see if they'll talk to me. See what else I can find out."

It's bizarrely hurtful, the idea of him going there, as if he's choosing to leave her side for the enemy. And she's scared, too, as if proximity to Chrissy is dangerous, as if secrets might be spilled or loyalties confused.

"Are you going to talk to her?"

He pauses. "Probably not the best idea at the moment."

Alice clenches her fists. "No."

"Like I say, I just want a word with Colella or Wright. They're the ones who are really on the inside of all this. And I'm pretty sure I can come up with a favor they owe me from back in the day."

"You usually can," she says, but can't muster a smile. Her heart is pounding and she isn't exactly sure why.

Peter at Chrissy's house.

You need to go with him.

The thought takes root and won't let go. At least if she's there, she'll feel more in control. And maybe she'll know the truth about the sign and the initials—and Leo—as soon as she sees her ex-friend. Maybe she still knows her well enough to read the secrets in her eyes.

"I'll come with you," she hears herself saying.

Peter's eyes widen. "To Chrissy's?"

Alice nods more decisively than she feels. "It's time."

TWENTY-EIGHT

GEORGIE

Saturday, December 9, 2023

"Rowena, can you hold the fort for a few minutes?" Georgie calls over to her, gesturing at the bar. "I just need a bit of a break."

Rowena looks up from talking with Ellen and Dave and gives her a thumbs-up. Georgie escapes into the back office to collect her thoughts, sitting in her usual committee meeting seat, stretching out her legs and letting her head fall back.

The conversations and events of the day replay on a loop.

Somebody in that church knows where Leo is.

My uncle peter helps peeple and peeple like him and ask him for things.

He catches bad guys like the man who made things go on fire.

Why is the sign back up?

Why is Alice talking to the police?

Avoiding his own stuff. And God, there's plenty . . .

I'd rather not take any trips down memory lane.

Outside this pub, there are ripples and movements she can't control. Alice talking to the police; Chrissy searching for Leo; Peter roaming around *sorting out other people's situations,* and Leo somewhere further afield, perhaps making his way back. Or perhaps never to return.

Her mind's eye starts turning the pages of Peter's scrapbook and she imagines Ethan looking over her shoulder. *What does that weirdo want with my son?*

Maybe she hasn't paid enough attention to Peter before now, or his ex-wife. It's all been about Chrissy and Alice. *The Inseparables,* Ethan used to call them. And Georgie's current search history, if she didn't clear it at least once a week, would be full of them. She sometimes wonders what someone in her position would've done before smartphones and the internet. How long would it have taken her even to find out her lover was dead? That awful limbo week of not hearing from him, thinking he was rejecting her, ghosting her, could've lasted months, even years.

She thinks of the day she waited in their usual hotel room, with a new dress, new underwear, reapplying her lipstick again and again as she waited.

The two room-service meals that turned up under their shiny silver domes, and sat there uneaten.

And the moment, several torturous days later, when she realized the alternative to being ghosted was a thousand times worse.

LOCAL HEAD TEACHER TAKES OWN LIFE

The photo they used was of him and Chrissy. That was a knife to Georgie's heart at the time, but later it became a flame to her anger: the *audacity* of her. Smiling beside him in all these tribute pieces, as though she hadn't neglected him, scoffed at him throughout their marriage. And the more Georgie agonized over it, the more convinced she became: There was more to it than work pressure and a looming inspection, of course there was. What if Chrissy had made things unbearable for him? Chrissy and her best friend and her brother? Maybe they'd found out Ethan was in love with someone else. Threatened him, made him feel he had no way out.

Drove him to it . . . or worse.

It was seeing Cromley back in the news, after Leo's arrest, that had really stirred the lurking doubts from the back of Georgie's mind. Seeing Chrissy's and Alice's faces, reading about the fight; thinking, *That village. Bad things happen in that village.* The googling and Facebook-stalking started then. Driving past and through Cromley, not yet daring to actually stop. Then the property searches, the first fragments of a plan. And then, like fate, the pub up for sale, the committee being formed: her chance to own a piece of Ethan's life. To find out why he ended it without any warning, not a *flicker.*

Now she sets her jaw as she types Peter's name into her phone. He doesn't seem to use social media but there are local news articles about his career, awards he's won, arrests he's made. There he is with his arms round other officers, an arrogant smile, slaps on the back, another promotion. *He's dodgy,* she thinks, all her instincts blazing. *He's dodgy as fuck.*

Her spine straightens when she spots his name in a report about Ethan's death. Has she seen this one before? Of course she has; she's seen them all, pored over them obsessively. But she reads it again, paying attention to the quote from Peter: "In my capacity as a senior police officer in the area, I can confirm that Ethan Dean's death has been ruled a suicide following a short inquest. In my capacity as a friend of the family, I'd like to say how devastated the whole community is by this tragedy."

Lies, she thinks, breathing hard. *Lies, lies, lies.*

She scrolls through a few more of the Google results, then tries some different search terms—*Ethan Dean inquest, Peter Lowe Ethan Dean, Peter Lowe cases, Peter Lowe fires* . . . And it's the final one—a wild card, really—that throws up a mug shot that stops her dead. The face blares out from the list of results, younger but recognizable, mainly because of his distinctively broken nose. It's the man from outside the pub a few weeks ago. The one who asked if she was Alice Lowe and then said, *Never trust a Lowe.*

She clicks into the article and scans for his name. Frank Jordan. She has never heard of him. She's about to google him separately when she hears shouts from the bar, voices raised in anger. She freezes as they climb in volume and intensity. Then she swears under her breath, jumps up, and hurries out of the room.

AS SHE TURNS the corner into the main bar area, she sees Janice, Ellen, and Sara standing in the corner near the fire extinguishers.

"No, Robbie was *here,*" Janice is insisting, gesturing at the floorboards. "And Leo was here . . . And Robbie literally just turned . . ." She demonstrates crudely. "And Leo punched him!"

Sara steps forward, vigorously shaking her head. "Jesus,

Janice, that isn't what happened! Robbie and Leo were both here . . ." She points to a spot further toward the bar. "And Robbie was up in Leo's face, saying something to him . . ."

"That's what I said!"

"*No,* you were making out like Robbie was minding his own business and then Leo just walked up to him and hit him. Did you even see a punch? Can you be sure it—"

Georgie rushes forward. "Hey, hey, what's happening?" She looks around, seeing everyone else staring at the unfolding argument, and no sign of Rowena.

Ellen turns indignantly to Sara. "Why are you defending him all of a sudden?"

"I'm just saying there was more to it. We all know there was, but nobody ever admits it. And now he's missing, and maybe . . . well, maybe it needs to be said."

"No, it does not! It's completely inappropriate! We're all on edge already, wondering what the hell is going on—"

"I wasn't the one who started talking about who was where and who saw what that night!"

"Well, we were all thinking about it!" Janice says. "It's impossible not to, being back here!"

Georgie thinks about intervening again, calming things down, but she is rapt. The electricity in the air feels like a release. And it's the first time she's heard anyone defend Leo. She holds her breath, lets things roll.

"Leo is a *murderer!*" Janice explodes.

"He was convicted of manslaughter," Sara hurls back.

"Why are you even here if you're on his side?"

"I'm not on his side! But the whole thing was a tragedy, a terrible, fluky tragedy—"

"Killing someone is *not* a fluke!" This is Ellen again now. She and Janice close in on Sara, and for a moment Georgie thinks someone's going to get hurt, again, in this cursed corner.

"Okay, everyone—" she finally speaks up.

"They were arguing," Sara plows on. "Robbie clearly said something to upset him—"

"You *can't* be suggesting he deserved it? You're as bad as Chrissy!"

"Well, to be perfectly frank," Sara says, chin jutting, "I don't think Chrissy *is* bad. I think she's had a bloody rough ride."

A murmur ripples around the pub. Now Georgie feels a dark wave of fury. Defending Leo is one thing, but she doesn't want sympathies to start swinging Chrissy's way. Undeserved. Uninformed. No, no, not on her watch.

She inserts herself into the middle of the jostling group. "Please remember that we're here to honor Robbie today!" she cries. "*Not* to dissect that terrible night!"

It's like pulling a plug. Shoulders sag. Heads go down. The three women look a little shamefaced, but their scowls are still in place, their bodies still bristling.

The toilet door bangs and Rowena comes back in. "Is Marianne—" She stops when she sees the cluster of pink-faced people. "Oh . . ." She looks puzzled. "Is everything okay?"

"Where have you been, Rowena?" Georgie can't help snapping.

"I popped into the toilet . . . I heard voices but I just thought things were getting lively in here . . ." The word *again* seems to dangle, unsaid. "I was only gone a few minutes . . ."

Georgie breathes hard, settling her mask back in place. "It's fine," she says, smiling thinly. "Nothing to worry about. Just an emotional day." She casts the smile around the room, forcing it wider.

"Well, yes, *quite* . . ." For a moment, it seems as if Rowena will say something along the lines of, *I told you so,* and Georgie prepares herself not to rise to it. Instead, Rowena blinks and raises the mobile phone she's holding in her right hand. "Is Marianne still here?"

People look around at each other.

"I think she went to get some air," Poppy says. "Although I can't see her from this window . . ."

Rowena starts typing clumsily on her phone. "Apparently the police want to talk to her."

Georgie looks at the table where Marianne was sitting. There is a half-empty wineglass still there, a plum-colored lipstick stain on its rim.

"I've had a message about that, too," someone else says.

"What's going on?" chimes a third person, across the other side of the room. "Apparently there are loads of police up at Chrissy's, and forensics, too . . ."

"I've just heard there's something happening further north."

"A helicopter." Everyone's phones are coming out now. "Some friends are saying there's a helicopter?"

Georgie wades into the crowd, asking them what they've heard, looking over shoulders at brandished phones. A few people are trying to contact Marianne. Others are looking at local news sites and social media. The noise level rises, voices bouncing off the bare floorboards and hollow furniture, the room warm, her heart beating fast. The sense of Ethan watching gets stronger, but more confusing: What would he want her to do? Among all the unexpected chaos, which way should she be looking?

"There's a fire," a voice looms out of the din, and Georgie spins around in alarm.

"*What?*" She can't see any smoke, can't smell burning, but she is already moving, heading for the fire extinguishers.

Rowena is gesticulating at her phone. "There's a barn on fire in north Derbyshire," she says, and Georgie stops in her tracks. Her mind shoots back to Robbie's piece about Peter catching bad guys—*the man who made things go on fire*—and then to her Google results from just now. She doesn't know how everything fits together. But Peter Lowe seems to be all over it.

"And helicopters, and police, and . . ." Rowena stops and puts her hand over her mouth. "Oh my God . . ."

"What?" Ellen asks. "What is it?"

"Someone says"—Rowena's voice dips—"that he's dead."

The whole room hushes.

"Who?" asks Sara, her voice also dropping to a whisper. "Who's dead?"

Rowena looks up, her eyes huge. Georgie's fingers close into tight, sweaty fists.

"Leo Dean," Rowena says. "People on Facebook . . . they're saying that he's dead."

TWENTY-NINE

ALICE

Saturday, December 9, 2023

Alice hasn't been this close to Chrissy's house since just after Chrissy moved in. The memory is foggy, as if she sleepwalked here with her thinly veiled blackmail folded in her hand. She was so angry, she remembers, so enraged that Chrissy *still* wasn't moving out of the village, even after she'd finally put her pub up for sale. Alice wouldn't be the one to leave. It should've been Chrissy.

The cottage's thatched roof looms ahead of her, in need of repair and dusted with frost. It's still odd to think of this place as Chrissy's home. Even after everything, Alice associates her with the flat above the Raven. So much happened there. Life, love, friendship . . . death.

The pub sign flashes in her mind's eye and she relives the shock of seeing it back up.

"Okay, Alice?" Peter asks as she stops on the lane, several meters from the cottage.

A police car and a large police van are parked just ahead.

Beyond Chrissy's front hedge, two scenes of crime officers work in silence, one dusting her wheelie bin for prints and the other shining a flashlight at the ground. Alice's heart starts to pump. There shouldn't be any traces of her from all that time ago, but still it makes her nervous.

The windows of the cottage are lit, several figures moving around inside. She recognizes the curly mass of Chrissy's hair.

"I . . . I don't know if I can go in." She takes a step back, drawing her jacket close around her body.

"It's okay if you can't." Peter sounds almost relieved.

"Are you going to?"

He purses his lips, his eyes darting. "I need to."

"Why?" As her resolve weakens, their reasons for coming here grow murky.

"I just need to talk to the officers."

She looks at him sidelong. "Pete," she says, "I'm going to ask you one last time." She slows her voice right down, keeping it low enough not to be overheard. "Is there something you want to tell me?"

Suddenly he grips her hand. His is freezing, like a slab of ice.

"Pete," she echoes. "Seriously. What is it?"

A beat of silence, then he drops her hand. "Nothing for you to worry about," he says in a tone that sets off every alarm bell in her body. "There's just something I need to do."

Before she can say anything more, he strides toward Chrissy's front garden. The SOCOs look up and watch him all the way to the door—in recognition or suspicion, it isn't clear. One of them calls out to him but Alice can't hear what's been said. She is rooted to her spot, shivering with cold, unable to follow him but unable to walk away.

THIRTY

CHRISSY

Saturday, December 9, 2023

Chrissy doesn't understand how it's happened. How *Peter* is in her house. He has barely looked at her in two years, has ignored all her attempts to reach out to him for help or understanding, has taken Alice's side so uncompromisingly. Her head is still reeling at the idea of his ex-wife visiting Leo in prison, and she is on the brink of a breakdown as she waits to find out about the barn fire. But here Peter is, looking calm, with Kiri and Ben treating him like an old friend, and she can't cope.

The detectives are a little more wary, more professional. Still, Peter's status as an ex-copper has allowed him into the house—*her* house—as if they've let him duck under the yellow tape of a crime scene.

"Sorry to intrude," he says, but still doesn't look at Chrissy. Doesn't explain, exactly, why he's here.

"Do you have some information for us?" DC Wright finally cuts to the chase.

"Is it true there's a fire?"

The detectives exchange a glance. "Where did you hear that?"

"Around," Peter says.

Nobody presses him further. How does he *do* that?

"We're still waiting for intel," DC Wright says, equally cagey.

"Is . . . is Leo involved . . . ?" Peter glances in Chrissy's direction, and with a jolt, she sees that he's not calm at all. His eyes are bloodshot, surrounded by creases of tension. He looks haunted. Terrified.

He looks how she feels.

For several moments, all she can do is stare back. Has she misjudged him? Does he care, after all? His eyes flicker to the stubby ends of her missing curls, and he frowns slightly.

"We still don't know," DC Colella says.

"Was there someone in that barn?"

"As I said, we're waiting for intel."

"Tell me what you've got." Peter's back in police mode, his voice turning brisk.

"You know we can't do that," DC Wright says.

Peter eyes her steadily. "I seem to remember you owe me a favor, Detective."

She arches her eyebrows. "Are you really playing the back-scratching card?"

"There was a problem with a case—back in 2015 I think it was? A problem with the evidence. And I believe I . . . *helped*." The euphemism rings strongly in the air but Chrissy still feels lost, feels as if she's watching an episode of a cop show.

"Pete," Ben says warningly. "That's not how it works, come on."

Peter swings round to eyeball him. "Isn't it, Ben? Really?"

Ben shakes his head and looks away. An uncomfortable silence descends and Chrissy feels a shot of impatience; whatever game they're all playing is getting them nowhere.

"There's speculation about Leo all over social media anyway," Peter says, turning back to DC Wright. "You may as well tell me the truth. I could help you manage what information gets passed around the village. I could . . ." He throws another glance at Chrissy. "I could help you find him."

Again, she stares back at him. *Now* he wants to help?

Chrissy doesn't understand him, never did. Her eyes trace the line of his stubbled jaw and the broad slope of his shoulders. She feels a dull pulse of hurt behind her rib cage, barely perceptible beneath her other emotions.

"You *can* help us," Wright says, and Peter's eyes glimmer. "By answering some questions. Down at the station might be more appropriate."

A phone rings. Wright pulls out her mobile. "Yes?"

The voice on the other end can be faintly heard: *DI Khan, calling from the scene of the* . . . Wright strides briskly out of the room. Detective Colella follows, and Chrissy watches them go in frustration, unsure if she should follow, too.

"Mate," Ben says to Peter. "Take it easy, okay? You know what Wright's like. Very by the book." He looks at Peter meaningfully, and Chrissy once again senses a subtext she's not party to.

"'By the book' doesn't seem to be working," Peter says curtly.

Nobody speaks for some time. Chrissy feels pulses of anger darting up through her like sparks of current.

"Why have you come?" she snaps at Peter. "Why now?"

He looks taken aback. She's already half-certain he won't answer. That he'll put up a wall, like he always did. His opaqueness used to drive Alice crazy, and in time Chrissy came to understand exactly what she meant.

Kiri peers between them with curiosity, until her phone lights up. Chrissy sees her blink twice, reading the message, then nudge Ben. He raises his eyebrows as she shows him her phone, and they both walk out of the room.

Chrissy is torn, again, between following them and staying with Peter. She doesn't remember when she was last alone with him. She can smell the outdoor air coming off his clothes and a faint tang of anxious sweat. She turns to meet his eyes. Unexpectedly, tears come into hers.

"I've been texting you," she says. "Calling you."

He sweeps a hand through his hair. "I know."

"I needed your help. Leo needed—*needs*—your help."

"I . . ." He exhales through his nose, continuing in a whisper: "I *have* been looking for him."

She jolts at this. "You have?"

"Every day since I heard he'd disappeared. I've been trying everything. Ringing round my old contacts at the prison, and in the force—only the ones I trust, of course . . ." He speaks even more quietly, eyeing the door. "I'd already asked a guard I know at the prison to call me when Leo was out, just so I could feel . . . I don't know . . . mentally prepared, I suppose. So I think I knew something was off even before you did, that he'd left earlier than expected . . . After that I managed to get into his Facebook, and I drove round all the places he used to hang out—"

"His Facebook?" she interrupts. "How?"

"He told me his PlayStation password, years ago, when we were having a gaming session with Robbie. Turns out he used the same one for Facebook. But there was nothing there, nothing useful. It was a long shot anyway."

She stares at him. This is exactly like him. Acting alone, no communication, never letting anybody know where they stand. She exhales, too, closing her eyes.

"Does Alice know?" she asks.

"Does Alice know what?"

"That . . ." She stalls as she realizes why her question seems ambiguous. "Does Alice know you've been looking for Leo?"

He looks down, shaking his head. "Alice doesn't know anything."

Chrissy puts her hands over her face, uneven lengths of hair tickling her fingers. She hears—feels—Peter stepping closer. "Chrissy . . ."

"Don't," she says, moving away. "I can't do this right now, Pete. All I can think about is where Leo is."

"That's why I'm here. I want to help properly. Want to be up front about it."

"Up front about . . . ?"

"All of it." His voice is urgent. "What's the point in keeping secrets now?"

She pushes back her hair, swearing softly, but she knows

he's right. Some secrets are like rituals; when they've been part of your life for long enough, you stop thinking about what purpose they serve.

But some secrets need to be taken to the grave.

"Why did Marianne visit Leo in prison?" she asks.

His whole face flinches. She wonders if this is new information to him. She can see thoughts running behind his eyes but can't tell what they are.

"She knows," he says.

Chrissy stiffens. "What?"

"After New Year's Eve . . . after what happened . . . I couldn't handle it. Couldn't keep it all to myself any longer. I told her."

Her head starts to roar as she follows the logic through. "Are you saying . . . Did she tell *Leo?*"

"I think so."

"Why the hell would she do that?"

"I don't know . . . The whole thing messed with her head, too . . ."

Chrissy starts to pace up and down her kitchen. "You didn't think to *mention* this, Peter?"

"I-I was angry with her for telling him. We'd been arguing . . . I was in shock myself, at the idea of him knowing. Then he went missing and—"

"And that's exactly when you should've told me! It might be important! Leo's cellmate said he'd not been himself in the last few weeks of his sentence. And no wonder, if Marianne dropped a *bombshell* like that."

"Keep your voice down," he says, nodding at the door.

"What's the point now? We need to tell them, too! You just said so yourself!"

"We should. We will. I just thought I'd try to find out what I could on my own first. Figure out if it was all connected . . ."

"*Shit.*" Chrissy turns her back on him. She can't believe Leo found out something so huge and didn't say a word. She imagines him stewing over it in the weeks leading up to his release. How could Marianne do that? She might've caused all this.

We *might have caused all this.*

She leans heavily against the worktop, splaying her fingers on its fake-wood surface. As she lifts her head, something catches her eye outside the window. She does a double take but she knows she's not mistaken. She'd recognize that tall figure anywhere.

"Alice is here, too?"

The kitchen door opens then, and the detectives stride back in. Chrissy is still staring out of the window. She is certain Alice can see her, but she can't make out her face clearly enough to know whether they're staring into each other's eyes.

"Ms. Dean," DC Wright says. Then again, louder, when Chrissy doesn't respond.

Chrissy snaps out of it, whirling around. *Leo. The barn, the fire.*

"Can we talk to you in private?"

They gesture toward the hallway. Chrissy glances back at Peter, then at the window, before she leaves the room and closes the door behind her. The hall feels dark compared to the kitchen, as if it's already night out here.

"What is it?" she asks, trying to focus. The PCs, Kiri and Ben, seem to have disappeared. And there is something different about the demeanor of the detectives, a sense that they are trying to appear calmer than they are.

"Our officers at the barn have been in touch . . ."

"What's happened?" Chrissy cuts through the preamble, her voice strangled.

Wright's expression is grim. She exchanges a glance with her colleague. "There's a body."

THIRTY-ONE

GEORGIE

Saturday, December 9, 2023

"Who says Leo's dead?"

"It can't . . . It doesn't . . . Are you *sure?*"

"Was it the fire?"

"Was it deliberate?"

"Where's he *been* all this time?"

Speculation pinballs around the pub as the villagers try to understand the escalating rumors. The mood begins to tip from one of frenzied information-seeking to something much graver. And there is guilt, too, Georgie can see. Guilt for every bad thought any of them ever had about Leo. Poppy starts crying and Janice won't stop talking, as if to detract from the names she was calling him only a few minutes before.

Georgie is still hovering near the fire extinguishers. Leo. Dead? The idea sits like a heavy mass in her chest but she can't tell what shape it is, what color. She never knew Leo.

But he was Ethan's son. Part of Ethan's other life, the one he always described in such unhappy terms. He loved Leo, though. All parents love their children; all children love their parents—isn't that a given?

She wonders if that's true of her own parents, for whom aloofness and disapproval seem to be natural states. Her thoughts move to Lola and she feels an unbalancing tug of longing and loneliness.

"Nobody wanted this," she hears someone say in the crowd, and the noise level dips in acknowledgment.

"No." It's Ellen who replies. "Of course not. Of *course* not."

Georgie feels her breath getting shallower. She pictures the empty flat above their heads, Leo's room with the flecks of Blu-Tack on the walls, the photo of Chrissy and Ethan with Leo between them. The initials behind these fire extinguishers taking on new meaning, now the marks of two ghosts, not just one. She thinks of Ethan's grave and the often powerful sense of him standing right beside her. Then with a small gasp she pushes through the pub, to the front door, out onto the square.

It is silent and crisp and still. The late afternoon light has a bleached quality to it, giving the outside world an air of surreal abandonment. Georgie takes deep breaths, the cold sharp in her lungs. She tries to calm herself with mantras from the yoga class she used to go to with Lo, but the question threads its way through them: Leo, dead? In the life she was supposed to have, she would've become his stepmum—in name at least. Stepmum to a boy who would end up in prison. Or perhaps he wouldn't have killed Robbie if his dad had never died. Perhaps everybody's lives would've been sent along a different course.

All the more reason to find out who was to blame. To hold them accountable at last.

She looks up at the Raven sign, right into the bird's eyes, and opens her mouth to scream. But she doesn't. She stops herself. And in that moment, she senses she is not alone. She turns and scans the square, spotting Marianne sitting on a low wall down the side of the chip shop, sucking on a vape that doesn't seem to fit Georgie's idea of her, though she couldn't say why.

Drawing herself up tall, Georgie walks over.

"Marianne," she says. "Are you okay?"

Marianne looks at her, seeming startled. "I'm fine," she half-snaps, then turns irritably away.

The wind picks up in the pause that follows. A greasy wrapper blows across the square, cartwheeling like something alive, and the Christmas tree quivers, unlit today out of respect.

"Apparently the police have been trying to get in touch with you," Georgie says.

Marianne turns back to her but says nothing. Her phone is in her hand, Georgie sees. There's no way she's been oblivious to any calls. She sucks on her vape and blows out a stream of fruity fumes.

"And . . . did you hear about Leo . . . ?" Georgie is unwilling to give up on Marianne this time. She knows something—she's sure of it. She's not as outside of all this as she first appeared.

"Hear what?"

"That he might be . . . I mean, there's speculation that he's . . . dead."

Marianne drops her vape with a clatter. She stares at Georgie, blanching. "What?"

"There was a fire and people are saying—"

"What people? How sure are they?"

"It's unconfirmed . . ." Georgie didn't expect the raw panic in Marianne's eyes. What does this news mean to her, exactly?

Marianne stabs at her phone and then holds it to her ear. Georgie can hear it ringing, wonders who she's calling. Nobody answers and Marianne shakes her head, jumping up from the wall.

"Are you okay?" Georgie asks again. "I didn't mean to shock you—" But she is distracted as she sees, out of the corner of her eye, the gleam of a fluorescent police uniform. Two constables stride across the square, determination in their step. Marianne bends to pick up her vape, twirling it between her fingers as the PCs spot them and swerve in their direction.

"We're conducting some inquiries into the disappearance of Leo Dean," the female officer says, looking at each of them in turn.

Georgie notes the word *disappearance*, not *murder*, not *death*. But she restrains herself from asking the question.

"Could you confirm your names, please?"

"Georgie Fallows," Georgie supplies after a moment's hesitation.

"Marianne Lowe," Marianne says, and Georgie is surprised to hear she's still using her married name.

Never trust a Lowe.

The female PC taps her pen against her notebook. "Marianne," she says. "Could we start with you?"

"Okay . . ."

"Is there somewhere in the pub we could use, perhaps? Somewhere private?"

Georgie steps in, recovering her hostess role with a shake of her hair. "I'll show you to the office." She starts walking briskly back toward the pub. "And I'll make sure you aren't disturbed."

Heads turn as she leads the police and Marianne through the pub. Conversations drop away and she keeps herself tall, shoulders pulled back, boots clicking on the uncarpeted floors.

"Will you be okay in here?" she says when they get to the office. "I can put the electric heater on . . ." She flits around the chilly room, half-wanting to stay, half-desperate to get out.

"This is adequate, thank you," the policewoman says.

Georgie knows when she's being dismissed. She shoots a glance at Marianne as she leaves. Marianne checks her phone one last time before tucking it away and perching on the very edge of a chair.

MARIANNE IS IN there for over half an hour. Georgie spends most of that time repeating the words *I don't know* as the other villagers ask why Marianne is being questioned, who else will be called in, whether Leo really is dead. Her head gets fuller and fuller, close to bursting, and she resists the urge to drink straight from the open bottle of red wine on the bar top.

She is about to escape outside for another dose of fresh air when the two officers and Marianne emerge. Marianne holds her handbag against her chest, her face drawn, her eyes tired. She walks out of the pub without a backward glance.

Georgie stares after her. Until she hears: "Ms. Fallows? Could you join us next, please?"

She whips her head back with a forced smile. "Of course."

THE OFFICE IS still freezing and she thinks about suggesting the electric heater again. But maybe it's better to be cold and clearheaded than flustered and over-warm. She finds herself in Peter's usual seat this time, because the police officers are sitting in hers and Alice's. She thinks of how preoccupied he always seemed at committee meetings, silent and disengaged until he would suddenly choose not to be. Georgie's attention was usually trained on Alice. Ethan hadn't trusted her and she'd assumed the stranger outside the pub had been talking about her, too. But it's all of them, she now thinks. *It takes a village to keep a secret.*

"We're PCs Lochland and Marley," the female officer says, pointing from her colleague to herself. "But most people round here know us as Kiri and Ben." She leaves a beat. "You're not from Cromley, is that right?"

Georgie uncrosses her legs. "I'm from London."

"So what brought you here?"

It's an answer she's trotted out many times. "I got tired of city living. And I love Derbyshire; I used to come here as a child." Both of these things are, in fact, true. They were the reasons a potential life here with Ethan had seemed like a call of fate.

"No other connection to this place?"

Georgie pauses, then shakes her head.

"And yet you bought into this pub? A substantial share, from what we've been told."

Georgie tries not to react, though she wonders who's been divulging. "Well, that was what clinched it, in the end. I've always wanted to be involved in something like this. Something . . . community focused. I worked in marketing and brand management in London, so when I saw what they were trying to do here, I thought I could help."

"And how have you got on?"

"Well . . ." Georgie lets her smile fade. "I didn't exactly expect . . . all of this . . ." She gestures at the two of them, and at the door that leads back out toward the bar.

"Did you know about the death that happened in this pub before you bought into it?"

Georgie pauses again. Then, in a moment of boldness, she says: "Deaths." Her voice is calm. Her hands are clasped in her lap.

"I beg your pardon?" Ben says.

"There have been two deaths in this pub."

They exchange glances. "You're referring to . . . Ethan Dean?"

"Yes."

"What do you . . ." They seem thrown off course. "Well, we're not currently . . ."

"You don't think there's any connection?" Georgie asks, still calmly, though her skin now has a sheen of sweat.

"Between a suicide and a bar fight?"

"In the same pub. Involving a lot of the same people."

They look at her strangely. Maybe this is her moment. Maybe she should've kept it this simple all along: herself and two police officers, in a room, with the right questions being asked.

But then Ben picks up his phone, taps a few times, and thrusts it at her. Grainy black-and-white footage is playing on the screen, and she frowns, confused by the diversion, until she realizes what she's seeing and she's back to ice-cold.

"Is this you?" Ben asks.

"What . . . ?" She still can't quite understand it. She can see it's her, all wrapped up in a hat and scarf, but it takes her a few more moments to place where she is, what she's doing. That night she walked up the lane to Chrissy's cottage. A moment of weakness, of wanting just to look at where she lived. She'd been out wandering anyway, unable to sleep as usual, and her feet had propelled her there. But where was the camera? One thing she'd always assumed about Cromley was a lack of CCTV. Not like in London, where you were forever being watched, whether you remembered it or not as you were going about your day. Being filmed in the village, unaware, feels even more unnerving. Where else might hidden eyes be spying?

"Chrissy Dean installed a privately owned camera outside her cottage," Kiri explains. "She's been receiving threats, so she—"

"I was just out walking," Georgie says. "I have trouble sleeping."

"Why did you go to Chrissy's house?"

"I just . . . wandered up that lane. Then realized where I was and turned back again."

"You linger there for"—Ben checks—"almost three minutes."

"It isn't a crime." She immediately regrets saying it. Nothing *she* has done has been a crime. She's been very careful about that.

"Do you know who replaced the pub sign?" Kiri plows on. "Or who might have defaced the pub wall?"

Georgie's heart hammers. *Deflect*, every nerve ending in her body urges her. *Play your card.*

She presses down through her long legs, into her heels, into the slight springiness of the linoleum floor. "I have something I need to tell you, actually, Officers . . ."

"Could you answer the question first?" Kiri's expression reminds her of the mock-strict schoolteacher look that Ethan would sometimes put on. It used to make her laugh, and there *is* something faintly ridiculous about Kiri's demeanor, like she's just playacting at being a police officer. But the atmosphere in the room is charged. If this is a game, it's a serious one.

"Was it you?" Ben joins in.

"Me? Why would I?"

"Why would anyone?"

"There is a lot of bad feeling in this village," Georgie says. "A lot of hatred. A lot of guilt."

"Guilt?"

Georgie nods slowly, glad Kiri has leaped on this word. "Guilty consciences all round is my observation. No wonder they're manifesting in strange ways."

They look at each other again, skepticism passing between them. In the silence, Georgie leans forward. "I saw Peter hiding something in the dumpster in the pub garden."

Now they swing back toward her, eyes wide. Kiri looks curious; Ben more concerned. But she has their attention, she has a bargaining chip, and she has the evidence, at home in her wardrobe, to back it up.

THIRTY-TWO

ALICE

Saturday, December 9, 2023

Alice watches her brother and her ex–best friend through the bright square of Chrissy's kitchen window. The police have disappeared, and Chrissy and Peter are absorbed in conversation. Alice wishes she could lip-read. What have they got to say to one another? It was always her and Chrissy before: the confiding, the closeness. Peter was just . . . around. And since Robbie's death, Alice and Peter have become the united ones, with Chrissy on the other side of a dark, uncrossable trench.

Now Alice sees Chrissy pushing her hands into her hair and Peter stepping near to her, reaching out as if he wants to touch her. Something stirs in Alice's core, almost like humiliation. Why is this so hard to watch?

Go in there. Find out what's going on.

Just as she's trying to unfreeze her feet from the ground, she sees Chrissy turn to face the window. Her head slumps forward, her hair cascading over her face, but then she straightens up and looks directly at Alice. Alice stops breathing as Chrissy keeps looking at her through the window, her expression inscrutable.

Then the detectives re-enter the kitchen and the spell is broken. Alice exhales, her breath a white mist in the air. Peter glances toward her but a stubborn fury prickles over her, stopping her from meeting his eye.

She keeps watching as Chrissy leaves the room with the police and Peter is left alone in the kitchen. He paces, clearly agitated. Alice keeps replaying it: the way he stepped toward Chrissy, the way she recoiled as if his proximity was painful. A different kind of painful from what she'd expect in this situation. Is she reading too much into it, or is she out here in the cold and the dark in more ways than one?

Suddenly the front door of the cottage flies open and Chrissy bursts out. Alice jumps back, even though she's still several meters away. Chrissy stands with her hands against her cheeks, her eyes wide and shining. Then she leans forward and vomits into a large plant pot.

Alice stares. Chrissy straightens slowly and Alice can make out tear tracks on her cheeks. Her burning instinct is to run toward her, comfort her, but she shuts it down. There is something agonizingly familiar about the look on Chrissy's face, though. The way her body stoops forward like it's trying to curl in on itself.

Grief. Alice knows it when she sees it.

A hard ball of dread forms in her gut. She takes two tiny steps forward, and her mouth opens but nothing comes out.

The movement is enough to make Chrissy turn in her direction. Curls are matted to the sides of her face and her upper body is shaking.

"Looks like you got what you wanted, Alice," she says, her words ringing across the garden.

Alice flinches. The raw anger in Chrissy's voice is familiar, too. She's spoken that way herself, many times in the last two years.

"How do you know what I want?" she retorts, but her own tone comes out meek and subdued.

Chrissy starts crying more violently, leaning forward as if to be sick again. Alice remembers vomiting in the pub toilet after she saw the initials in the wall. She thinks of how much weight Chrissy lost after Ethan's death because she couldn't keep anything down. And she herself after Robbie's.

"Chrissy," comes Peter's voice from the house. He runs out of the front door, his eyes flicking to Alice but hardly seeming to see her. "What's happened? Is it Leo?"

He looks just as wretched. Alice watches him intently as he fixates on Chrissy.

"They've found a body," Chrissy sobs.

Peter's face contorts. "Leo's?"

"They don't know yet. A man. They think he died in the fire. And they . . . they . . ." Chrissy doubles right over with her hands on her knees. "They found a coat, too, nearby. The coat Leo was wearing when he came out of prison."

"Fuck," Peter says, his hand shooting up to his mouth. "Oh, fuck."

Alice is still frozen several paces away, watching them

as if she's on the other side of a screen. Chrissy's tears are tapping into a dark place inside her. Peter's stricken face is scattering her thoughts.

"We don't know anything for sure yet," Peter says, touching Chrissy's shoulder. "We shouldn't jump to conclusions."

We? Alice's head feels thick. The dark garden swims, the lit cottage swaying in the background. "Peter," she says, fighting to keep it together. "Tell me what's going on. I mean, *really*. All of it. Please."

He looks at her through a sheen of tears. Close to Chrissy, distanced from her. Consoling Robbie's killer's mum. Crying, it seems, over the killer himself.

"He's my son, Alice," he says in a broken voice. "Leo is my son."

THIRTY-THREE

CHRISSY

Friday, March 5, 1999

Chrissy was late opening the doors to the pub that evening. She was clearing up broken glass in the upstairs flat, trying not to make any noise as she picked the shiny, sharp flecks out of the carpet. Even when she cut her finger, she bit her lip to stop herself from whimpering. Ethan was marking exam papers at the desk in the corner, and she couldn't disturb him any more than she already had.

Taking the dustpan through to the kitchen, she allowed herself a quiet sob as she tipped the glass into the bin and wrapped a plaster around her fingertip. On nights when his stress levels were this high, her very existence made him furious. She would try to be small, silent, invisible, but it was never enough. Her stomach churned as she put the dustpan carefully back in the cupboard, closing the door with barely a clunk. An impossible task lay ahead of her: stopping the bustle of the pub from rising through the ceiling as the night went on.

She glanced around to make sure the kitchen was spotless, then crept back through the living room. Ethan was muttering to himself, calling his pupils stupid and lazy, but she knew he'd be writing all the right things on the papers, all the encouragement and guidance a model teacher should provide. He muttered the word *idiot* more loudly as she passed, but didn't show any outward signs of noticing her leave.

Downstairs, she took a moment to recover. To become Chrissy the smiling hostess again. She raked her hands through her hair, imagining flecks of glass caught in her curls, then unbolted the front doors of the pub.

To her surprise, Peter and two other men were already waiting outside.

"Oh!" she said, finding a grin. "You're keen tonight!"

Peter grinned back sheepishly. One of his friends leaned forward, clapping him on the shoulder. "We're celebrating!"

Chrissy's mood lifted just a little. It was hard not to get swept up in their cheer as they barreled through to the bar. The older man bought the round, tipping Chrissy generously, then proposing a toast: "To Pete!"

Chrissy joined in with the Diet Coke she'd poured for herself. "So what's the occasion?" She winked at Peter. "Don't tell me you're making an honest woman of Marianne?"

He looked a little coy and shook his head. Maybe an engagement *was* in the cards, given the tinge in his cheeks, but that apparently wasn't the cause for celebration tonight.

"Thought not," Chrissy teased. "She's out of your league."

"I know it," Peter said without any hint of bitterness.

"Pete closed a major case today," the older man finally supplied. "Nasty fucker we've been trying to get for ages. 'Scuse my French . . ." He held up a hand to Chrissy, who laughed and shrugged, then he clapped Peter on the back again. "The boy done good."

"It wasn't just me," Peter said.

"And modest, too." Chrissy kept up the teasing, knowing it was water off a duck's back to him.

"You took charge," the older man said. "Stepped up. I was proud to have you on the team."

Peter looked quietly thrilled, and Chrissy felt a warm buzz of pleasure on his behalf. She wondered what time Alice would be in tonight. She'd be proud of her brother, too.

"Well, that *does* sound like a big deal," she said, dropping the mockery. "Nice one, Pete." She raised her glass again. "Next round's on the house."

The three men cheered loudly. Chrissy remembered Ethan upstairs and winced. The sound of male voices in the pub annoyed him more than female ones; he would accuse Chrissy of having too much fun with men she shouldn't even be talking to. Gone were the days when her outgoing, flirty nature had been a turn-on for him. When he'd stand at the bar, drinking her in as she sparkled for everybody else. He'd bought her this pub, called her his queen of the Raven, and then punished her for all of it—the stress of running the place, her friendships with her punters, the daily disappointment of the life he'd claimed to want.

"What was the case?" she asked Peter as he sipped his beer.

There was something lovely about the way his face brightened, pleased to be asked about his work. A contrast to the curl of Ethan's lip when she tried to talk to him about teaching. Apparently she just wouldn't understand.

"Can't say too much. A bunch of crimes—arson, mainly. Murder. Should have enough evidence to go to court now."

"That's great," she told him.

"Yup." He seemed to remember he was rubbish at accepting compliments and ducked his head back to his pint.

"All sounds a bit action-packed for round here," she added with a smile, gesturing at the field outside the back window.

"You'd be surprised," he said. "Rural crime's on the up. It wasn't actually in Cromley, though. Further north, more toward Yorkshire. Not *our* village."

"God forbid." She laughed. "No crime in Cromley. The village elders see to that!"

"Ah, no need to talk about your husband that way," he joked, without seeming to notice the freeze of Chrissy's smile.

Ethan *was* a lot older than her. The gap seemed to widen every day. And it was true: He did act as if he was in charge of Cromley, as if everybody should fall at his feet every time he walked into the church or the pub or the school. Nobody would believe her if she told them the truth. Or perhaps everybody would assume she was at fault.

Everybody except Alice.

As if on cue, the door opened and her friend swept in. Her near-black hair was long and loose and she was wearing a purple velvet blazer over a black-and-white striped dress. Just looking at her made you think, *I bet that woman is bloody fasci-*

nating to talk to. And she was, she really was. Chrissy couldn't keep up with all the things she knew and read, but Alice never made her feel as if she needed to.

"Oh my God, I need a drink," Alice said, collapsing elegantly onto a bar stool. She launched into an anecdote about an older male academic who'd spoken down to her while staring at her legs, then partway through remembered to hoist herself over the bar to give Chrissy a hug. Dropping back down, she rounded off her story with a matter-of-fact summary of how she'd subtly destroyed the man in return, then turned to her brother. "You're here early, Constable Lowe!"

"He's celebrating," Chrissy said. "He's been single-handedly taking down Derbyshire's most dangerous criminals."

"And I thought *I'd* achieved something taking down one misogynistic bloke." Alice grinned. "Congratulations, bro . . . Wait, was it the case you were telling me about?"

Peter darted a warning glance at his boss. "I told you nothing," he said out of the corner of his mouth to Alice.

She tapped her nose, then glugged from the glass of red wine Chrissy had poured her without needing to ask. "Just the job," she said, beaming at Chrissy. "Thanks, lovely. I'm only having one, though. Got an abstract to write." She twirled the glass. "Just. One."

"Maybe two," Chrissy said, mimicking Alice's usual follow-up.

"See how this goes down," Alice agreed, smiling again. Then she leaned toward Chrissy and flicked her eyes at the ceiling. "Ethan?" she inquired in a lower voice.

"Marking papers," Chrissy said. "And . . . stressed."

"Okay," Alice murmured, her eyebrows knitting. "Well . . ." Concern spread across her face like a cloud. "Call me later if you need me."

Chrissy nodded, her stomach corkscrewing at the thought of what might be in store for her tonight, after closing. It all depended on how noisy the pub got, and to what extent he decided it was her doing.

"You know you can *always* call me, right?" Alice said more forcefully, reaching past the pumps to squeeze Chrissy's hand. "I'm not just saying it."

"I . . ." But the door swung open and more customers came in—Dave, Ellen, Janice, and Rowena—so Chrissy moved away from Alice to serve them. She could feel Alice's gaze on her, though, as she often did. Sometimes she suspected Alice was checking for signs she was physically hurt. But sometimes she just seemed to be observing admiringly; Alice would comment that she made pint-pouring look like an art form. Maybe she was trying to make Chrissy feel better about the fact that Alice was the high achiever, *and* the looker, while all Chrissy had was her pub and her regulars.

That wasn't nothing, though, she mused as she saw Dave threading coins into the jukebox, swaying to the first few bars of "Breaking the Law."

"One for the coppers," he said over his shoulder, and the three police officers laughed raucously.

Chrissy relinquished any hope of a quiet night. She poured herself a whisky and knocked it back before serving Peter and his colleagues another round.

———

ALICE LEFT AFTER two glasses of wine, hugging Chrissy as if she didn't want to let her go.

"Come and stay at mine," she whispered into her ear. "Come and *live* at mine."

Chrissy's eyes filled with tears. She could do that, couldn't she? She could leave Ethan. But there was always the possibility that he would be sad and sweet and sorry when she got back upstairs. That he would hold her even more tightly than Alice was right now. Those nights happened more often than Alice seemed willing to believe. And they meant more to Chrissy than she could ever explain.

"I'll be fine," she whispered back. "He'll probably be asleep when I go up."

Alice drew back, holding Chrissy by the elbows. "*Call me,*" she said with feeling. "I'm only round the corner."

AFTER ALICE HAD left, Chrissy threw herself into her work. She couldn't predict or change how Ethan would behave, but she could make the people around her happy. There was joy in knowing their little preferences—who liked dry-roasted peanuts instead of salted, who appreciated two straws in their vodka and Coke—and in the music and the flushed faces and the jokes she'd heard many, many times before. There was joy in seeing Peter let his hair down—a rare sight since he'd been trying hard to get a promotion—and in flirting a little with him and his colleagues; also a rare occurrence since Ethan had told her it made her look desperate and cheap. She kept ducking behind the bar to take sips of whisky, which heightened the joy, softened her fear. As long as there were customers in the pub, her life upstairs was on pause. In short snatches she could even believe it didn't exist.

But the customers wouldn't stay forever. Every time a group said good-bye and wandered out into the spring night, Chrissy's fear would notch back up. She wanted to grab hold of her neighbors, beg them to stay. But eventually, inevitably, the pub was empty.

She cleared the glasses slowly, her body becoming heavier, limper, as all the energy and bravado of her hostess persona trickled away. When two wineglasses slipped through her fingers and shattered on the floor, she was right back to earlier. Ethan knocking the glass of wine she'd brought him straight out of her hands, snapping that he couldn't drink while he was marking papers; was she a fucking idiot? The fact that he normally *did* drink while marking wasn't worth pointing out. She'd just cleaned up without a word, and she did the same now, crying at her own clumsiness.

"Chrissy?"

She jumped at the voice from behind, whipping round with the sweeping brush brandished.

"Don't shoot!" Peter said, holding up his hands.

She breathed out, lowering the brush. "I thought everyone had gone!"

"I was just in the toilet," he said, looking around the empty bar. "Clearly for several hours . . ." Then he stepped toward her, studying her face. "Hey, are you okay? Are you . . . crying?"

She shook her head, turning away. "Just tired."

"Chrissy . . ."

"Honestly, I . . ." She darted a glance back at him, seeing genuine worry in his eyes. Had Alice said something to him? Hinted about Ethan? Chrissy had begged her not to; the last thing she wanted was a police officer knowing the complexities of her marriage. "I'm fine," she finished lamely, concentrating on the last of the tidying up.

He started helping her and they worked in silence for a while, just the clink of glasses and the soft pad of their footsteps. The air smelled of beer and furniture polish, falling into gradual shades of darkness as Chrissy went round switching off the various lights.

She paused behind the bar, watching in surprise as Peter closed the glass washer and pressed two buttons to switch it on. "How do you know how to do that?"

He shrugged and flushed. "I've seen you do it loads of times."

The idea of him watching her—enough to know which buttons to press—sat strangely, but not unpleasantly.

"It's kind of impressive, the way you basically run this place by yourself," he said. "Alice always says so . . . and I agree."

"Not by myself," Chrissy said. "Ethan's my business partner."

"But it's you," he said, pointing at her as if she wouldn't know who he meant. "It's basically . . . you."

More tears filled her eyes. "I love this pub," she croaked. "It's what keeps me . . ." Now she stopped. She wasn't sure whether she was going to say, *keeps me going* or *keeps me here*. Either would be giving away too much.

Suddenly she felt his hand on her arm, gentle and light. Goosebumps formed under his fingertips. Her heart pounded as her eyes slid up to his. His pupils were dilated and she wanted to ask him how much he'd drunk, then wondered how much she had, then stopped caring as he moved in closer.

"Peter," she said warningly, as he nudged his nose against hers like a question.

"Sorry," he said, slurring slightly. "Is this okay?"

"We . . ." Her stomach flipped as she imagined Ethan coming down the stairs. Peter kissed her cheek, then her neck, sweeping aside her mass of curls. Chrissy's body fired up in a way it hadn't in a long, long time. "We can't," she whispered, putting a hand on his chest. He inhaled and pulled away from her, but his fingers hovered softly on her arm.

The end of his kisses felt like being pushed out into the cold. Chrissy breathed hard, fighting with herself. She couldn't do this. But why shouldn't she? She got punished most days for doing nothing wrong. This was something she wanted, something just for her. In this moment, she seemed to want it more than anything.

"In here," she murmured, pulling Peter toward the cellar.

THIRTY-FOUR

ALICE

Saturday, December 9, 2023

Alice strides through the woods, shoving branches aside with her cold, numb hands. She can hear a rushing sound but doesn't know if it's the river, deeper within the trees, or just the hiss of shock in her ears. She fled as soon as Peter said the words *Leo is my son*, yelling at him not to follow her. Now she has never felt so alone, so unconvinced he was even planning to.

The woods are like a dark, frozen maze rather than the place where she walks Beech every morning, where she used to bring Robbie for picnics and hide-and-seek. Noises seem distorted, thrown about among the trunks, and the patches of frost on the ground glint like fragments of glass. When her foot skids and she stumbles over a tree root, she lets herself fall. Then lies panting, winded, staring up at the starless sky.

Twenty years of her life, completely reframed.

She imagines herself getting flatter and thinner until she

is part of the forest floor. Then she wouldn't have to *try* anymore. Wouldn't have to be angry or in pain, or wrap her head around the secret her brother and best friend have kept from her. She wouldn't have to confront all her ugly little emotions: jealousy, exclusion, embarrassment. How *stupid* she must've been not to have realized. To have assumed she and Peter were fighting the same fight. He let her rant and rage about Leo, let her express the darkest, nastiest feelings toward him . . . and all this time, she was talking about Peter's *son*. She is ashamed of herself but she is furious, *furious* with her brother for allowing that to happen. And somewhere in the chaos of it all, she is desperately sad for Robbie. He looked up to Peter like a dad, while his real son was living just around the corner.

Leo is my nephew.

My nephew killed my son.

Peter's son killed his nephew.

Whichever way she puts it, it feels like a sick joke the universe has played.

"Alice!" she hears somewhere in the distance, then feels the tremor of footsteps in the ground she's still lying on.

It's Peter's voice. She doesn't want to talk to him but she can't move. Everything that has been keeping her functioning seems to be seeping into the cold earth. Maybe when he reaches her, she will just be bones.

"Alice?" The footsteps come closer. As far as she can tell, it's just him, and that's something at least. She can't face both of them, now that she knows they *are* a "them."

She remembers that Leo is suspected dead, and a wave of something else goes right through her. A son and a nephew, both gone. Even from her place of self-loathing and self-pity, it's too awful to contemplate.

"Alice! Are you okay?" Peter rushes toward her and then he's crouching beside her, rubbing her left hand between both of his. "You're bloody freezing! Are you hurt?"

There are lots of answers she could give, she thinks, but she shakes her head. Feeling ridiculous now, she moves her feet and fingers to bring back some sensation, then slowly sits up. Peter takes off his hat and puts it on her. It's warm from his head and too big, sinking comfortingly over her eyes. After a second, though, she rips it off and hands it angrily back to him, letting the cold resettle in her scalp.

"I'm sorry, Al," he says, looking sadly at the hat. "You . . . you must be pretty shocked."

"Why didn't you tell me? Before . . . and after . . ." She can't decide which hurts more. Chrissy and Peter keeping this secret while they were all close, or Peter keeping it after Leo killed Robbie.

"It was a one-night stand," he says, bundling the hat into his pocket. "We didn't want Ethan or Marianne to ever find out. Even when . . . *especially* when Chrissy realized she was pregnant. She wanted Ethan to believe Leo was his—"

"But Ethan was a *monster,*" Alice breaks in, unable to contain herself. She feels another rush of baffling emotion: a different kind of anger toward Peter, justified or not, for letting Chrissy stay with Ethan rather than whisking her and their baby away.

She knows it isn't that simple but she wishes it could've been. There's another life there, somehow, which they all could've had.

"I didn't realize what Ethan was like until much later," Peter says, bowing his head. "But Chrissy was insistent he should never know. She wanted to make it work with him."

Alice thinks back to that time. Chrissy was at her happiest when she was pregnant. Hopeful for the future, hopeful that life would be different. It's agony to think about it now.

"So, we just never spoke of it . . ." Peter shifts around, struggling to get comfortable on the ground. Eventually he stands up and holds out a hand to help Alice to her feet, too. She takes it reluctantly. When they're standing face-to-face, he puts his hands on her arms, makes her look at him, and she feels as if he's tricked her again.

She can't get her head round how he managed it, all these years. Socializing with Chrissy and Leo. Marianne there, too. Never giving anything away, even though it must've been on his mind constantly.

Watching Leo grow up alongside Robbie.

Watching him attack him and kill him and get sent down for manslaughter.

"How the *fuck* did you keep that to yourself?" she says, pulling out of his arms.

Peter flinches and steps back. "I don't know. I don't know how either of us did it. I think, for the most part, I was just glad I got to see Leo. I hated the fact he was being brought up by that bastard . . . especially as I came to realize how much of a *bastard* he really was . . ." Veins protrude from his neck like tree roots. "But . . . at least I was in his life. And I did what I could to feel closer to him. I even kept a scrapbook . . ." He pauses, as if remembering something, and looks off into the trees with a sudden deep frown between his brows.

Alice fends off a barrage of images. Peter and Chrissy together. Where? How? She doesn't want to know, yet her brain keeps suggesting different possibilities, different scenes. She sees Leo's face but can't bear to analyze it for resemblances to her brother. She sees Ethan's fake smiles and private sneers and his lifeless, staring eyes.

"After Ethan died . . ." she chokes out. "Even then, you didn't . . ."

"I couldn't tell Marianne," Peter says. "I *did,* eventually. That was why we split up. Why we've got so much to work through now, on top of everything else. But for years I was too scared to tell her—"

"But you could've told *me!*" Alice says, shoving her hand into his chest. "Why were you both too cowardly to tell *me?*"

He staggers and grabs a tree trunk to keep from losing his balance. She must've shoved him harder than she thought. He looks at her steadily and there is anger in *his* face now. She's crossed a line but she won't be the one to apologize.

"I think you know why, Alice," he says crisply, and she stares back at him in confusion.

They both startle as his phone buzzes in his pocket. Peter doesn't move for a moment, his eyes still fixed on Alice, then he sighs and pulls out the insistently ringing phone.

"Hello?" he says into it, sounding as weary as Alice feels. "Yeah, it's Peter . . ."

She takes the chance to wipe under her eyes and brush the dirt off her coat. What now? What next? The idea of returning to the village, of talking to the police, to Chrissy, finding out about the body . . . It makes her want to lie on the ground again and never get up.

Peter talks in one-word sentences into his phone. *Yes* and *no* and *nearby* and *okay*. When he hangs up, he draws in a breath that seems to come up from his boots.

"I need to go back," he says. "The police know about my scrapbook. I've got no idea how. I . . . I got rid of it . . ."

"What do you mean?"

"I chucked it in the dumpster at the back of the Raven. I was worried it would look weird if the police found it in my house. It was full of cuttings about Leo, even about his conviction and everything, so I panicked that it would look like I . . ." He sighs and presses his temples. "Now I've got some explaining to do."

"Just tell them the truth," Alice says, shaking her head. "Like you should've done from the start."

He looks at her piercingly. "You're one to talk, sis."

"I have never lied to you!"

"Haven't you?"

"No! You know me, Peter. You're the only one who does anymore. And I thought I knew you—"

"No, Al," he breaks in, holding up a hand. "I don't know you. I don't understand the person you are now, if I'm honest. I don't think anybody does . . . and I think that's the way you like it."

"Fuck you," she yells, and goes for him again, but this time he catches her wrists, stops her from hitting him.

"Alice!" he says. "Please!" His voice cracks and she sees it again, the same stricken look he wore outside Chrissy's house. It pulls her up short, makes her deflate in his arms. It's a look she knows. The look of a parent who thinks their child might be dead.

Alice steps away, eyes hot with tears. Peter is breathing hard, too, and just as deflated, his head hanging forward with his hand over his face.

"I can only hope it isn't him, Alice," he says, half-muffled by his palm. "The body in the barn. I know you might . . ." He stops and she stares at him again, wondering if he's really going to say it out loud, going to suggest that she might wish Leo dead. His eyes meet hers, then cast down. "I know you understand," he says instead. "This is a mess, a fucking awful mess, but I know, deep down, that you understand how I'm feeling."

The worst feeling in the world, Alice thinks. But she doesn't trust herself to say it out loud and not start howling.

THIRTY-FIVE

ALICE

New Year's Eve 2021

The tequila slammers began twenty minutes before the chime of the new year. Alice already felt tipsy, soft with a wobbly combination of happiness and unease. She was happy to be surrounded by friends, talking drunken politics with her brother, popping behind the bar to help Chrissy, popping back out to gulp more wine. But uneasy to see Robbie and Leo still acting tetchy with each other, sitting together, then moving apart, picking up their guitars, squabbling about which song to do, then putting them back down again.

The worst part was, Robbie didn't seem to want to sit with her, either. Was he annoyed she hadn't said the right things earlier?

She leaned in toward Peter. "Do you think he's okay?" She nodded toward Robbie. "Do you think he's pissed off with me?"

"I thought it was me he was being off with, to be honest,"

Peter said. "But I don't know why. I'll go say hi, offer to get him a tequila."

Alice smiled at him gratefully as he stood up. She thought about going with him, giving Robbie an early new year's hug, maybe Leo, too. But she held back and watched Peter click into Fun Uncle Mode, miming a suggestion of shots, Leo and Robbie both gazing up at him with habitual earnestness. Just for a moment she saw them as younger boys, twelve, not twenty-two, both with their own dad issues, both looking to Peter to fill that gap. Her heart strained as her mind rewound the years. But as she blinked back into the present, Robbie seemed to remember he was in a mood—with the universe, or with specific people, she still wasn't sure—and dropped his eyes to the table. Leo continued laughing at whatever Peter was saying, gloom half-clearing from his face, but Robbie scowled as if his laughter was offensive.

Alice rose to head over there—seriously, what was going on?—but then Chrissy appeared with a batch of tequila shots on a tray.

"Cheers, my love," she said to Chrissy, tapping her glass against hers.

"Cheers, Alice."

"To 2022." It sounded as futuristic as every new year did. "And good things to come."

"Here's hoping," Chrissy said with a note of apprehension in her voice.

Alice desperately wanted them both to count down to midnight with a sense of positivity. She glanced at the clock. Fifteen minutes to go. "Any resolutions?"

"Haven't really thought about it."

"Let's do another trip!" Alice touched her locket, wishing she could see Chrissy's, but it was underneath her T-shirt as usual. "Paris was incredible, wasn't it? In fact I think that was my resolution last year, to take you somewhere, get you out from behind that bloody bar even if it was just for a weekend. This year we could do longer; we could go to New York or somewhere sunny and tacky like—"

"Your new year's resolution was to get me to go on holiday?" Chrissy interrupted, looking at her strangely.

"Well . . ." Alice felt suddenly embarrassed by this, though she wasn't sure why. "Yeah, kinda . . ."

It was true that her priorities seemed to have shifted in the last two years. She used to start each January with ambitions for herself and her career, but since Ethan's death it was like all her focus had gone toward Chrissy. She clasped her locket again, sliding it left and right on its chain. Waited for Chrissy to laugh affectionately, to call her a dope for making such a lame-ass resolution.

"I need to go change the barrel on the Guinness," Chrissy said flatly, her eyes following the locket's movement.

Alice raised a smile and watched her go, the aftereffects of the tequila humming in her head. It was nearly midnight. There were lots of people she wanted to hug and kiss on the stroke of the new year but her best friend had disappeared into the cellar just as the clock was ticking toward twelve. She looked around for Robbie. He and Leo were playing darts now, over in the other corner, and she hoped that was a good sign. Still eleven minutes to go. She left her handbag on her chair and followed Chrissy down to the cellar.

THIRTY-SIX

CHRISSY

Saturday, December 9, 2023

Sometime between twilight and midnight, a knock on the door makes Chrissy turn from her kitchen window. She is alone now, apart from Amrit, the family liaison officer who arrived after the detectives left to consult with the pathologist. The house feels quiet, but not peacefully so; it feels like it's holding its breath.

Amrit looks over at her, halfway through making yet another cup of tea. "Want me to get that?"

Chrissy is about to nod, then changes her mind. "I'll go."

Her heart booms as she walks to her front door. Is this it? The moment she'll know? She opens the door, expecting police officers, and instead is utterly thrown.

"Tess!"

Her sister is standing there. Hair as wild as Chrissy's; scruffy blue jeans to Chrissy's scruffy black ones. She's holding a green casserole dish under one arm and has an overnight bag slung over the other. Yet she still manages to fold Chrissy into a hug, and Chrissy cries on her shoulder at the unexpectedness of her presence.

"What are you doing here?"

"What do you think?" Tess says. "Is there"—she pulls back, looking at Chrissy searchingly—"any news?"

Chrissy shakes her head. "Nothing since I called you. I wasn't even sure if my voicemail would make any sense, to be honest. I was so . . . I could barely . . . How did you *get* here so quickly? I didn't mean for you to . . ."

"Hey, hey, it's okay, Chris. Take a breath."

Tess hugs her again, and this time it's a crush of an embrace, and Chrissy's tears soak into her fleece. "We're still waiting for ID on the . . ." She can't bring herself to say *body*. She considers saying *man,* then shudders and gives up.

Chrissy lifts her head from Tess's shoulder eventually, and they go through to the kitchen. She introduces Tess to Amrit, her voice cracking again on the word *sister*. Tess lives miles away. Has a family of her own to look after. She and Chrissy don't keep in touch as often as they should, both busy, Chrissy sometimes unable to face it. But Tess is *here*.

"When did you last eat?" Tess flicks the oven on and shoves the casserole dish inside. Chrissy hasn't the energy to explain that her oven takes an eternity to heat up and that the huge pot of food might never actually cook. But there is something comforting about seeing the light glowing through the oven door.

"Tell me," Tess says, taking Chrissy's hand. "Tell me what's been going on."

"I don't know where to start."

"The beginning," Tess says.

"I don't . . ." Chrissy rubs her face. "I don't even know what the beginning is."

The first time Ethan chatted her up in the Raven? The day she married him, ignoring the churn of misgiving in her stomach? The night with Peter? The night Ethan died? The night she argued in the cellar with Alice while Leo and Robbie were arguing, fatefully, above?

"Tess . . . you visited Leo in prison sometimes, didn't you?"

Tess nods. "He was always my favorite nephew."

"Only nephew," Chrissy says, but a smile tugs at her lips. It's true that Tess and Leo have always got on well. His moods never fazed her.

"Did he ever say anything to you?" Chrissy asks. "Especially toward the end of his time in there. Did he seem different? Did he seem . . . upset? Afraid?"

"He seemed"—Tess pushes her hair back from her face, mirroring Chrissy, who is, as ever, doing the same—"haunted," she says finally.

"*Haunted?*"

Tess tilts her head to one side and her curls flop heavily. "By what he did."

"Yes . . ." Chrissy feels a deep twist of sadness and guilt. Always the guilt, even when she can't connect it to anything specific. "He never stopped hating himself for it."

"But it seemed to get worse, not better, don't you think?"

"I'm not sure." Chrissy feels panicked, again, that she may have missed something important; that other people have seen things in her son that she hasn't.

"Especially toward the end," Tess says. "I suppose that's

natural. He was being released early for something he was still punishing himself for."

"Maybe . . . maybe it wasn't just that," Chrissy murmurs.

"What do you mean?"

"He found out . . ." Chrissy glances at Amrit, who is discreetly finishing her tea-making but clearly listening. It's still a huge thing to say aloud, an admission of a long-term lie. She still hears Ethan's voice in her head calling her a liar and a bitch. "Leo found out, a few weeks before his release, that Ethan . . . that Ethan wasn't his dad."

Tess raises her eyebrows, but her reaction is mercifully low-key. "Oh?"

"I . . . I always knew he wasn't. But I never told him. Never told anyone, except his real dad."

"And that is . . . ?" Tess prompts gently.

Amrit puts the teas down on the table in front of them and retreats. Chrissy reaches for hers, scalding her hands.

"Peter," she whispers into the steam.

"*Alice's* Peter?" Now there is a stronger note of surprise in Tess's voice.

Chrissy nods, closing her eyes. She's had every regret it's possible to have in the last few hours. Never telling Leo. Never telling Alice. If it had been someone else—a stranger, an anonymous one-night stand—she probably wouldn't have hidden the truth. But something about the tangle of relationships always made it feel too hard.

Even after Ethan's death.

Especially after Ethan's death.

And in the end, Leo had found out at the worst possible time.

"Are you shocked?" she asks Tess. Then she puts down the mug and starts crying. "It doesn't matter if you are. Nothing matters now except . . . except him being okay." She buries her face in her hands and Tess touches the back of her head.

"That *is* all that matters," she says, stroking Chrissy's hair. "And I wish I could promise he's going to be okay. I really do."

A phone rings and Chrissy jolts upright. In the corner of the room, Amrit pulls it out of her pocket and answers it. Chrissy stares at her. Is *this* it, now? Amrit isn't saying much, just listening. Chrissy starts to get to her feet, but Amrit is wrapping up the conversation, nodding and saying, "Understood."

She hangs up and comes over to the table. She looks serious, yet calm, but this is her standard look, Chrissy is coming to realize.

"That was the SIO," Amrit says. "Sorry, that's senior investigating officer. The barn fire and Leo's disappearance are still being treated as two separate cases at the moment, but they're being overseen by—"

"Please," Chrissy says. "Just tell me, is Leo alive?"

"Still no ID on the body," Amrit says apologetically.

Chrissy lets out a moan.

"I'm sorry," Amrit says. "I know it's awful, the waiting. I do have some information for you, though, if you feel able to hear it?"

"Yes." Chrissy straightens herself up. "Yes, please, whatever you've got."

"The men who were in the white car—the driver and the passenger—are in custody."

Chrissy leans forward. "Who are they?"

"Their names are"—Amrit picks up her phone and swipes sideways—"Ryan Fuller and Paul Jones." She looks at Chrissy over her glasses. "Ring any bells?"

"No." Chrissy racks her brain, just in case, but draws a blank. "No, I've never heard of them."

"You're sure?" her sister asks, as if willing Chrissy to find the memory in the depths of her mind.

Chrissy tries, she really tries. She's so desperate to be of some use. But she can't magic up a connection that isn't there. "No, I don't know who they are."

"They've been arrested on suspicion of car theft," Amrit says. "There's nothing else we can link them to at the moment—not the fire, or Leo—but the officers at the nearby station will hold them for as long as they can. Apparently Fuller has a minor criminal record, but apart from that, there isn't a lot we can go on."

"Could they have crossed paths with Leo in prison?" Tess speaks up.

"Neither of them has ever served a custodial sentence," Amrit says. "But they *are* local to the area. Both have residential addresses within ten miles of the barn, and thirty miles of Cromley."

There is silence for a moment. Chrissy stares at the table. Amrit shifts and clears her throat as if she has more to say, so Chrissy lifts her head and nods for her to go on.

"Scenes of crime officers have been inspecting the barn now that the fire has been put out," Amrit tells her.

"Is there . . . There *is* just one . . . ?"

Amrit nods quickly. "Just the one fatality. No other people on the scene. As you know, they found Leo's coat nearby . . ." She hesitates, then taps her phone and shows Chrissy a photo. "This is his, isn't it?"

Chrissy forces herself to look. The navy parka lies in a crumpled heap, as if Leo has disappeared from inside it. It is covered in streaks of dirt and other stains that might be charring, might be blood.

"That's his," she chokes out, closing her eyes. "He's had it for years."

"Forensics are analyzing it, too." She hears Amrit tapping again at her phone. "Chrissy . . ." she says gently. "Can I show you something else, or do you need a break?"

She breathes in deeply. She can smell the casserole now, but it's too meaty, too strong. She opens her eyes to see Tess and Amrit watching her with concern. "I'm okay," she says.

Amrit holds out the phone. Unsure what she's looking at, Chrissy takes it from her and zooms in on the picture. Everything looks dark and burned and indistinct. For a moment she fears she's being shown the body, and almost throws it back at Amrit.

"Can you see it?" Amrit leans over to point at a paler shape among the charred debris. "This was found in the barn."

Now Chrissy starts to make it out. A half-blackened heart. The snake of a silver chain.

A locket. It's a locket.

She leaps up and runs to the drawer where she normally keeps hers, fumbling open the velvet drawstring pouch. It's empty. She got it out earlier, didn't she, alongside the note?

Swiveling back to the table, she sees the corner of the note under the cookbook she threw on top of it when Amrit first arrived. She had forgotten, in all the madness, that the locket should also have been there. And it's not. The locket is gone. The locket was in the barn, in the fire, and she has no idea how or why.

THIRTY-SEVEN

GEORGIE

Saturday, December 9, 2023

Something bad's happened to him, hasn't it?"

Ben looks up from his phone when Georgie asks the question.

"Leo," she clarifies, her eyes wide. "Can't you tell me?"

She and Ben are alone in the pub's office now, and have been for some time. Kiri has gone to make a phone call—Georgie presumes to alert someone to track down Peter—and has been absent longer than expected. After Georgie told them about Peter and the scrapbook, there were questions. Lots of questions. Georgie was surprised and slightly irritated by how many were about her—why she was in the pub the morning she saw Peter, which window she was looking out of, why she didn't go straight to the police.

In the end, though, Georgie didn't give any of the answers she'd intended to. For once, she didn't stick to her own plan.

Is that why Ben seems uncomfortable in her presence now—because she veered in such an unexpected direction?

I saw him from the upstairs flat, she told them, abandoning her original, safer lie about seeing him from a downstairs window. *I . . . was exploring.*

Exploring?

And I didn't take the scrapbook straight to the police because Peter is . . . one of you. I didn't know whose toes I might be treading on. What I might be walking into.

She'd wanted to see their reaction to that. And it was Ben who seemed to react most strongly, frowning and starting to protest. Kiri cut across him with the professional line: *I understand, Ms. Fallows, but I can assure you this will be investigated in the same way as any other important lead in this case.*

The phrase *important lead* fed Georgie's confidence. Now she looks steadily at Ben as she waits for him to answer her latest question.

"He's missing," Ben says, scratching his beard. "That's all we know at the moment."

"There are rumors that he's dead."

"They're unfounded."

"Does that mean you can't say?"

"It means we don't know anything for sure."

Georgie nods. Somehow, she feels calm and agitated at the same time. She is trapped in this room, Ben is trapped with her, and it's a bind or an opportunity, depending on how she plays it.

"How long have you been a police officer?" she asks him, flashing a smile as if she suddenly just wants to chat.

He still looks wary. "Twenty-odd years."

She lets her smile twinkle just a little. "You don't look old enough."

His eyebrows twitch but he doesn't respond. He seems humorless, she thinks, but then she remembers seeing him in photos, laughing and backslapping with Peter and other colleagues.

"So you've worked with Peter a long time?"

He nods and fidgets with his beard again. Georgie thinks of Ethan's chiseled jaw, always silky-smooth. She never saw it get even a tiny bit stubbly because they never spent more than a few snatched hours together. She never saw him with the flu, or in his slippers, or strolling round a supermarket. He will always be, to her, a beautiful man in a suit, or naked under hotel-room sheets, and she treasures those images but she feels robbed of all the other parts of him. Robbed of their chance to be together in the real world.

She couldn't even go to his funeral. She can't even shout it now: *I loved Ethan Dean and he loved me.*

She wants to. God, how she wants to. What's stopping her?

"Did you work on the Ethan Dean case?" she asks. It's the second time she's allowed herself to say his name today. Each time more boldly, with more ownership, though she doesn't know if anybody else can tell the difference.

"Well, it wasn't really a case . . ."

Georgie bristles. "Wasn't it? A man died. He was only forty-eight."

He blinks at her. She stares him down: *Yes, I do know how old he was.*

"But . . ." He looks confused. "It was straightforwardly—"

The door swings and Kiri comes back in. "Sorry about that. Got tied up. We'll try not to keep you too much longer, Ms. Fallows . . ."

"It's fine," Georgie says smoothly. "I'm happy to help."

Kiri looks between them, as if sensing tension, then sits back down and checks her notebook and her watch.

"Where is the scrapbook now?" she asks Georgie. "At your house, did you say?"

"Yes."

"And that's in the village?"

Georgie hesitates, trying to remember how she left the place looking. It seems a lifetime since she went to visit his grave early this morning. "I can take you there," she says.

Kiri glances at Ben. "We'll need to collect the scrapbook as evidence. So, yes, once we've got everything we need here . . ." She flips backward in her notebook, her eyes zigzagging. "It would be helpful if we can do that."

"I can do it," Ben says, stirring. "You should get home to your kids once we've wrapped up here, Kiri. It's late."

"You've got a little one to get back to as well," Kiri says.

"He's long asleep." Ben sounds tired himself. "I'll just swing by Georgie's on my way home. You've got further to travel."

Kiri seems reluctant and Georgie recognizes a fellow control freak. She eyes Ben again and thinks, *No, I wouldn't trust him with this, either.* But she likes the idea of continuing their chat. She feels as if they were only just scratching the surface.

THIRTY-EIGHT

CHRISSY

Saturday, December 9, 2023

The second phone call comes twenty minutes later. It comes to Amrit's phone again, but Chrissy can tell from her body language that it's the one they've been waiting for, and all the breath seems to leave her body.

"Okay," Amrit says into her mobile, nodding and glancing at Chrissy. "I'll tell her . . . Could you repeat that, please?" She draws a pen out of her pocket, uses her teeth to pull off the lid, and scribbles something down on a piece of paper.

She hangs up, turning to Chrissy.

"The body has been provisionally identified," she says. "Pending a formal ID from the next of—"

"Is it Leo?" Chrissy stands up, blood rushing to her brain.

Amrit shakes her head. Chrissy's legs fold and her sister holds her up—already braced, it seems, to do so. *It's not him. It's not him.* She wants to check, make sure she hasn't misunderstood, but her throat has closed completely.

"The deceased's name is Frank Jordan."

Chrissy manages to take in the name but she doesn't recognize it. Does it ring a faint bell, somewhere in the fog of her thoughts, or is it just a pealing of gratitude to this dead stranger for not being her son? *It isn't him. Isn't Leo.* She stumbles back over to the table, sinks into a chair, and releases a body-racking sob into her palms.

Tess and Amrit sit down quietly either side of her. Tess is crying, too, her cheeks shiny. Amrit touches Chrissy's arm, and then she says, "He was in the same prison as Leo."

Chrissy shakes herself alert. "At the same time?"

Amrit nods. "Frank had been in prison much longer. Over twenty years, in fact, but he was transferred to Leo's prison five years ago and their sentences overlapped."

"Jesus," Chrissy says, alarmed at the thought of this person living alongside Leo. And dying, it seems, in a place where Leo may also have been, not so long ago. "What did he do?"

"Murder and arson, among other offenses. He was released three weeks before Leo."

Chrissy's heart gallops. Arson. And a barn fire. It can't be a coincidence. "Could he have . . . harmed Leo? Gone after him once he was out?"

"We don't know. We've sent some officers to the prison to conduct interviews with staff and inmates. We need to establish if there was any kind of relationship between Frank and Leo." Amrit pauses. "He never mentioned anything to you, Chrissy?"

Her head is throbbing with relief and worry. "I don't think so. I don't remember him ever talking about a Frank."

She'll ask Izzy, she thinks. See what Cliff knows about him. *Frank Jordan.* She rolls the name around, checking whether it bumps up against anything. He sounds like a serious criminal. Could he have been the reason Leo was so distressed, not because of Marianne's revelation? Or is she trying to absolve herself?

"But where is Leo?" she asks, appealing to Amrit as though she has all the power, the knowledge. At the moment, she's all Chrissy's got. "We're no closer to finding him." She feels Tess's hand on her arm, firmer this time, and realizes she's shaking.

"We're looking," Amrit promises. "We've got a full-scale national search underway."

"It isn't his body," Tess says softly, pressing Chrissy's hand. "That needs to be enough for now."

Chrissy reaches for her cigarettes with trembling fingers. Leo is still out there. She believes that; she has to.

"I . . . should tell Peter," she says, and it feels strange, the acknowledgment, finally, that he's Leo's parent, too. She picks up her phone but everything she thinks of typing sounds either too casual or too dramatic.

"Peter is at Derby police station at the moment," Amrit says. "Being interviewed."

Chrissy is half-ashamed of her own rush of nerves. All she wants is for them to find Leo, but the investigation is stretching to include all the complications of the past.

"What about Alice?" she asks tentatively. "Is she being interviewed, too?"

"I'm not sure," Amrit says. "I haven't been told that."

Chrissy wonders about Alice's state of mind. How angry is she about Chrissy and Peter's secret? Enough to start spilling others?

Her breath quickens as her mind races on. Alice must resent not knowing something as important as the identity of Leo's real father. But the thing she *does* know is huger by far. And Chrissy can no longer gauge if she'll keep a lid on it. A lid that is already being nudged at, lifted in tiny fractions, every time Ethan's name comes up.

She needs to swing the focus back to the present. But how? The prickle on the back of her neck has returned. The feeling that still, after all these years, Ethan is casting his shadow.

It's not him, she keeps reminding herself, clinging to a splinter of hope. *The body isn't Leo.*

But still, nothing is resolved. Nothing feels safe. She can't remember the last time it did.

THIRTY-NINE

CHRISSY

New Year's Eve 2021

Chrissy had had anxiety attacks before, so she knew the signs of one coming on. She sat on the edge of a barrel and took deep, slow breaths, inflating and deflating an imaginary paper bag. What was so triggering about this evening? Why couldn't she look forward to a new year, sparkly and full of promise, like everyone else?

Just for one night, why couldn't she forget?

"Need some help?" came Alice's cheerful voice as the cellar door creaked and high heels clip-clopped down the steps.

Alice stopped when she caught sight of Chrissy—not changing the barrel but sitting on top of one, empty hands cupped around her mouth. "Chris, you okay? Shall I get you a bag?" She knew the signs, too. She'd rubbed the small of Chrissy's back through what felt like a hundred attacks, during her marriage and after. She'd even started carrying a paper bag in her handbag after a while, folded up neatly, in case Chrissy needed it.

Always there. Looking after her. Like a mum with spare clothes in a rucksack—like they both used to do for their mucky, muddy boys. Sometimes Chrissy wished the dynamic was different. Wished she wasn't the one always making the call. *Can you help me patch this window up? Can you help me cover this bruise with your good foundation?*

He's dead, please help me, he's dead.

The breathlessness was ebbing now, though, so she stood up and tossed back her hair. "I'm fine."

"Sure?"

"Sure."

"Peter's looking after the bar for a minute," Alice said. "So take your time."

"Is he?" Chrissy flashed back to the night, *that* night, when he'd helped her tidy up after closing. The way he'd set the glass washer going without needing to ask which buttons to press. She glanced to the left and pictured two figures messily entwined against the wall of the cellar. Sometimes she was able to think of it as a happy memory. The night two friends made a baby. But that kind of romanticism seemed ridiculous right now. The memory had jagged edges and a painful core and she had nobody to blame except herself.

She was the one who'd wanted to pretend Leo was Ethan's. She'd regretted it, oh how she'd regretted it, once Leo was older and Ethan's attentive-husband act had dropped away yet again. But she couldn't retract all the things she'd forced Peter to promise. Couldn't break their vow of silence, even when she'd wanted to run screaming to his door.

Plus, he had Marianne. Chrissy kept waiting for them to announce they were having a child of their own, kept preparing herself for it. But they never had.

Was that what was haunting her tonight? The things that might've been different if she'd left Ethan all those times she'd come heart-thumpingly close.

"It will get easier," Alice said, as if reading her thoughts.

"Why should it?" Chrissy said, too tired to go along with the new-year-new-start relentlessness, even for the sake of her best friend's obsession.

Alice smiled, undeterred. "Because it'll have me to answer to if it doesn't." She flexed her skinny biceps and Chrissy saw the shimmer of some kind of body cream or powder on her skin. Alice was shiny and sweet-smelling. Chrissy felt grubby and ugly and scarred.

And angry. She felt the anger swelling, even as she knew that it wasn't fair, really, wasn't aimed at Alice. But, as so often, Alice was the person in front of her.

"Why did you get me this locket?" she asked.

Alice looked startled. "What?"

"Why did you give me a locket identical to yours? Tell me we should wear them all the time? This isn't primary school."

Alice flinched like she'd been slapped. "Because . . . because . . ."

Chrissy felt as awful as if she *had* hit her. But with the guilt came the defensive urge to dig her heels in, to double down.

"You think I like wearing this round my neck as a constant reminder?" she flung out.

"Reminder? Of us being friends?"

"Of us having this . . . thing . . ." Chrissy couldn't even say it because they never talked about it, except in a weird code that had nothing to do with Ethan's death and everything to do with friendship and lockets and *looking out for each other*. "This shared . . . *thing*."

"Matching lockets," Alice said. "Matching fucking lockets. That's all they are."

"No, they're not!" Chrissy raised her voice. Her hair tumbled into her face and she pushed it back but it fell forward again, with an infuriating will of its own. Alice had not a hair out of place, never did. Even that night, the Ethan night, she had only looked a little paler than usual, her pupils bigger and darker. She had been the calm one, as usual, but wasn't that what Chrissy had needed?

Wasn't Alice *always* what she needed? And didn't she know, deep down, that this would be the case forever, and that Alice would be on her side forever, no matter what she hurled at her on bad days like this?

"*Chris . . .*" Alice reached out to tuck her hair behind her ear for her. But a thud overhead made them both stall. The ceiling tremored and they frowned, glancing at the closed cellar door.

"Sounds like things are getting rowdy," Alice said. "Is it twelve already?"

"I don't know." Chrissy wasn't ready for "Auld Lang Syne" and kisses on each cheek. There was more she wanted to say.

She watched Alice turn back to face her, locket winking from her flushed throat, and she blurted again: "Sometimes I think you like having something over me."

Alice's mouth fell open. "*What?*"

"I don't mean . . . I just mean, I think you like being the . . .

the *keeper* of my guilt. My secrets. It's like . . ." Her mouth seemed to be moving without instruction. "It's like you've put them inside these lockets and now we carry them round and . . ."

"Fucking hell, Chris!" Alice yelled. "They're just necklaces! With pictures of our sons inside. Our sons who grew up together, who we—"

This time, the thud was much, much louder. And there were shouts that seemed to roll across the ceiling like a giant bowling ball. The two of them froze, eyes locking, chests moving up and down.

Then the cellar door flew open.

"Alice! Chrissy! You need to come! You need to come *now*."

FORTY

ALICE

Saturday, December 9, 2023

Alice sits on the edge of her chair in the police station waiting room. The central heating is intense, trapped by the nylon carpet and the stuffy air. The chill of the woods replaced by sweat running down her back beneath her clothes.

She remembers sitting here with Chrissy in the aftermath of Ethan's death, holding her clammy hand until their palms were stuck together. And after Robbie was killed, she must've come here, too, to make a statement. She can't remember whether anybody held *her* hand, whether she let them even if they tried.

She wonders how many lies have been told in this building. Imagines them all swirling in the air: the bigger the lie, the stronger the trace.

Peter has been in the interview suite for almost an hour, and she doesn't know what to make of that. She's been half-anticipating getting called in herself, but so far they seem focused on Peter. Her stomach still contracts when she thinks about him and Chrissy and the secret they kept, but he is her brother. She'll wait.

On the drive over, they talked a little more. He explained how Marianne had told Leo that Peter was his real dad a few weeks before his release. "I don't know why," Peter said, shaking his head. "I don't know why she did that." Now Peter and Chrissy are worried there's some link between that and Leo's disappearance. Alice had felt another petty urge to say, *This is what happens when you aren't honest,* but swallowed it. She was no stranger to keeping secrets.

Talk to Chrissy, Peter had urged her as she squirmed in the passenger seat. Alice shook her head, turned her face away, but she knows she will have to, at some point. It's like a weight she's dragging around, getting heavier the longer she leaves it. But what would they say to each other? How can any of this, ever, be fixed?

A young guy sits down opposite her and she does a double take. He reminds her so much of Robbie, she can't stop looking at him. The same long fingers—great for playing bass, great for gaming, he used to say—and the same near-black hair, so similar to her own, and to Peter's.

The question inevitably follows: *Does* Leo resemble Peter, too? But she just never saw it, never looked for it? And what about his temperament? It always went unsaid, each time Leo flew off the handle, that he might've got some of his less favorable traits from his dad—from Ethan. Alice always suspected Chrissy was thinking it, and was careful not to imply it herself, back when they were friends. But now she has to reframe those memories, too: It can't have been genes Chrissy was worried about.

She is still sneaking glances at Robbie's lookalike when Peter emerges. He stands over her, shoulders drooping with tiredness, and she wants to hug him but she's still stiff with the remnants of her anger.

"How was it?" she asks.

"Let's get going," Peter says.

As they start to leave, a door swings open somewhere behind them, and her breath hitches: Is it her turn?

"Peter," says a deep voice. Peter freezes, then turns slowly around. "Sorry, could you pop back in for a moment?"

Peter looks half-wary, half-impatient. The man who has come out to call him back isn't familiar to Alice. He is a similar age to her brother, with an air of authority about him, and she wonders if he's the SIO.

"I thought we were done," Peter says.

"Just one other thing. If you could . . ." He jabs his thumb back the way Peter came.

Alice senses her brother might lose his temper. But she also sees the familiar signs of him reining himself in, doing a lightning-quick assessment of the pros and cons of getting cross. Eventually he sighs, throws a glance at Alice, and strides away with the man.

So, she waits again. The Robbie double is gone and she stares at the empty seat where he was. She picks at the ragged skin around her nails, remembering the distant days when she used to get manicures and rub nutty-smelling hand cream into her fingers. Members of staff leave in their warm coats, waving to the desk sergeant, letting in gasps of cold night air as they go.

When Peter re-emerges, his exhaustion has taken on a twitchy edge. Alice asks again if everything is okay, but he just gestures at the automatic doors, diving through them as they slide open. He walks quickly to his car, Alice taking long strides to keep up, but once they're inside he doesn't turn on the engine. He leans his head against the steering wheel and lets out a long sigh.

"Did they give you a hard time?" Alice asks.

"It was so weird being on the other side of it. After all the interviews I've done in that room. I explained about the scrapbook . . ."

"Why did they call you back in?"

"Oh . . . no reason, really. Just dotting the i's, crossing the t's . . ." He lifts his head from the steering wheel but curls his large fingers around it.

Alice squints at his profile, sensing there's more to it than he's telling her. But then he turns to look at her, and she sees his eyes damp and shining. "It wasn't Leo, Alice. The body wasn't him."

She feels a surge of emotion, so powerful that she jerks forward and her seat belt tightens across her chest. She isn't sure what emotion it is, exactly. A soaring release with a heavy drag of something darker.

"That's . . ." She can't find the words, so she just reaches out to touch her brother's shoulder, reminding herself how much this must mean to him. If she'd seen Robbie beginning to stir as he'd lain on the pub floor, it would've felt like a miracle.

"It was a guy called Frank Jordan," Peter says.

Alice sits back. "Why does that name seem familiar?"

Peter rubs at his stubble. It's more than stubble by now, actually. It's a beard that looks as if it hasn't been washed in a week. She looks at the bags under his eyes and feels another ripple of guilt. She's been blind to the fact that, in the last few days, he's been suffering more than she has. *It's not a competition,* he would say, but Alice turns it into one sometimes; she knows she does.

"I was the one who arrested him," Peter says. "I'm basically the reason he went to prison."

Frank Jordan . . . Alice casts her mind back over Peter's career, remembering the names and cases he would sometimes mention, the articles he would show her in the local paper.

"The big arson case from about twenty years ago," he says.

It starts to come back to her. It was one of Peter's first high-profile arrests.

"You were celebrating . . ." she says as a faint memory surfaces: him and two colleagues getting drunk in the Raven. "Breaking the Law" on the jukebox. Wanting to stay and celebrate with them—and make sure Chrissy was okay—but knowing she had an abstract to write for the next day. Back when her career meant almost as much to her as her friends.

"Yeah." Peter's hand drifts up to his greasy hair. "That was . . . that was actually the night that me and Chrissy . . ."

Alice blinks twice. Another reframing. She toasted her brother's success that night, then went home to write twenty drafts of a two-hundred-and-fifty-word abstract. Oblivious to the fact that her best friend and her brother were having sex. Conceiving the baby that would go on to kill hers.

"Chrissy was upset, and I was a bit drunk, a bit full of it . . . We ended up—"

"I don't need the details!" Alice breaks in. She knows she sounds prudish, bitter, but she doesn't want to hear it, picture it.

"Sorry." Peter shrugs. "It's just a weird coincidence. I've often thought about that night . . . but I haven't thought about Frank Jordan in years."

"Do you think it could be significant? That you were the one who got him sent down?"

Peter is frowning hard. "Maybe. He was released a few weeks before Leo. Wright and Colella have sent some people out to do interviews at the prison. And they're looking for a link between Jordan and the guys who were in the car they were tracking." He puts a hand to his stomach. "I've got a bad feeling, though, Alice. A really bad feeling."

Alice swallows and says nothing. Peter starts the engine, turns on his headlights, and reverses out of the parking space. Alice stares out the window at the dark, damp streets gliding past. She hadn't noticed it raining, but it looks as if it's been heavy, and she thinks of what she's heard in numerous TV crime dramas, about evidence being washed away, stormy weather making manhunts harder. She can't work out how she feels about the idea of Leo somewhere out there in the darkness and rain.

She opens Peter's glove box and rummages around for tissues. It's full of old CDs, their scratched covers reminding her of happier days. Just as she's about to give up, her fingers close around something at the back. For a second she thinks it's the neck of a bottle, and her stomach clenches; she thought Peter had stopped stashing alcohol in his car. But it's too slim for that, and made of plastic . . . She pulls it out and turns it in her fingers, then drops it back inside and slams the compartment shut.

Sitting back in her seat, she glances at Peter, whose attention is fixed obliviously on the road. She tries to slow her pulse by closing her eyes and breathing steadily. It doesn't mean anything, she tells herself as her thoughts start churning again. It isn't that unusual to keep a red marker pen in the glove box of a car.

FORTY-ONE

GEORGIE

Saturday, December 9, 2023

It's pitch-dark by the time Georgie leads Ben toward her rented cottage. She lives in the least "villagey" part of the village, she often thinks. Two of the houses on her small street are empty and most of the rest are occupied by commuters who leave early in the morning and come back late at night. As she unlocks her door, ushering Ben inside, she still feels as if Ethan is watching. She imagines him jealous—maybe *wants* him to be jealous?—though she isn't sure why. Sometimes she sensed that he could be a jealous man. His questions about what she got up to when they weren't together, the way he would watch her talking to the room-service guy or the hotel barman.

Nothing to worry about here, my love, she reassures him in her mind. *At least, not on that score.*

She remembers the kindness of the hotel receptionist on that final night, the many times she went downstairs to ask if he'd seen the man who was supposed to be joining her. "My husband hasn't arrived," she kept saying to the staff, and maybe they knew he wasn't her husband but it comforted her, somehow, to call him that.

Shaking off the memory, she wipes her boots on her door-mat, scattering the last few clumps of earth from his grave. She takes Ben through to the living room. The fireplace is cold and dark. Last night's wineglass sits next to her armchair, her checked blanket thrown over the back. A sad scene, she thinks, looking around. No photos on display. None of the expensive scented candles and potted plants she used to have in her London flat. She hasn't unpacked anything personal or beautiful, can't make this a home until she's done what she came here for.

"I'll go and grab the scrapbook," Georgie says, leaving him in her living room.

Going upstairs to the heavy wooden wardrobe, she pushes aside her new array of countryside-appropriate clothes and reaches to the back. She's about to leave the room with the scrapbook when she pauses, turns around, and opens one of the drawers on the right-hand side of the wardrobe. Inside is a cardboard box. She hesitates, a faint flutter in her chest, then takes it downstairs with her, too.

Ben is inspecting her wood-burning stove. "What make is this?" he asks, suddenly conversational.

Georgie looks at him blankly. "I have no idea."

"My wife wants one like this. We've got an open fire at the moment but it's messy and she thinks a burner would be—"

"Here," Georgie interrupts, thrusting both the scrapbook and the cardboard box toward him.

"This is the . . . ?" he says, accepting the scrapbook.

She watches him turning the pages, the muscles around his eyes getting tighter. Eventually he snaps it shut. "Well, thanks. I believe Peter's been taken in for questioning at Derby police station. I'm sure there's an explanation."

"Are you?"

"Well . . ."

"Because he's your buddy?" She mimes a playful cuff of his arm, but her smile is a grimace.

He doesn't answer. He nods at the cardboard box she's still holding. "Was there something else?"

She hesitates again, cradling the box. When she finally hands it to Ben, she feels as if she's passing over a baby or a pet. *Be gentle,* she wants to say.

Ben looks more like she's handed him a bomb. He peels the lid off nervously and peeks inside. Georgie hears the items moving as he puts his hand in and shuffles them around; she knows what they are just from the sound of each one. He lifts out a silver ballpoint pen with a hotel name on the side. A cloth napkin. A black cocktail stirrer. A cuff link that Ethan left by the bed once, when he had to leave in a hurry. Then Ben gets to the photo. The only one Georgie has of the two of them: a selfie she begged him to pose for.

Ben stares at it as the wall clock ticks in the silence.

"You . . . and Ethan Dean?" he says at last.

Georgie nods without dropping her gaze.

"You . . . you should've mentioned this earlier," he

says, sounding unsure of himself. "We're investigating the disappearance of his son."

"Well . . ." Georgie's pulse pounds in her ears. "I suggest you also investigate Ethan's death. *Properly* this time. Otherwise I'm going to take my concerns higher. As high as possible."

"It was suicide." Ben looks at her as if she's unhinged. "There was no doubt."

"According to who?"

"A coroner, of course."

"Based on what?"

"He was found hanged!"

Georgie flinches and closes her eyes. Not that image. She never lets herself picture that.

She opens her eyes, lifting her chin. "Did you see him?"

"Yes, actually. I . . . I was one of the first responders. And I can assure you—"

"You and Peter Lowe, by any chance?"

Ben puts the box down on the arm of a chair. There is a glow to his skin now. A new heat in the room.

"Look, Georgie. I'm here about Leo Dean. If you've nothing else to add on that subject, I'm going to take the scrapbook to the station and then I'm going to go home."

She steps forward. "He *wouldn't* have killed himself. Not without severe provocation. Or . . . force."

His expression flounders between sympathy and frustration. "I know it must be hard to accept—"

"We were supposed to meet that night. In our hotel. He wouldn't have let me just sit there. He even ordered room service in advance; it arrived while I was waiting. Lobster and chicken supreme." She almost breaks, thinking of the two meals congealing under the metal domes. "Why would he, if he knew he was going to die?"

Ben passes a hand across his eyes. "I don't know what you're trying to—"

"He had no reason to do it," she presses on. "We had *plans*. And not just for that night."

"Clearly, his state of mind—"

"You know nothing about his state of mind! I did!" She thumps her own chest. "He loved me, and he wouldn't have just abandoned me. He left no note. Gave no signs."

"He was a troubled guy, Georgie."

She falters slightly. "What?"

Ben lets out a heavy sigh. "I know you probably don't want to hear this, but maybe he wasn't the person you thought he was. How do you know you saw the real him?"

Her chest heaves. "Because I *know*."

He steps closer now. She feels him swinging the power balance, using his stockiness, his uniform, trying to close her down. "It was a suicide, Georgie. I'm sorry for your loss. But there was nothing more to it than a man with . . . problems. Big problems."

She won't have it. She makes herself as tall as possible and looks directly into his face. "I think someone killed him."

He laughs. He actually laughs. She feels rage clawing its way up her throat.

"Do you have any evidence?"

"Chrissy was *awful* to him." Her words pour out too fast

now. "Alice resented him. Peter does whatever Alice needs him to. It's not hard to see how, between the three of them, they might have got away with it."

Ben shakes his head. "This is an actual conspiracy theory!"

Georgie resists the urge to grab his jaw, push her nails into his skin, make him see how serious she is.

"He had you fooled," Ben adds, his laughter disappearing. "He had you totally fooled."

She goes very still and gazes up at him. "No," she says crisply. "Chrissy and Alice and Peter had *everybody* fooled. And I'm going to prove it. I'm going to get it reopened as a murder case—"

"He was a bad guy!" Ben erupts, his whole face turning bright scarlet. He winces, as if he hadn't intended to say it, then jerks his shoulders resignedly. "He was . . . a shit." His voice quietens. "And he probably knew it. And that was probably why he took his own life."

Georgie stares at him, speechless for a second. She touches her ring. Glances at the photo jutting out of the top of the cardboard box. "That's really unprofessional," she says coldly.

"Well, I think this whole conversation has gotten a little—"

"Everyone loved Ethan! *I* loved him! He was a wonderful man and his family didn't deserve him, didn't want him—"

"He was a *brute!*" It's another eruption. But this time he doesn't look shocked or sheepish in its wake; he looks exasperated, wild-eyed, his hands in his hair.

Georgie breathes hard. "What would you know about it?"

"I . . . I heard things. Saw things . . ."

"You're lying!"

"Why would I? That night, when I saw him hanging there,

saw the state Chrissy was in, blaming herself, hiding old bruises . . . I understood the whole situation like that . . ." He clicks his fingers in her face. "I've seen the likes of it before. A fucked-up guy, an abuser who couldn't live with himself anymore—"

"*No!*" Georgie's insides burn, bile flooding her mouth. She shoves his chest and he staggers but he's still talking. *He won't stop talking.*

She is overtaken by fury. All she wants is to stop the poison spewing out of his mouth. Evil, he's calling Ethan. Brainwashed, he's calling her. Suicide, he's still insisting, but he doesn't sound sorry about that anymore.

She backs toward the fireplace, fending off the words. She almost trips over the edge of the hearth but her hand finds the metal poker in its holder, something to anchor herself with. As she pulls it out, black ash flurries in the air. Ben is talking, still talking. People talk too much when they're guilty, when they're lying, when they're in the wrong but too far gone to take it back. She knows this but she just wants him to stop, wants to keep his lies from burrowing into her brain. She screams and lifts the poker, swinging it into the side of his head.

FORTY-TWO

CHRISSY

Sunday, December 10, 2023

In the early hours of the next morning, after Tess and Amrit have fallen asleep, Chrissy opens Facebook on her phone. The blue glow of the screen is the only light in her living room. She finds Izzy, adds her as a friend, and sends her a direct message.

> Frank Jordan. Does Cliff know anything about him? Could you ask him next time you speak to him? Grateful as always. Chrissy x

Then she puts down her phone and stares across the room at the shape of her sister asleep on the sofa, flinching every now and then as if she's having bad dreams.

Chrissy has spent the last hour or so googling Frank Jordan. She now remembers him, the fires. They were in the local news a lot, around twenty-five years ago. She wasn't paying much attention to the outside world back then, locked into an increasingly abusive marriage, but she does recall all those fires in north Derbyshire, the police convinced they were all linked, all arson, and a particularly bad one in a hotel, which turned out to be a deliberate attack on three people who were staying there. Frank Jordan got careless over that one. He went on the run and Derbyshire Police spent years trying to track him down. He'd been suspected of other crimes before, drug dealing and burglaries, but this was the first one the police knew he'd committed, and they were desperate to nail him for it.

Chrissy got a shock when she found the news piece about his eventual arrest. There was Peter, looking young and earnest in his uniform, with a statement underneath about how the arrest and charge of "one of the area's most wanted criminals" had been secured by "an officer with a promising career ahead." She jolted as she remembered. *That night.* Peter's celebratory drinks. The cellar, afterward, her legs wrapped tight around his waist, her arms pulling him closer. It feels so strange that the two things are connected: Leo's conception and Frank Jordan's arrest.

An arsonist who died in a fire. There is a dark kind of justice there, but what does it mean? How is it going to help them bring Leo home? She thinks of her charred locket among the debris. Now in a sealed evidence bag in the police station, she presumes. Chrissy told Amrit it was hers, but not that it had been a gift from Alice, a gift that had sometimes felt like a padlock around her neck.

Her phone lights up and she stirs, hoping it's Izzy. It isn't a Facebook message, though; it's a text from Peter.

We'll find him.

She swallows hard as she looks back over all the other, ignored messages she's sent him this week. For some reason, this one makes up for his silence. She feels irrationally reassured, and no longer so bleakly alone.

CHRISSY WAKES TO light streaming in through half-open curtains. It's dawn. Tess is gone from the sofa and she can hear the kettle boiling in the kitchen, the noise that has punctuated the long stretch of the last twelve hours.

There is a searing pain down one side of her neck. She fell asleep in the armchair with her phone glued to her hand. It's starting to feel like they're imprisoned here—Tess, Amrit, and herself—even though they could venture out whenever they want.

Chrissy checks her phone, panicked to have potentially missed something, and sees that Izzy has replied.

Will ask Cliff when he calls today. Stay strong,
babe. Been thinking about you and Leo
constantly xxx

Amrit and Tess come into the room carrying three cups of tea between them. For once, Chrissy feels like drinking hers, her mouth bone-dry from the long night. "Anything?" she croaks to Amrit, a shorthand question that's become as regular as the kettle clicking on.

"Officers spoke to some of the prison inmates and staff first thing this morning."

"Already?" Chrissy glances at the clock.

"A lot of them were quite reluctant to say much about Frank Jordan," Amrit says in a tone that's as close to frustration as Chrissy has heard from her yet.

"People were . . . afraid of him?"

"It seems that way. But one person, a staff member, said they thought Frank and Leo were friends."

"*Friends?*" Now Chrissy's eyes pop. "Surely not? I'm amazed they were even in the same prison, given . . ." She's about to say, *given the difference in what they did,* but falters. In her mind, her son is not really a criminal, not like Frank Jordan. But other people don't see it that way.

"Well, this prison guard had noticed them whispering together sometimes. Talking in the yard. He started keeping an eye on their budding friendship, sensing something potentially dangerous about it. He was even thinking about reporting it internally, but then Frank was released, so—"

"What do you mean, 'potentially dangerous'?" Chrissy breaks in.

Amrit consults her phone. "'It looked kind of intense,'" she reads from the screen. "The guard seemed to think . . . they might've been plotting something."

Chrissy puts down her tea, no longer able to swallow. *Plotting something?*

"But . . . it might not have been a friendship," she says. "It might've looked like one, but it might've been . . . something bad."

Amrit says nothing, and Tess looks across at Chrissy with worry in her eyes.

"Someone should've intervened," Chrissy adds, fighting tears. "Someone should've kept him safe."

She doesn't add herself to that judgment, but she thinks it for the hundredth time. *She* should've kept him safe.

HOURS LATER, WHEN Chrissy is outside smoking yet another cigarette, Tess sticks her head out of the cottage door and calls to her. "Chris, Amrit's had some more news."

Chrissy throws away her cigarette and hurries back into the house.

"Two forensic reports, just in," Amrit says. She has both her phone and a laptop in front of her, and her glasses on, looking more businesslike than usual.

Chrissy perches on the sofa arm, then stands up again, restless. Tess stands beside her, placing an arm around her shoulders. Chrissy is aware that she must smell—of cigarettes, of sleepless nights and showerless mornings—but Tess stays close.

"We have the full report on how the fire in the barn may have started," Amrit goes on, leaning toward the laptop. She scrolls with the mouse, her eyes moving. "Remnants of a metal lighter were found at the scene. It wasn't possible to ascertain much about it, though, because it exploded . . ." She shows Chrissy a photograph, but it is just of a mangled piece of metal that might once have been the shell of a Zippo. "Does Leo smoke?"

"Yes," Chrissy says.

"Does he own a metal lighter?"

"Not that I . . . He used to buy the plastic disposable ones."

Amrit swivels the laptop back to herself. "Fragments of rope were also found . . . Experts were unable to conclude whether the fire was started deliberately or accidentally . . . Lots of dry hay in the barn would've caught easily, and the fire would've spread quickly . . . The pathologist's report on the deceased should indicate whether he was killed by the fire or other means . . ."

There are more photos of the burned-out barn, of blackened beams and a half-collapsed roof, and Chrissy stares at them all, searching for signs of Leo, for the things a team of expert strangers might have missed. Why her locket was there. Why any of this has happened.

"So . . . they don't really *know* how it started?" she says, sinking down next to Amrit.

"It's very hard to be sure."

"Or whether Leo was there?"

"Most of the forensic evidence was destroyed, of course. But . . ." Amrit minimizes the photos of the barn and opens another document instead. "That brings me to the other report . . ." The document flashes onto the screen and Chrissy jumps at the words *traces of blood*.

She grabs the edge of the laptop.

. . . confirmed as Leo Dean's . . .

"What's this?" she says. "Leo's blood? Where?"

"This is from the forensic analysis of the stolen car," Amrit says.

Chrissy tries to read it quickly over her shoulder but can barely see past the word *blood*. She can hear Tess murmuring, standing behind her now, as if she's reading under her breath. Amrit subtly moves the laptop out of both their eyelines.

"Traces of Leo's blood were found in the trunk of the car," she says.

Chrissy puts her head between her knees. Amrit's voice continues but it's muffled now, as if she's underwater.

"It wasn't a lot," Amrit says, as if this will reassure her. "But enough to confirm that Leo was in the car—"

"In the *trunk?*" Chrissy says to the floorboards.

"And perhaps injured—"

"*Bleeding.*"

"But the good thing is . . ." Amrit pauses. "Chrissy, are you okay?"

Her head swims and waves of hot and cold shimmer over her.

"Chrissy?" Tess says. "Can you look at me?"

Slowly, Chrissy uncurls. Amrit is holding out a glass of water. She takes it and drinks and wipes her mouth. "What's the good thing?" she asks, hearing how desperate she sounds.

"This means we can hold the driver and passenger of the car for longer," Amrit says. "We can arrest them on suspicion of abduction and question them properly."

Abduction.

"Can I see the car?" Chrissy hears herself saying. "Can I go to the barn?"

"Chrissy, is that a good idea?" Tess says. "Think how you'd feel—"

"I want to see them for myself," Chrissy says, putting down the glass of water with a thunk. "Please, Amrit. I need to get a sense of where the barn is, what's around it. I need to see the trunk they put him in. I think I'd be able to . . ." She falters because she doesn't know, exactly, what she hopes to achieve. "I just think it might trigger something. There's a piece missing to all this and I'm not going to figure it out sitting here."

Amrit looks dubious, but not unsympathetic. "I don't know if that will be possible, Chrissy," she says. "But . . ." She shrugs and picks up her phone. "I can ask."

Chrissy nods emphatically, rubbing her fingers along the seams of her jeans. Her head is a swirl of painful images: Leo's coat in a crumpled heap, Leo's blood spattered in a car, a barn roof collapsing in on him. Her imaginings will only get worse, she knows, until she sees something real.

Maybe it's the same contrary logic that has kept her in this village, even after everything; that kept her living in the flat above the pub after Ethan died, and for a while after Robbie did. Running away from places doesn't help her. Wherever she lived, she would wake up every day still believing she was in Cromley. Always, inescapably, her home.

FORTY-THREE

ALICE

Sunday, December 10, 2023

Where are we going?" Alice asks as Peter drives straight past her house. "Pete . . . ?"

After a night at the police station, then his place, she is desperate to go home, shower, see Beech, *think*. When she realizes where he is taking her instead, she slams her foot on an imaginary brake.

"Peter," she says. "I can't."

"Yes, you can," he says. "You have to."

She shakes her head, thinking about jumping out of the moving car. "You're supposed to be on my side!"

It's all so much more complicated now that he has a stronger link to Chrissy, arguably, than to her. Is that what's hurting her the most? She looks over at him, steering determinedly up to Chrissy's cottage. He feels far away, as if she's losing him.

He brings the car to a stop but neither of them moves.

"You go in, if you want to," she says, folding her arms. "I'll walk home."

"*I'm* not going in," he says. "You are. You need to talk to her. This has gone on long enough."

"You can't force me."

"No. But this is all going to be so much harder, Alice, if you two stay at war."

"Being friends with her was the hard part. It's brought nothing but grief."

He shakes his head. "It's *not* being friends with her that's tearing you apart."

Her anger flares, tears rising with it. "Losing my *son* tore me apart. And she . . . she—"

"You don't need to tell me how that feels."

"Your son is still alive!" she half-screams, banging the dashboard. As she hears herself, she knows they're the words she's wanted to scream at Chrissy for the last two years. The unfairness of it. The injustice. To hear Peter talking about making things easier is an insult.

"Neither of us knows if that's true," Peter says softly, bringing her anger back down.

Alice buries her face in her palms, unable to look at him. Then she gets out of the car, slams the door, and marches toward Chrissy's house.

SHE THINKS IT'S Chrissy who's opened the door, until she realizes it's her sister. Tess looks shocked to see her, and Alice is thrown, too, memories of Christmas drinks with Chrissy and Tess flashing through her mind, Leo bantering with his aunt, playing in the pub garden with his younger cousins.

"I . . ." She flounders as Tess gazes at her, not quite friendly and not quite hostile. "Is Chrissy here?"

Tess pauses. Alice wonders how much Chrissy has told her about the way things have been between them. "I'd better ask if she . . ."

But then Chrissy's voice comes from behind. "It's okay, Tess. Let her in."

Tess stands aside and Alice walks slowly through. Her heart is beating fast and she wants to change her mind, run away. Chrissy looks disheveled and unslept, as she probably does herself. The house is spotless yet there is a bodily smell of stress and fear.

In the kitchen, a woman she's never seen before is making tea, but Alice's eye is drawn to a collage on the wall, a patchwork of photos of Chrissy and Leo. She remembers the Dean family photos all over the flat above the pub, the wide smiles and huggy poses telling a different story from the truth. And she remembers the photo of Alice and Robbie that Chrissy used to keep in a frame next to her side of the bed. It annoyed the hell out of Ethan. He always hated Chrissy's closeness with Alice, wanted everything to be about him. But Chrissy refused to take the photo down.

Alice is left hanging for a moment, until the woman offers her a cup of tea, seeming to have a spare ready-made. Alice accepts, just for something to hold.

"Could you give us some privacy?" Chrissy says to Tess and the other woman.

The tea-maker leaves politely. Tess lingers, like Chrissy's bodyguard, until Chrissy nods at her and she retreats, shutting the door behind her.

Alone for the first time in two years, they stare at each other. Alice's legs feel soft and she longs to sit down, but she's afraid of acting too familiar, maybe of looking weak. Silence wraps itself around them, as if neither wants to be the first to say something.

"Any news on Leo?" Alice asks finally.

"Do you care?" There's an edge to Chrissy's voice, a challenge, but it's not entirely aggressive. It's as if the question is genuine. Alice decides to treat it that way.

"Yes," she says, and knows that it's true, but complicatedly so.

She sees Chrissy swallow. "No news, really. Some leads, I suppose, but nothing . . ." Her voice cracks. "Nothing good enough."

Alice looks down, worried she might cry, too. She wants to get through this without tears, though she doesn't know why it feels important.

"I'm sorry," she says, "about that."

"*Only* about that?"

Alice raises her head. Chrissy looks back at her, unblinking, her tears gone now, too. Alice never thought she would apologize to Chrissy. She's been living, every day, with the need to make Leo and Chrissy hurt as much as she has. But she's got that wish now, hasn't she? And it feels disgusting. Layers of hurt on top of hurt.

Still, she can't answer the question. The anger is part of her now; it's in her blood.

"Did you write Robbie's and Leo's initials on the pub wall?" she blurts.

Chrissy's head snaps back. "What?"

Alice falters. Saying it out loud has burst the bubble of her own certainty. She's been imagining Chrissy smug about Leo's release, defiant of all her haters in the village, but now that she's in a room with her, the image crumbles. She's not a troll, is she? She's a terrified mum.

"Someone's . . ." Alice feels lost. If Chrissy didn't do these things, she has no idea why they're happening.

"Have you been sending me threatening notes?" Chrissy counters.

Alice freezes. She doesn't want to lie but she can't bring herself to tell the truth. She stays silent and knows that's worse, a cop-out.

"You've been trying to drive me out of my home," Chrissy says, visibly shaking. "Even if you didn't send the notes, you've been trying to ostracize me anyway, with your fucking committee, your emails, your . . . *cruelty*."

The last word swings hard into Alice. Her own anger flies up like a shield. "*I'm* cruel?" she says, lifting her arms. "You think it was a kind idea to bring Leo back here? To rub it in my face that . . ." She thinks of what she half-screamed in the car—*your son is alive*—but stops short of saying it, closing her fists at her sides.

"I wasn't doing that to taunt you! I was just bringing him home! You were supposed to be my best friend, Leo's godmum—"

"But it *felt* like a taunt. Everything did! Have you *any* idea,

Chrissy? You being around, a constant reminder. You trying to excuse what he did . . ."

"I didn't!" Chrissy cries. "Alice, I wasn't trying to excuse it. I was just trying to understand."

Alice shakes her head. "No, no, you were trying to . . . you implied that . . ." She is choking with the effort of not crying; why can't she just let it happen?

"I'm *sorry*," Chrissy says. The first genuine, meaningful apology that's passed between them. Alice closes her eyes, feeling a blast of shame. But then the fury rears back up, like a monster she can't control, and she realizes this isn't what she wants the apology for.

She wants Chrissy to say sorry for Robbie's death. Wants *somebody* to.

"He's my son," Chrissy says. "I *have* to defend him. Stick by him. He was tortured by what he did, Alice. Felt guilty every day. He needed me. You would do the same."

"But I *can't!*" Alice says as the tears erupt. "I won't ever get to!"

Chrissy starts crying, too. "I know." She steps closer and Alice steps away, scared of how hard she might sob if Chrissy touches her. "I'm sorry for that. I'm so, so sorry."

"I'm sorry, too," Alice chokes out, and the release of it is huge.

They cry for a few moments, standing near each other but not touching. It's impossible to stay that way, though. It feels unnatural. Alice isn't sure whose arms reach out first, but the brush of Chrissy's curls against her face is achingly familiar. They are careful with each other, as though they're both bruised, and the hug feels like a transgression, like lifting a ban that was in place for a reason.

Alice is the first to pull back. They wipe their faces, blinking as if they've just woken up.

"I sent the first note," Alice says in a low voice, her heart skipping. "But . . . not the others."

Chrissy looks at her for a long pause. A memory flickers anxiously at the back of Alice's mind: the red marker pen in Peter's glove box.

"I—" she starts to say, but Chrissy walks away from her.

Alice falls silent, wondering if she's blown it, whatever reconciliation they might've been edging toward. Chrissy opens a drawer, reaches right to the back, and pulls out a piece of paper.

"This note?" she says, walking back to Alice.

She unfolds it and thrusts it at her. Alice winces at her own spiky, livid writing in black pen.

EVERYBODY KNOWS WHAT YOUR SON DID. EVERYBODY SAW IT. HATES HIM FOR IT.

The writing gets messier, the sentences tapering down the page.

BUT WHO KNOWS THE TRUTH ABOUT YOU?

WHAT HAPPENED BEFORE

WHAT HAPPENED ABOVE

"You can probably see why I held this one back from the police," Chrissy says.

Alice swallows and nods.

To her surprise, Chrissy shoves it into her hands. "Take it to them, if you want," she says, her eyes wide. "You must've thought about telling them?"

"Lots of times," Alice says, remembering all those sleepless nights, rehearsing what she would say, fantasizing about Chrissy's arrest.

"Well . . ." Chrissy is trying to look stronger than she feels, Alice can tell. "Why don't you?"

Alice looks down at the note. Sees the small hole where her pen went through the paper, she was pressing down so fiercely. Writing it was the only thing she could do, because she knew, really, that she would never tell the police Chrissy's secret. And she knows it now, too.

She tears the paper in half, then in half again.

FORTY-FOUR

GEORGIE

Sunday, December 10, 2023

The roads are quiet and Georgie drives instinctively, almost blindly, somehow gliding over potholes and patches of ice. She feels sick and she thinks, irrationally, that she can still smell Alice's vomit from that day in the pub, as if it's clinging to her skin. The craggy hills on either side of the road feel nearer than usual. These Dales, which she's driven through so many times, seemingly closing in on her flimsy city car.

What has she done? *What has she done?*

She is so far from her original plan that nothing makes sense. She sees Robbie's and Leo's initials carved into every tree she whizzes past. Sees ravens up in the branches, leering down at her. Closing in. Pushing. Isn't that what she was trying to do, with the initials, the pub sign, all of it? Push Alice enough that she'd break under pressure and give herself away. Take Chrissy with her. And anyone else with a guilty conscience.

Right now, though, as she yells at the trees and the birds to be quiet, to let her think, she fears the only person she's pushed to their limit is herself.

She is so overwhelmed she almost misses her turnoff. She brakes and screeches up a narrow back road, her little BMW groaning and wheel-spinning as she urges it up the hill. Lola would be horrified at what she's putting it through. Lola would be horrified by what she's *done*. She gasps out a panicked sob as she reaches the car park and steps into the force of the wind.

His grave is right on the edge, in an exposed, even windier spot. She runs toward it, weaving between the other graves, doing her usual checks to see if anybody else is here. Her fear, always, was that she'd run into Chrissy, her cover blown. But she realizes now that she needn't have worried. Chrissy never visits him. The fact that he's buried all the way out here says it all.

She drops to her knees in front of his headstone. The cold seeps through her laddered tights and bites at her skin. A steep valley falls away to her right, and on its far side a tall viaduct rises into the sky, the focal point her gaze is always drawn to.

"Help me," she begs him. "Tell me what to do."

But she can't feel him as strongly as she usually does. It's as if Ben has taken that from her, too. She touches his engraved name, trying to reconnect. *I don't believe anything he said, my love. Of course I don't.*

She had to shut the idiot up, didn't she? Couldn't let him keep saying those things, spreading that poison. She thrusts away the image of him thudding to the floor, eyes rolling in shock.

Then she notices something. Little spots of red on the pale gray headstone. At first she thinks she's hallucinating, haunted by the spattering on her white carpet, the memory of trying to clean it up, wash it away, closing her eyes to the much bigger problem lying motionless beside her. She leans in closer. She isn't hallucinating. It is blood. There is blood on Ethan's grave.

FORTY-FIVE

CHRISSY

Sunday, December 10, 2023

Chrissy sits behind a desk in front of a room full of murmuring people. Her palms are clammy and she keeps wiping them on her jeans, firing glances at the camera even though it's not yet recording.

Her gaze drifts to the second row. To Alice, sitting there, head and shoulders above the other women in the room. There is still a wariness between them, a distance they might never close. Part of Chrissy is braced for Alice to jump up and start yelling, or to shoot her a soul-crushing look, like she did when their eyes met across the courtroom during Leo's trial. The detectives seem to be expecting the same, glancing questioningly between the two women from their own seats behind the desk. But the expression on Alice's face is more like the one she was wearing when Chrissy came out from making her statement about Ethan's death. *Get through this, just get through it and everything will be okay.*

Chrissy doesn't know if that's true, but she clings to her hope that doing this will make a difference. Her eyes move from Alice to the door, then to the clock on the wall. Two minutes till the press conference starts, and Peter isn't here. Maybe she pushed him too hard, asking him to sit beside her and make a public appeal for their son to come home. Maybe this isn't the right moment to start acting like co-parents.

Her phone buzzes with a message from Tess: Good luck. I love you. x

Chrissy swallows. She asked her sister to stay at home just in case. She has a fear of leaving the house empty in case Leo turns up there. Part of her is still consumed with hope that the next message from Tess will be He's here, he's here!

There's no time to reply. Chrissy silences her phone as Detective Wright opens the press conference with a statement about the search for Leo, appealing for anybody with information to call the hotline. She details what Leo was wearing and the area of Derbyshire they're particularly interested in. Chrissy battles to sit still, sips her water, glances at Alice again as she waits for her turn. The detectives think Leo may have gone on the run or be in hiding. That an appeal from her might encourage him to turn himself in. Chrissy still can't quite tell if they think he's guilty or scared. Is it better to imagine him out there with no protection, no food, no bed, than in a car trunk or a burning barn? Marginally, yes, but she is still more terrified than she's ever been.

Detective Wright gives her a signal. Chrissy shuffles in her chair, takes a deep breath. Then there's a noise at the back of the room. The door opens and Peter rushes in. Heads swivel as he strides to the front and sits down beside Chrissy without apologizing. He smells freshly showered. He's had a shave. There is no time to adjust to him being here when she'd given up on him; the green light on the camera is winking and Chrissy begins to speak.

AFTERWARD, CHRISSY CAN barely remember what she said. What *they* said. But Alice and the police tell her she did well, that it was perfect, that having both of them there made it stronger. Chrissy doesn't care about perfect. Alice was always the strong public speaker, not her. She just cares that there's the tiny possibility of Leo seeing it and knowing he's desperately loved, by both his parents. She wishes she could've given him that assurance years ago.

As she stands with Alice and Peter in the car park, snow falling onto their coats, Kiri comes rushing up to them. She has a harried look about her and her braids are loose over her shoulders.

"Hi," she says, a little breathless. "Have any of you heard from Ben today?"

They glance at each other and shake their heads. Kiri looks to Peter in particular.

"Not since I saw you both yesterday," he says. "Why?"

"He was supposed to be here for the press conference. But he hasn't shown. I've been calling him but he's not picking up."

Peter frowns. "You tried Jenny?"

"Yeah, no answer from her mobile, or their home number." She frowns, too, then shrugs and says: "Well . . . I'm sure he'll rock up at some point . . ." Her eyes betray more worry than her voice. "Thanks anyway."

"Let us know?" Peter says, his face screwed up in thought.

Kiri nods a little vaguely, bites her lip, then walks back into the building.

Left alone again, the three of them don't seem to know what to do with themselves. Chrissy looks down at their shoes getting dusted with snow and can't quite believe they're standing here together, so outwardly calm.

"I can't go back to the house," she says. "Can't just sit there and wait anymore."

"Then let's go and look for Leo," Peter says.

"Where?" Chrissy asks, gesturing at the sky.

Peter is already pulling his car keys out of his pocket. "We'll start with the barn. Follow our instincts from there."

Chrissy nods, recognizing the same compulsion she had herself: to go to the barn, hoping inspiration would strike. Amrit had asked on her behalf but was told Chrissy should stay away; it was still a crime scene under investigation. But now her blood fires back up: Amrit isn't here.

"Do you know where it is?" She thinks of the moving blue dot on the police officers' laptop screen. "I've a rough idea, but . . ."

"We'll find it," Peter says. "We'll get as close as we can. If Leo's on foot, he can't have got far from there."

Chrissy pushes her hair behind her ears. She knows there are whole teams of people out looking for him. But she wants to be one of them. Wants to be sure she's doing everything, absolutely everything, she can.

Nobody has said, outright, that there is a possibility they're searching for a body. Every time the thought enters Chrissy's head, she thrusts it away.

———

THE SURREAL FEELING returns as they pull off in Peter's Land Rover: the strangeness of being in a car with Peter and Alice. Chrissy tamps down a fear that this is a trap, that they're taking her somewhere she won't come back from. She messages Tess to tell her their plan so that at least someone else knows. How long will she keep suspecting that their truce is a lie?

Alice has got straight into the backseat, as if still keeping herself cautiously separate, and is sitting with her long legs drawn up into her body, staring out of the window in pensive silence. From the driver's seat, Peter hands Chrissy his phone.

"Keep an eye on this, will you?" he says. "In case Kiri contacts me, or Ben when he turns up."

"Okay . . ."

"The passcode's one-zero-one-one."

Chrissy raises her eyebrows. Ultra-private Peter, giving her his passcode? As she commits it to memory, she realizes the code is Robbie's birthday. She wonders, distantly, whether he would've used Leo's if everything had been out in the open. And it hits her again, how complicated the last two years must've been for Peter. She resented him for never reaching out to her after Leo went to prison, but it must've torn him apart, knowing his son killed his nephew but being unable to talk about the horrible mess of it. *Because* of the horrible mess of it.

As they snake up through the outer edges of the Peak District, hills rise on either side of the road, pierced by jutting boulders of dark stone. Chrissy always liked the contrast between the White Peak with all its limestone and the Dark

Peak—her home—shaped out of millstone grit. It felt like the difference between a bright, clean, shiny pub, and one more like her own, dingier and rough round the edges. She closes her eyes as memories of her former life reel through her mind. Ethan's face looms inevitably among them. She opens her eyes and concentrates on the road.

"Where might he go?" she says aloud. "If he *was* hiding, or running? Where might he go?"

"Family?" Peter says.

"I've been in touch with anyone who might've heard from him."

"Familiar places? People often gravitate toward places that mean something to them, in my experience."

Chrissy's legs start to twitch. "What if he's in another car trunk somewhere?" she says. "Or . . ." She's about to say, *worse*, but she still can't allow herself to go there.

Nobody has an answer. Peter flicks on the radio, but the cheery song that blares out seems to make him wince, and he turns it off again.

Then, suddenly, he indicates left. "Let's make a stop-off," he says.

Chrissy looks out of the window in confusion. "Where?"

She hears Alice moving in the back, leaning forward so her face appears between the two front seats. "Marianne's?" she says, and Peter's silence seems to be all the confirmation they're going to get.

Chrissy takes a breath. She didn't know where Marianne had moved to. But it makes sense to talk to her. She prepares herself to hear about her conversation with Leo at the prison.

Why she chose to upend his life without asking anybody else it might affect.

Keep your cool, she tells herself. *An argument won't help Leo.*

Can't promise anything, another part of her bites back.

MARIANNE'S COTTAGE IS in the middle of nowhere. The wheels of Peter's Land Rover grind through the snow, already much deeper up here. Smoke spirals from a chimney and the snow leading up to her front door is undisturbed, their footsteps the first to mark it. Chrissy pulls up her hood, then feels guilty for trying to keep herself warm and dry when Leo might be far from it.

Peter seems to steel himself before knocking on the door. When she appears, Marianne looks shocked to see the three of them, shrinking back as if it's an ambush. "Pete . . ." she says. "Alice, Chrissy . . ."

"We're searching for Leo," Peter says without preamble. "Can we talk to you?"

She hesitates, then opens the door wider, letting them in. She offers them hot drinks but they shake their heads.

"We haven't got long," Peter says. "Time's ticking."

Chrissy's eyes roam the small living room, the thick wooden beams sloping low overhead, but stop when she sees a framed photo crammed with familiar faces: Peter, Marianne, Leo, Robbie, Alice, and herself. A gig night at the Raven, all of them laughing, arms around each other. Why would Marianne keep this in a frame when most of those relationships have fallen apart?

Marianne seems to notice where she's looking. "I've been trying . . ." She starts and then falters. "Trying to adjust to the idea . . . To think of us all as . . ." She trails off, her cheeks turning pink.

"It wasn't your place to tell Leo the truth," Chrissy snaps.

"Well, it wasn't *your* place to . . ." Marianne gestures at Peter, then looks away in distress. Chrissy shuffles uncomfortably, but the guilt of sleeping with Marianne's partner fails to outweigh her anger. She thinks of the times, in the past, when she would catch Marianne looking at her questioningly, almost hostilely. She always dismissed it as paranoia; it was during a period when every look, every whisper, felt like a sign that people knew all her secrets. But was it possible Marianne had always had a nagging suspicion about her and Peter?

"I didn't intend to," Marianne says after a while. "That wasn't why I visited him."

"Then *why?*"

"I just wanted to see him. Talk to him. I was trying to get my head around the fact that he's Peter's son . . ." She glances at her ex-husband, pursing her lips, and he looks back with sadness in his eyes. "I was trying to accept it. But he seemed so confused about why I'd come. Seemed to think I'd been sent by Alice or Peter as some kind of spy, or to make him feel bad. So . . . I ended up telling him the truth."

"How did he take it?" Peter asks Marianne.

"I don't think he believed me at first. Thought I was just trying to stir up trouble . . ."

You were, Chrissy thinks, like a reflex, but her guilt has grown bigger now, the scales tipping back toward self-blame.

"But then . . ." Marianne stares into the fire as it spits out sparks. "Then he went very pale, as if what I'd said had sunk in. And he said, 'It makes sense now.'"

Chrissy stiffens. "What makes sense?"

"I'm not sure exactly. Maybe he always suspected something? But . . . I don't know . . . There seemed more to it than that. It was as if I'd really drawn back a curtain."

"You didn't tell me this part," Peter says.

"Well, we weren't doing a great job of talking to each other around that time, Pete."

He looks away. Nobody speaks for a few moments and the heat from the fire becomes intense. Chrissy's eye is drawn back to the framed photo. All of them so oblivious to what was to come. The idea of Marianne trying to "accept" Leo makes her feel prickly, like another woman trying to lay claim to her son. But if Marianne can help them, Chrissy has to put everything else aside.

"Did he say anything that might tell us where he is now?" she asks, breaking the silence. "Or what happened to him when he left the prison? Did he mention Frank Jordan?"

Marianne thinks for a moment. "He said nothing about Frank. He was quiet for a long time, actually. I expected him to ask more questions . . ." She pauses, tilting her head. "But the only thing he asked was whether Robbie knew."

Chrissy sees Alice react to the mention of her son. "He didn't, though, did he?" Alice says, her posture suddenly alert.

Marianne looks again at Peter. Something flickers back and forth between them. Chrissy scrutinizes Peter as he shifts from one foot to the other, his Adam's apple moving in his throat.

"I think . . ." Peter says. "There's a possibility he might've figured it out."

"What?" Alice says. "How?"

Peter pushes a hand through his hair. "I don't know for sure. It was only afterward that I started thinking about it. You know how you go over and over little details? I was trying to figure out why Robbie seemed off with me, right before he . . ." He glances at Alice, who has a frozen, pained expression on her face. "He was, though, wasn't he, Al? Nothing seemed quite right that night."

"It's hard to remember," Alice whispers. "It's hard to remember anything except . . ." But she does, Chrissy can see. She does remember; she just can't think around or beyond the big thing, the awful thing.

"A couple of days before, Robbie went up into my loft to dig something out," Peter says. "I think he was going to sell my old Nintendo games for me, something like that. When he came back down, he seemed a bit distracted. He kept bringing up Leo, asking me weird questions . . ."

"What was in the loft?" Alice asks, her voice thick with anxiety.

Yes, Chrissy thinks, her heart in her mouth. *What was in the loft?*

"The scrapbook," Peter says, with another guilty glance at Marianne. "All my cuttings and mementoes about Leo. There was a baby photo, too, tucked in the back of it. I . . . I took that out before I threw it in the dumpster. Couldn't bring myself to chuck that away forever."

Chrissy gazes at him. He kept a baby photo of Leo? Where did he even get it from? And cuttings. *Mementoes.*

"You think Robbie saw the scrapbook?" Alice asks.

Peter shrugs again. "Perhaps he had suspicions already. Maybe he put two and two together . . ."

Chrissy's pulse speeds up and she catches Alice's eye. It's still a taboo subject between them, the word *provoked* still dangerously contentious. But could this be why the two boys—*cousins*—argued so badly that night?

And is this one more reason to wish they'd never kept their stupid, misguided secret all this time?

AS THEY'RE TRAIPSING out of the house, Marianne grabs Chrissy's arm at the doorway. Her eyes are so intense that Chrissy's instinct is to pull away. She sees Peter glancing back as he gets into the front of the car. Feels Marianne's hand tighten on her arm, detaining her.

"I've been so angry with you," Marianne says, her voice low and raspy.

Chrissy doesn't know what to say. There isn't time for this. She hears Peter starting the engine and gestures toward him.

"But I *am* sorry," Marianne continues, not taking the hint. "It was reckless to tell Leo. I've been beating myself up about it."

Chrissy sighs and relents a little, inclining her head. "There are a lot of things we all should've done differently, Marianne. Maybe there's no point in—"

"I'd been in the dark all that time." Her eyes get even wider. "My husband had a *son*. My husband had this deep, important connection with other people that I knew nothing about. I wanted to make myself part of it, talk about it . . . get back some control, I suppose. It sounds awful when I put it like that."

No, Chrissy thinks reluctantly. *It sounds familiar.* That powerless feeling of uncertainty, of shifting sands. Isn't everybody afraid of that?

"I was even desperate to talk to *you*. I kept . . ." Marianne flushes. "Kept calling you and then chickening out . . ."

Now Chrissy's attention is seized. "Wait. *Calling* me?"

"I imagined asking you stupid questions. Like, what's Leo's favorite color? Like, how did it feel when you found out you were pregnant? Like, why did you sleep with my boyfriend and have his baby and—"

"Did you call me on my home phone?"

Marianne blinks. "Yes. I don't have your mobile number."

Chrissy flattens her palm against her forehead. "Jesus, Marianne. I thought it was Leo. Or someone who'd got him. I was going to get the police to try and trace the calls . . ."

Marianne flushes deeper. "I'm sorry. I stopped when I found out Leo was missing. I just wanted to . . ."

Chrissy screws her eyes shut. "I have to go. I have to find Leo. I can't waste any more time."

"Look, I meant it when I said . . ." But Chrissy is already walking away, shaking her head. "I hope you find him! Chrissy, I really hope you do!"

She glances back, seeing Marianne framed in her doorway, scrunching the lapels of her long black cardigan. Chrissy nods, exhaling heavily, then ducks her head into the car and closes the door behind her.

FORTY-SIX

ALICE

Sunday, December 10, 2023

They drive away from Marianne's in silence. Alice is back in the days just before Robbie's death, the dark swirl of memory threatening to pull her all the way down. If he *did* figure out Peter was Leo's dad, how might he have felt about it? She thinks of his idolization of Peter, his issues with his own dad. And the rivalry that always simmered between Leo and himself, even when they were almost inseparable.

She's startled from her thoughts by a phone ringing in the front of the car.

"It's yours," Chrissy says to Peter. "Hang on, I put it in the glove box . . ." She opens it and starts rooting around.

Alice tenses, remembering what she saw in there yesterday. She is sure she sees Peter's shoulders stiffening, too, from her seat behind him. Chrissy's rummaging seems to go on for a long time. The phone keeps ringing. Two CDs fall out and there it is, the red marker pen, tumbling out alongside.

There is a moment of stillness. Chrissy frowns at the pen that has landed in the well between her feet. The phone rings and rings. Peter stabs at a button on the car's control panel and Kiri's voice comes through the hands-free.

"Pete? Can you talk?"

Peter clears his throat. "Go ahead," he says with something like relief in his tone.

"It's . . . it's about Ben."

"What about him?"

"He's . . . hurt," Kiri says, her voice strained. "Pretty badly. He's been attacked, or so it seems."

Alice sits forward. Chrissy, leaning down to retrieve the pen and the CDs, straightens up quickly.

"*What?*" Peter says, the car juddering as it pops out of gear. "What do you mean? Who by?"

"That's . . . the strangest part." Kiri leaves another pause and her breathing comes through the speakers. She sounds like she's walking, hurrying. "I found him at Georgie Fallows's house. Lying on the floor with a head injury. Conscious, when I got there, but only just."

Alice's brain seems to flip over on itself. *Georgie?* She can feel the same stunned confusion radiating from Chrissy and Peter, the red marker forgotten. Georgie is odd, sometimes a little fake, hard to read. But why on earth would she attack Ben? In her own home?

"I don't follow," Peter says. "Do you think it was her? Why would she do that?"

"We're still trying to work it out. Ben went there last night to pick up"—she clears her throat—"some evidence. When he didn't show up for work this morning, I thought I'd go round there and check with her. But there was no sign of her, her car was gone, and when I tried Ben's mobile again, I could hear it ringing in the house. So I called for backup and we got inside. Poor Ben, he was . . . he was in a bad way."

"Jesus," Peter says, glancing at Chrissy. "Is he going to be okay?"

"I fucking hope so." It's the first time Alice has heard Kiri swear. She wonders if she knows she's on speaker, that she's got an audience. Alice keeps quiet and Chrissy seems to be doing the same.

"Is he talking?" Peter asks. "Can he remember anything?"

"He's sedated. They're checking his brain function. He said a few things on the way to the hospital, though. He seemed a bit muddled, but . . . he kept mentioning Ethan Dean."

Another baffled silence fills the car, but this one has a vibration to it, an undertow of dread. Chrissy turns in her seat to look at Alice. Alice stares back at her, struggling to understand.

Peter says, more quietly: "Ethan?"

"Yeah. I know. It's odd. From what I could make out, Georgie was making accusations of some kind, and Ben said something she didn't like . . ." She pauses and there's the sound of a door opening and closing at her end. "I'm really not sure. Hopefully he'll be clearer next time he wakes."

"But . . . she didn't even know Ethan," Peter says. "Did she?" He looks at Chrissy again, and Chrissy puts a hand up to her mouth, her face pale.

"We're looking into it," Kiri says. "And we're trying to track Georgie down. If you hear anything, you'll let me know?"

"Yes," Peter mumbles distractedly. "And likewise?"

Kiri hangs up and the car is silent again. Alice keeps opening her mouth to speak, then closing it. She hears Chrissy taking a breath as if she wants to say something, too, but nothing comes out.

Then she sees Chrissy pull out her phone, open Safari, and type in Georgie's name. Pictures of Georgie fill the screen, most of them corporate headshots. Alice can sense Chrissy's anxiety, can hear her breathing more quickly as her finger taps and taps.

Then Alice sees her go still.

She leans even further forward. "What is it?" she asks softly.

"This hotel . . ." Chrissy holds up her phone to show Alice a photo of Georgie and some other smartly dressed people having cocktails in a swanky lounge. "In London. Ethan used to stay there when he traveled for work. And Georgie . . . by the looks of it . . . used to take clients there. This is from her old company's website."

Alice studies the picture. Georgie is wearing more makeup than she does around the village, and a designer suit with high heels rather than the indigo jeans and knee-high boots she's adopted for her country life. She's beaming at the camera, holding a martini. The caption reads, *Cocktails with some of our amazing clients*.

"Do you think she knew Ethan?" Alice asks.

"Yes," Chrissy says with more certainty than Alice is expecting. "Yes, I do. I think she wears a ring that he gave her. I think . . . I think she's been watching me."

Alice pulls her seat belt away from her throat, suddenly feeling it cutting right in. She knows Chrissy suspected Ethan of having affairs in the past. And Georgie would be just the glamorous type he'd go for, to make himself feel important. Her stomach contracts with renewed hatred for him. She thinks of Kiri using the word *accusations* and heat spreads up her neck and into her face.

Georgie sat in all those committee meetings, throwing around her marketing jargon, her shiny smile. Why had she really been there? What does she want?

"We're near the graveyard," Chrissy says, looking out of the window.

Alice looks, too, realizing how far they've come. The turning for Shirebrook is only a mile or so ahead of them along the snowy road.

"Let's make another stop-off." Now there is hard determination in Chrissy's tone.

"Are you sure?" Peter asks.

"I have a feeling," Chrissy says. "I just have a feeling."

Peter says nothing more, but when he reaches the junction, he turns in the direction of Shirebrook and the church. Alice sits back in her seat, feeling faintly sick. It isn't the winding roads, but the sense of drawing closer to Ethan's grave. She tries not to think too often about that night, when Chrissy called her in floods of panicked tears, saying, *I did it, I did it, I couldn't stand any more.* Tries not to recall rushing to the Raven, heart clanging as she climbed the stairs to the flat. Ethan was sprawled on the living room floor, looking both bigger and smaller, somehow, than he had when he was alive. His face was blue and there were thick red stripes around his neck. A purple dressing gown cord lay coiled on the carpet nearby.

Chrissy was hyperventilating and Alice knew it was bad, so bad, and it was up to her to make it okay, she *had* to make it okay. For Chrissy. For the person she loved more than she could even admit.

What they did after that haunted her for years. He was heavy and unwieldy as they hoisted him up. It took so long to fasten him to the beams in the ceiling, to make it look right; he kept flopping back down and his eyes were open, watching them the whole time. He'd been sick down his work shirt but all Alice could think was that it would make it look more realistic. Her mind seemed to separate into two: the half that was appalled and terrified; the half that saw a job that needed to be done. Both halves, later, would go into shock. And even later than that, would unite in one consoling thought: Chrissy deserved better than Ethan.

Now they are climbing the slope toward the churchyard where he's buried, and Alice feels chilled to the bone. She reaches forward, instinctively touching Chrissy's shoulder. Chrissy's hand immediately rests on top of hers. It's ice-cold, too. But Alice's skin starts to thaw and her courage trickles back as Chrissy's fingers press against hers.

FORTY-SEVEN

CHRISSY

Sunday, December 10, 2023

Chrissy stands in front of Ethan's grave and waits to feel something. Waits for the shame, the hatred, the anger, the guilt, the fear. She runs her eyes over his name on the headstone, over the words *beloved husband of Chrissy and father of Leo,* remembering the bad taste they'd left in her mouth as she'd commissioned them.

The feelings won't surface. She is as hard and cold as the headstone.

She hears a rustle, and Peter comes to stand beside her. Alice is across the other side of the churchyard, staring out over the valley.

"I'm sorry," Peter says, looking at the grave. "I should've realized what he was like. Sooner. *Much* sooner."

She shakes her head. "I didn't want you to know."

"Why?"

"I suppose . . . I was ashamed."

"You have *nothing* to be ashamed of." He says it with

such vehemence that she looks toward him in surprise. Does he know anything? Does he suspect? She has held it so tight inside all this time. Has drawn the smallest possible circle around it, and even that has felt hideously vulnerable since she and Alice have been driven apart.

"This thing with Georgie is . . . so strange," she says carefully, with a shake in her voice.

He nods. "Yes. It is. It's okay, though. It's . . . going to be okay."

It's what he always says. And she always wants to believe him.

"Accusations?" she whispers, huddling into her coat.

Peter shakes his head. "She's attacked a police officer. She's clearly not in her right mind."

"But they might be obliged to at least—"

"Even if they do"—he looks at her meaningfully—"there's nothing to worry about."

She shakes her head, slightly befuddled as to what he's trying to say. She wants to take comfort from it, from *anything*, but it only adds to the butterflies in her belly. Her eyes go back to Ethan's grave and a shadow of memory passes across the stone. That night was the worst he'd ever been. He was angry and stressed—all the speculation about Ofsted wasn't so far from the truth, after all—and intent on hurting and humiliating Chrissy beyond anything he'd done before. She remembers the weight of him on top of her, crushing the breath out of her—

"There's something else I need to apologize to you for," Peter says, breaking the memory apart.

Chrissy turns and looks at him. As he looks back with

shame all over his face, she suddenly knows what he's going to say.

"The notes," she says, her voice flat.

He presses the heels of his hands into his eyes. "I'm so sorry."

Chrissy inhales, then exhales strongly. Feelings are building now, starting in her sternum, but she doesn't know which ones are about Ethan and which are about Peter.

"*Why?*" she asks.

Peter is stooped, as if he has something heavy around his neck. "It was only ever when I was drunk."

Chrissy feels a rush of anger, thinking of Ethan making the same excuse. "That isn't a reason," she says fiercely. Did she ever say that to Ethan? Ever tell him it was the oldest excuse in the book, and not a good one?

"I just . . ." Peter makes an effort to straighten up. "It messed with my head so much, that you were so nearby, and Leo was in prison, and my nephew was . . . was dead. Because of him. Because of my son. But I couldn't even call him that. Round and round I'd go . . ." His voice weakens, almost disappears, then comes back: "Whenever I was drunk, I found ways to blame you. For being a reminder. For not letting me tell Alice before it was too late . . ."

"It *wasn't* my fault," Chrissy growls. Another thing she should have said to Ethan but never did. She feels the release, the power of saying it, even to the wrong person.

"I know," Peter says. "Sober me knew that, I swear. I was always so ashamed when I remembered. But I couldn't take it back, and then it would happen again; it was like my only outlet . . ."

"You think *I* had any outlets?" Chrissy's voice rises, and she looks over at Alice, but she hasn't moved. "I was alone. I had shit to deal with, too. Like being threatened in my own home. Hated by all my friends . . ."

"I'm sorry. Chrissy, I really am. We're getting to a good place and I wanted to tell you. I don't expect you to forgive me . . ."

She sees Ethan, begging for forgiveness, groveling at her feet. She fell for it every time. But she won't this time, she'll make him—

"What's going on?" Alice sprints toward them, looking concerned.

Chrissy steps back, unable to speak. She feels caught between past and present, fizzing with anger but confused about who it's for.

"I told her . . ." Peter says, sounding bewildered, too. "It was me . . . the notes . . ."

Alice is silent. Chrissy wonders whose side she'll take. Maybe she already knew? She wrote the first one, after all. Maybe this was all a huge mistake, trying to reconcile.

"What's *that?*" Alice says in an incongruent tone of voice. Chrissy is thrown, thinking she's missed a beat.

Then she sees that Alice is pointing at Ethan's grave. Her head whirls and she tries to focus. Alice shines the flashlight of her phone over Ethan's headstone, illuminating what she's spotted. Little drops of red on the edge, and a faint spatter over the word *beloved*.

"Is that what I think it is?" Chrissy says.

Peter leans in, inspecting it more closely. "I'd say so," he says, glancing at her warily. "And in this weather, it can't have been there long."

"What the . . ." Chrissy scans the area around her, then weaves between the graves, glad of an excuse to move away from the other two. The graveyard feels as dead as the people buried in its ground. There aren't even any birds in the leafless trees. And yet there are flattened patches of weeds. *Spots of blood on Ethan's grave.* Only Ethan's, as far as Chrissy can see.

She feels her fury ebbing, turning into something different, something more like that prickle on the back of her neck.

She goes to the church and tries to open its large wooden doors. They give a little when she pushes them, but seem to be bolted. She walks down the side of the church, but can't see in through the stained-glass windows. Then Peter calls to her from the far side of the building: "Chrissy! There are some footprints."

She hurries round. Alice comes over to join them, too. Peter points at the ground, where there is a faint set of footprints in the small bank of snow that has collected against the church wall. Chrissy crouches down to examine one. It's chunky, the toe wide and round. It makes her think of Leo's Doc Martens, but she's conscious of clutching at straws. Then she sees, just behind it, another two tiny specks of red against the white snow.

She lifts her head to look at Alice and Peter. The prickle on her neck is more like a hand now, pressing insistently.

"I think we need to get the police up here."

FORTY-EIGHT

GEORGIE

Sunday, December 10, 2023

That was close, Georgie thinks as she accelerates along the twisty road that leads east from the church. She spotted Peter's Land Rover in her rearview mirror just after she'd turned off the road that slopes down from the churchyard. He was turning up the same road, surely heading for the place she'd just left, but he didn't appear to recognize her car. As she breathes out and eases her foot down a little more, relief sours into something darker. She's pretty sure Chrissy was in the car with him. Those curls are unmistakable. Why are they going up there now?

Her hands tighten on the wheel as she pictures Chrissy trampling all over Ethan's grave. She thinks of the blood on his headstone: How could it have got there? It feels like a sign, a bad omen. Her phone keeps ringing from the passenger seat, calls from Lola and from a number she doesn't know.

She ignores them. Keeps driving. But where to? She considers fleeing south, to London, to her old home or perhaps Lola's. But she can't face having to explain how it all went wrong.

A couple of miles on, she gets stuck behind a tractor. She cranes forward in frustration, trying to overtake it but unable to see. She can't risk a crash; it would draw too much attention. Resigned to slow progress, she takes the chance to look at her phone, and the first thing she sees is a text message from a sender calling themselves *DerbysPolice*.

Her hand quakes slightly as she taps it.

This is a communication from Derbyshire
Police. Please contact us as a matter
of urgency. NO REPLY TEXT. Visit
Derbys.police.uk for more information.

Georgie inhales, reads it again, then deletes it in a panic. The next message in her inbox is from Lola.

Derbyshire Police just rang me, Gee! They're
looking for you! What the hell is going on? I
saw some stuff in the news about your village.
It is Cromley isn't it? Please please call me. I'm
freaking out.

Tears spring into Georgie's eyes but she blinks them away and deletes that message, too. Perhaps she should turn off her phone. The idea troubles her, like severing her last connection to anybody or anything. As the traffic starts moving, she holds down the power button until the screen goes dark. Then she leaves the main road at the next turning and barrels along a dirt track. If she sticks to the back roads, she's less likely to be spotted. She'll get as far away as she can, find somewhere to hide, then decide what to do next.

It's only when she stalls the car that she realizes she's violently shaking. She jerks to a halt and sits there panting, wheezing, her lungs caving in. She tries to imagine Ethan beside her, soothing her, but the only voice in her head is swearing at her, calling her a fucking idiot for stalling the car. And it's his, it's Ethan's, but not as she knew him, not *her* Ethan. Ben has planted a new version, angry and abusive—Ben and Chrissy and everyone else. They're twisting her memories, turning his spirit into a shadow rather than her only light.

With a growl of fury, she turns the key in the ignition. The engine sputters briefly and then dies. Georgie swears and revs it again, but the same thing happens. She screams, hitting the steering wheel, trying to start the car with more and more pointless force. Nothing. She has broken down in the middle of nowhere, wanted by the local police. She hears Lola saying, *Well, if you will drag your poor car to the countryside and then put it through hell . . .* Then Ethan, the new version of Ethan: *Look at the state of you, Georgie. This isn't what I signed up for.* She roars even louder and snaps off her seat belt, jumping out of the useless car and storming down the road. At the last minute, she doubles back for her phone, leaving it turned off but shoving it into her pocket. There are sirens in the distance. She puts her head down and hops over a stile into an overgrown field.

———

GEORGIE ISN'T SURE how long she's been walking when she sees it. Twilight is descending and her vision is turning hazy with tiredness. She's just starting to think she needs to find somewhere to sleep when she squints ahead and sees the most incredible view, so striking it jolts her awake.

Several sets of hills sweep down toward each other, crossing over like arms in a dance. In between two of them, an enormous stone structure of pillars and arches seems to hold the rest of the landscape on its shoulders. A river flows underneath, glinting pale in the fading light. It's the viaduct she always sees, in the distance, from Ethan's grave. She hasn't got this close to it before. She keeps walking toward it, feeling humbled, insignificant, awed.

And then she freezes. There is a figure on the top of the viaduct. A man standing right on the edge, silhouetted against the lilac sky, looking down at the huge drop below.

FORTY-NINE

ALICE

Sunday, December 10, 2023

The churchyard crawls with scenes of crime officers. Alice stands at the edge, feeling overwhelmed. It makes her nervous to see police officers swarming around Ethan's grave, as if they'll be able to tell, somehow, that they didn't investigate his death as thoroughly as they should have at the time.

Chrissy comes over and they stand together, united now in their anxiety. Alice thinks about taking her hand but it still feels like a leap of faith.

"What have they found?" she asks Chrissy. "Anything?"

"Some fibers from a navy jumper," Chrissy says. "Which may match the one Leo was wearing when he left prison. They're sending them off for fast-tracked analysis."

"Really?" Alice turns toward her. It's hope that she feels, and she is happy to recognize it. Hoping that Leo is alive feels a thousand times better than wishing him harm.

Chrissy's eyes are glassy. "The blood-spatter experts think the blood is from someone with an injury, walking around the churchyard. They're trying to get DNA from it but . . ." Her chest rises. "I think he was *here,* Alice. I think Leo was here, not so long ago."

Alice swallows. "That's good, Chrissy. That's good news, isn't it?"

"But where is he now? And if he's hurt . . ." Chrissy closes her eyes, and Alice feels the old desire to take her friend's pain and absorb it into herself. The opposite of what she's felt for the last two years. It's like waking up from a spell. Except not everything is magically fixed, not everybody can wake up.

"If he was here, it must've been because . . . he felt compelled," she says to Chrissy. "So where else? Where else might he be drawn to?"

Chrissy stares toward Ethan's grave, cordoned off now with fluttering yellow tape. "The village?"

"Would he go there? If he doesn't want to be found?"

"It wouldn't make sense. But he's taken a risk coming to *this* place. If he *did* come . . ." Chrissy trails off as though there are too many *ifs* to contend with.

"Well, maybe that tells us something about his state of mind," Alice says. "Maybe . . ." She stops abruptly. Thinks of what Chrissy said when they finally had their showdown, about Leo feeling guilty about Robbie every day. "Maybe he'd go somewhere linked to Robbie, too? Somewhere that—"

A familiar expression has overtaken Chrissy's face. The one that lights up her features when her thoughts and Alice's suddenly synchronize.

"The viaduct," she says, pointing into the distance.

Alice is already moving. Peter is talking to one of the SOCOs and she grabs his car keys out of his hand. He looks at her, confused, but she doesn't explain as she rushes away. It's only when she reaches his car that she realizes he's followed, and she throws the keys back over to him. She says the word *viaduct* and he starts the engine.

FIFTY

GEORGIE

Sunday, December 10, 2023

Georgie struggles to find a way up, at first. But then she sees a narrow path to the right of the viaduct, cutting steeply through brown roots and slippery rocks. She trips several times, grazes her hands, and eventually ends up on her hands and knees, scrambling like an animal.

When she reaches the top, she can see the figure properly. Her breath catches: It *is* Leo Dean. He is alive. He is here. But he is dangerously close to the edge of the viaduct, swaying and looking down at the valley.

Her nerves soar as she edges forward. She stops a few feet away from him and tries not to glance at the dizzying drop. The hills on either side of the viaduct seem to cradle it, bringing a false sense of protection, but it's so high that stepping off it would feel like stepping off the end of the Earth. And Ethan's son, her should've-been stepson, is inches away from doing just that.

"Leo?" she says softly, then has to repeat it more loudly to be heard over the wind.

He jolts and she gasps in alarm, but he keeps his balance and turns only his head. He frowns at her, unrecognizing. His face is covered in bruises and his sweater and jeans are dirty and torn.

"Oh God, Leo," she says again. "Are you okay?"

"Who are you?"

"Why don't you step back a little?"

"Who *are* you? How do you know my name?"

"I'm . . ." She wonders whether to tell him or pretend to be a stranger who's heard about him on the news. Which would encourage him to trust her more? "I'm . . . a friend. Who would love for you to step back so we can talk . . ."

He turns away. "Leave me *alone.*"

"I can't do that."

"You really can. If you knew what was good for you, you would."

"What do you mean?"

Keep him talking, she thinks, *keep him talking.* Her eye flickers to the sky stretching out behind him, the stars just beginning to show.

"I'm not a good guy," he says angrily.

"I'm sure that's not true."

"You don't know me."

"Everyone's good, deep down." She pauses, shaking off a fleeting image of the blood running from Ben's head. "Everyone's got something to—"

"I'm wanted by the police." He turns again, challenging her to react.

She keeps her face neutral. *So am I*, she thinks, wondering whether to say it, create some common ground.

"Well . . ." she says, shuffling forward, "let me tell you a secret . . ."

"I don't want to know your secrets!" He waves his hands, seeming to panic. "I have enough of my own!"

"Okay!" She stops where she is, terrified of unbalancing him. "Okay . . ." When his shoulders sag and he lowers his hands, she dares to ask: "Why don't you tell me about yours?"

He is silent for a long time, still staring down the bowl of the valley. His upper body starts to shake. "It doesn't matter now," he says through tears. "There's no going back."

"There's always a way back," Georgie says, but wonders if she believes it. What is the way back for her? Has she thrown away her last hope of unraveling the truth? Or could this be it; could Leo be her chance to make sure it wasn't all for nothing?

"I'm a KILLER." He shouts it into the sky like he's trying to hurl the word over the viaduct's edge.

Georgie jerks backward, even though she already knows this. Leo's whole body is rigid now, his fists clenched at his sides. One foot nudges forward so its toe hangs over the edge. Georgie pulls herself together and inches toward him again, her hands hovering without touching him.

"But you've done your time for that," she says.

He swings round to stare at her. "How do *you* know?"

"I . . . I recognize you—"

"Have you been sent here to bring me in?" His eyes turn wild. "Are you a cop?"

"No, no . . ."

"I'll jump!" he yells, flailing his arms. "I can't go back to prison. I can't."

"I'm not a cop! I promise! I'm a friend, I knew your dad—"

He freezes, one hand stuck out in front. Slowly, almost robotically, he swivels to glare at her again. "What?"

"I . . ." Her face burns hot. Was that a mistake? "I . . . I knew Ethan." She says his name tenderly and she's relieved to feel a sweep of untainted love. She won't tell Leo about the things Ben said. Whatever their family dynamic, Leo must know, as she does, that Ethan was good. And maybe, like her, he has questions about his death. All that time to think in prison; maybe he wondered.

He retracts his hand and rests it against his chest.

"Ethan wasn't my dad."

Now it's her turn to stare. "What?"

"He wasn't my dad. He *wasn't* my dad." He grows frantic, stamping his feet. "But it doesn't matter now. None of it fucking matters. I killed him for no reason . . ." He shakes with fresh sobs, and Georgie's head starts to roar.

"Killed . . . who?" she shouts back as the wind picks up again.

"Robbie. My friend. My . . . cousin. Did you know him, too?" He barely pauses for her answer. "Whatever, it doesn't matter. I killed him because I thought . . . I thought . . . *Fuck* . . . " The pain in his voice is like cracking glass.

Georgie swallows, trying to stay composed. She doesn't know which part to focus on. Leo *isn't* Ethan's son? On a delay, she registers the fact that he called Robbie his cousin, and shock rockets through her.

Peter is Leo's dad?

Chrissy slept with Peter?

Anger surges again, peppering her vision with black spots. Is there anything Chrissy didn't put Ethan through?

Then it strikes her: It's further motive, perhaps. Another reason Chrissy might have wanted him out of the way.

"Because . . . you thought what?" she asks, returning to Leo. He is rocking now, shaking his head; she wants to tell him to stop, be still, but maybe breaking his rhythm would be worse.

Then he murmurs, barely audible: "I thought he meant something else."

"Robbie?"

He stops rocking and glances over his shoulder. His face is white, his eyes bloodshot. "Who *are* you?"

"It's okay," she says. "You can trust me."

He scrutinizes her so intently she wants to look away. But she gazes back at him, nodding encouragement, trying to project kindness.

"Well, it doesn't matter now anyway," he says, like a repeated mantra. "You may as well know. Then you can tell people, after I'm gone. You can tell them the truth 'cause I'm too much of a coward to do it."

Georgie's throat hurts and she feels her pulse in her skull. She inches another step closer. "Yes. You can tell me. But then we can sort it out together . . ."

"This can't be sorted out! I've killed *three people*. They'll send me straight back to jail and I can't . . . I can't . . ."

Her legs feel like vapor. "Three people?"

"See? I'm a bad guy—"

"No," she says quickly. "No, I'm just trying to understand . . ."

"Two of them were for a reason. Two of them I can *just* about . . ." He squeezes his eyes shut, bashing his fist between them. "But Robbie . . . that was senseless. That didn't have to happen, shouldn't have happened. And when I realized that . . ."

"Why was it senseless?"

"He kept saying things, that day. Kept hinting. I told myself there was no way he knew, but it felt relentless, the little mentions, and I was spooked, I felt sick. Then in the pub . . . playing darts . . . he got right up close . . . he called me 'Daddy's boy.'"

Her gaze snaps to his face. "What?"

"Robbie did. He said he knew my little secret. That was what sent me into a panic, made me so mad . . . He called me 'Daddy's boy' and he looked over at the door to the flat, or at least I thought he did, and I thought he meant . . . thought he knew . . ."

"Knew *what?*" Georgie's pulse is like a current now, electrifying her skin.

"I thought he was talking about Ethan. That he'd figured out what I did." More tears stream down his face and he turns back toward the drop, wiping them roughly away. "And I snapped. I went for him . . ."

"Wait . . ." Georgie's mind spins, scrambling the pieces together.

"But when Marianne came to see me in prison, I realized it wasn't that at all. He'd figured out Peter was my real dad.

He was jealous. It was Peter he looked over at, not the door. Not because he knew—"

Georgie can't stop herself from yelling. "What did you *do?*" She wants to grab him now. Shake the answers out of him.

"I killed my dad . . ." His confession is thrown to the valley. "The man I thought was my dad—"

Georgie feels as if she's falling. "You? It was *you?*"

"He wouldn't stop hurting my mum and—"

"No!" She slams her hands over her ears. "No, no—"

"LEO!" comes a shout from behind, making them both freeze.

They stand there for a moment, locked in place, breathing hard. Footsteps approach. More than one set. Georgie has her back to them, her hands still over her ears, but she sees Leo's eyes leave hers. Sees them widen, his face crumpling.

"Mum."

Georgie drops her arms and turns. Alice, Chrissy, and Peter are running toward them. All three, together—of course—charging at her. She looks sideways at Leo. One push. There is time before they get to her. She looks back at the Inseparables and her rage is so strong she can hardly breathe.

"Get away from him!" Chrissy shouts.

Georgie plants her feet, lifting her chin. *Never trust a Lowe.* Or any of their friends. She has nothing left to lose but she still can't let them win.

FIFTY-ONE

CHRISSY

Monday, December 16, 2019

Ethan had been in a terrible mood since Chrissy had questioned him about the gold ring on his computer screen two weeks before. He hated to be challenged. Wanted to act like the spotless one in their marriage, despite overwhelming evidence to the contrary. It amazed Chrissy how he could exist in two opposite states at the same time: behaving like a monster while seeming genuinely convinced he wasn't one.

And now he was furious that she had made salad for dinner. She'd made it because he'd announced over the weekend that they needed to start eating more healthily, all three of them, said Chrissy had to stop making stodgy pastas and so much red meat—was she trying to give them heart disease? But apparently, in the ever-changing rule book she was expected to understand, it was just as important that he ate a hot meal on a Monday, after a difficult day at work. He moved the salad around on his plate with the sharp tip of his knife, and she could feel the build of his temper, the charge in the air. His school had had the dreaded Ofsted call that morning. Three teachers were off with stress already. And Chrissy had served a fucking salad.

Leo was at the table, too, glancing between his parents. Chrissy's heart squeezed as he tucked into his dinner with forced gusto, telling her it was "Nice, Mum, really, really nice."

Ethan stopped eating entirely, shaking his head in disgust.

"Why don't you go have a pizza with Robbie?" Chrissy said to Leo, as cheerfully as she could muster.

He looked worried. "This is fine, Mum."

"Oh, this can just be a starter! Go on, go hang out." She tried to flash him a reassuring smile. *Go,* she willed, as she always did when she sensed Ethan was about to erupt. *Please just go and be with your friends.*

Leo didn't move. He frowned down at his plate, then back up at her, clearly confused about what she really wanted him to do. She nodded encouragingly, pleadingly, and he shrugged and stood, picking up his plate.

"I'll clear up," Chrissy said. "See you later, love."

He put the plate back down. With one last look at her, he went. He didn't look at Ethan and Ethan didn't look at him.

Chrissy breathed out as she heard the flat door close behind him. Ethan had never turned on Leo but it was always, always her fear. Dread replaced relief as the silence settled between her and Ethan. Her mind started buzzing with all the things she could do to rescue the situation. Apologize? Grovel? Cook him something else? She ran on adrenaline these days, trying to anticipate his reactions, dodge and deflect his moods. She caught herself shaking with it even when he wasn't around.

You have to get out of this marriage. The thought grew bigger every day. Things were only getting worse, only going in one direction. But it felt so hard. So huge. He would come after her, use everything at his disposal, all the power and respect he did nothing to deserve. And everything was in his name. The pub, all of it. Even if she managed to get away, she'd have nothing. He would squash her like a fly and then he'd suck her back in and have even more reason to punish her.

"So he gets pizza, does he? Golden boy?"

Chrissy closed her eyes. It was the thing that astonished her most, sometimes—that Ethan was even jealous of his own son. Had been since the moment he was born. Occasionally she wondered if he suspected Leo wasn't his, but other times she thought, *No, it's not that, he just can't stand that I love him more.*

Ethan picked up the salad bowl and upturned it over her head. Pieces of lettuce and tomato fell all over her clothes, catching in her curls, homemade dressing dripping into her eyes and down her neck. He banged his fist on the top of the bowl, then walked off and left her sitting there, wearing it like a dunce's cap.

AFTER SHE HAD cleaned up the mess in the kitchen, Chrissy went to the bathroom and stared into the mirror. She smelled of the dinner nobody had finished. Strands of her hair were stuck together with oil and the crown of her head was throbbing. Leaning on the edge of the basin, she dissolved into heaving, humiliated tears, trying not to make any noise. When she was calm enough, she took off her messed-up jeans and fleece and put a dressing gown over her T-shirt.

Emerging from the bathroom, she looked toward the flat door. She could walk out, run to Alice's, never come back. But what about Leo? This was his home, too. He had his exams; so much going on. She had to hold on just for a while.

She became aware of Ethan murmuring in the living room, and turned that way with a frown. Was he on the phone? Who was he talking to? It seemed like he was ordering food—something about chicken, lobster?—but when she edged into the room, he was sitting motionless in his green armchair, his mobile out of sight. His hands were splayed on each arm, legs crossed at the ankles. Chrissy approached him warily. "Shall I make us something else?"

"Like what?"

"Well, we haven't got much in but I could pop out and—"

"You're clearly not going out, are you?" He gestured at her dressing gown. "Don't say things you don't mean."

Rage bubbled up, faster than she could stop it. "I'm only wearing this because you chucked salad all over me!"

There it was. Her big mistake. She made one at least once a week, these days. Her tongue was sore from biting it so often, yet still not often enough. He stood up and his hand flew out, hitting her across the face with one smooth whip-crack.

She stumbled onto the sofa. Her cheek flamed and her anger blazed even hotter. How dare he? How fucking dare he? So often she froze, but sometimes she went into fight mode, and both had the same outcome, she had come to realize, but she still never knew which she would go to in the moment. She howled as he leaped on top of her. Another slap across her face. Hands around her neck and nothing but terror now, struggling for her life, not her pride, kicking and pushing but he was so much stronger. His left hand ripped open her dressing gown and the untied cord came out, flicking snakelike to the floor. Chrissy was panting. Was she screaming out loud or just inside her head?

And then she saw him. Leo, coming into the room. The horror in his eyes. His mouth moving but she couldn't hear his words; she was close to fainting, Ethan's hands still at her throat. Then suddenly there was blissful release, Ethan's weight lifting off her, air rushing into her lungs. His face floated as if he was levitating. But he was spluttering, turning purple. As she came back to herself, she understood. The dressing gown cord was around Ethan's throat and Leo was behind him, pulling, pulling, pulling.

"Leo!" she said. "No!"

Pulling, still pulling. Ethan went slack and rolled sideways, crashing to the floor. Leo froze, staring at him. Chrissy's ears rang with a high-pitched tone.

"Oh my God," Leo said, flinging away the dressing gown cord as though it had bitten him. "Oh my God. Oh my God."

He fell to his knees next to Ethan. Chrissy came to life and jumped up from the sofa. For a moment the whole room rotated and she thought she was going to be sick.

"Oh my God." He was crouching over Ethan, trying to shake the life back into him. "Oh my God."

Chrissy grabbed him and pulled him away. He crumpled against her and she held his head and rocked him as he howled. She glanced at Ethan and bile rose into her mouth. He was gray. He was gone. Just like that, he was gone.

She propped Leo up and looked into his eyes. "You need to go, Leo. I'll handle this. Just go."

"No, Mum—"

"Please. I love you so much. Please go."

"Where?" He looked at Ethan and another strangled sob escaped. "How can I—?"

"Go somewhere where there are other people. The park or the chip shop or somewhere like that. Act normal. Be safe—"

"I can't. I can't."

"You can." She held his face in her hands. "Leo, please, it needs to be now."

"But . . ."

"It *will* be okay."

He was still weeping as he got to his feet and she ushered him to the stairs, wiping his cheeks with her sleeve. "I'll call you later, okay? I love you."

"I love you," he choked out, and then he ran.

She looked out of the front window and saw him hurrying across the square, pulling up his hood and disappearing into it. Her shoulders started shaking, her body convulsing with shock, but she breathed through it, cupping her hands around an invisible paper bag.

Then she stumbled through to the bedroom and grabbed her phone. *Call Alice* was the first icon in her shortcuts screen. Alice had programmed it in herself: *Just one tap if you ever need me.* Chrissy tapped it. Alice picked up on the second ring.

FIFTY-TWO

CHRISSY

Sunday, December 10, 2023

Chrissy tears across the grass toward her son. But the huge relief of seeing him is caught up in confusion. How is Georgie here? *Why* is Georgie here? She stops short of diving at Leo and pulling him away from the edge, fearing it might send them both flying over. She is desperate to touch him, gather him in, but she staggers to a halt. Alice and Peter come to a stop on either side of her.

"Leo," Chrissy chokes out. "Oh, Leo, I'm so happy to see you. Please, will you—"

"Get away from here, Mum!" he shouts.

She recoils as if he's thrown something. "Leo—"

"Leave me!" She sees he's crying, that he's been crying for a while. "All of you . . ." His eyes dart to Peter. "Leave me alone."

"Leo, everything's okay," Chrissy says, her own tears still thick in her throat.

"No, it isn't," Leo says. "Everything's *fucked*. It's over."

Chrissy starts to protest again, but Georgie speaks. "You're right." Her voice is so cold it sends a shiver through Chrissy. "It's over."

Chrissy turns to her. "Stay *out* of this, Georgie! Why are you messing with my family?"

"Leo just confessed something to me," she says, her face muscles clenched so hard they seem to spasm.

Dread lodges in Chrissy's chest. "Confessed?" She glances at Leo. "Leo, you're not thinking straight . . . Please step back, come with me . . ."

"He killed my Ethan!" Georgie cries.

"*Your* Ethan?"

"Your son took him from me."

"No," Chrissy says frantically. "No, that's not true—he doesn't know what he's saying."

"It doesn't matter anymore!" Leo yells, turning to face the valley and bracing himself as if to jump.

"No!" Chrissy screams. "Leo, don't!"

He freezes with bent knees. She knows it's the sound of her distress that has stalled him. That night with Ethan, he couldn't stand it any longer. Now it feels like the only way to make him think twice about this. "Please," she begs. "I love you, Leo. I can't lose you again."

She is aware, as she says it, of Alice beside her. Of the fact that she has lost her son forever and Chrissy has a second chance with hers. If she can just get him away from the drop, if she can just stop Georgie from unleashing the secret she has kept, for his protection, all these years.

"Jump, if you want to," Georgie says viciously. "It won't stop me from telling everyone what you did."

"Leo didn't kill Ethan," Chrissy says. "I did. It was me."

"Mum." Leo shakes his head. "Time to stop pretending. I killed Ethan because he was . . ." His voice breaks. "He was hurting you. I killed Robbie because I thought he'd found out. And then I killed Frank Jordan. I left him to burn because I'd trusted him with the truth and then he wanted me to . . . to . . ." He stretches his hands out on either side of him, as if he hopes to fly off the edge now, rather than jump. "I'm a killer and it'd be better if I just . . . didn't exist."

"No, it wouldn't!" Chrissy strains her vocal cords trying to get through to him.

Next to her, Peter comes to life. "No, it wouldn't," he echoes, with so much feeling Chrissy aches behind her ribs.

And then Alice, quieter, but clearly in tears, too. "No, it wouldn't."

Leo's hands sink to his sides and he turns to look at them, as if registering, properly, that they are all here for him. Chrissy opens her arms and for a moment thinks he's going to come to her. But then there is Georgie, vibrating with fury, stepping between her and Leo with hatred blazing in her eyes.

"It *would* be better if you didn't exist," she hisses at Leo. "You should be in the ground instead of Ethan. None of you deserved him. You're still lying about him now—"

"We're not lying," Chrissy says. "Georgie, I don't know what he was to you, or what he did to you, how he brainwashed you—"

"Don't insult me!" Georgie turns toward her. "Don't insult *him!*"

"But he was a bad man. An abuser. I'm sorry if—"

"You're sorry? You're *sorry*? Your son killed your husband and you just stood by? Covered it up, even? Exactly how many lies *have* you told?" Georgie flings a look at Peter and Alice, too. "Did you all know? Of course you did. And your little friend Ben, so desperate to defend you all. Cromley's most fucked-up clique. Pathetic. Incestuous, I'm willing to bet. I don't know why I bothered trying to mess with your heads. You're already doing a good enough job yourselves."

She backs away, toward Leo, toward the edge. Chrissy's heart vaults into her mouth, seeing her so close to Leo, waving her arms around, more and more out of control. Chrissy steps forward and Peter is with her, Alice, too, but she fears they're closing in too tightly, surrounding Georgie and Leo and the drop.

"Be careful," she says in a croaky whisper. "Everyone, please . . ."

Georgie swivels back to Leo, shouting into his face. "I'll make you pay! I'll make you pay for what you've done!"

Leo puts up his hands, shielding himself, his features screwed up in despair. Chrissy can't bear it. All she's ever tried to do is protect him. She would take the blame for Ethan's death in a heartbeat if suspicions were ever raised. Even more so after he killed Robbie; she'd known that if anybody found out about Ethan, too, Leo's sentence would become longer than he could stand. And she'd thought Alice was the danger. The one to fear. She hadn't even thought of Georgie.

In a burst of desperation, she reaches out to yank her back from Leo. But somebody knocks against her shoulder, there is a confusing jostle of bodies, and her hands grasp at empty air. She hears a scream. Then she sees that Georgie is falling, limbs flailing, hair haloing out around her. Chrissy gasps and closes her eyes as Georgie is swallowed up by the dark valley below.

FIFTY-THREE

ALICE

Sunday, December 10, 2023

The four of them sit on the frozen grass and wait for the police. Alice is trembling and shivering, numb and wired. Peter puts his arm around her and she leans into him, shaking even harder. Opposite them, Leo lies with his head in Chrissy's lap. The beam of a helicopter sweeps over the valley and sirens wail somewhere below.

"I can't believe it," Chrissy keeps murmuring. "None of this feels real."

Alice wants to tell Peter he should go and sit with Chrissy and Leo, put his arms around them instead of her. But a selfish part of her clings to him, desperate not to be alone. She replays Georgie's fall, her hands lifted to the sky, mouth open in one long scream for help. Her body somewhere below them: Where did it land? What, if anything, did she feel?

Suddenly, Leo lifts his head, looks straight at her. "I'm sorry, Alice," he says. "I'm so sorry about Robbie."

Habitual anger stirs and a familiar bitter taste comes into her mouth. Maybe it would feel good to lash out one more time. Maybe it would help to fend off the thoughts of Georgie—her broken body down there in the darkness—and of Ethan, Robbie, everything that has been revealed. But she is tired, so tired, of hating and punishing.

"I forgive you," she says.

Leo shakes his head. "How can you?"

Alice glances at Chrissy, then at the black sky. "Because . . . Robbie would." When it comes down to it, she realizes, it can be as simple as that.

Leo rubs his palms over his face. "I miss him."

"So do I," Alice says, "so much."

She sees Chrissy nodding, then sees her stop herself, as if she doesn't think she has the right. Alice catches her eye but can't work out how to communicate that it's okay; she knows she misses him, too. She has always known.

"I'd do anything to take it back," Leo says.

"So would I. But we can't. We just have to"—Alice forces herself to say the words, though they still catch in her throat—"try and heal." She sounds like her therapist, and she doesn't know if she'll be able to follow through, but it's a start. Peter squeezes her more tightly, but she shuffles away from him and tilts her head toward Leo, indicating that he should be with his son. Peter gazes at Leo but doesn't move.

"What happened, Leo?" Chrissy finally asks the question. "When you left the prison? Frank Jordan . . . ?"

Leo is quiet for a moment, staring into space.

"It's okay if you're not ready to—"

"It started before I left the prison," he cuts her off.

Now Chrissy falls silent; they all do, waiting. Down in the valley, the sirens seem to be getting closer.

"Frank and I got kind of friendly when we realized we were from the same neck of the woods," Leo says. "He'd heard I was from Cromley; he was from a bit further north. We . . . bonded over it. Pathetically, looking back, I think he became yet another dad figure." He laughs humorlessly. "You know I'm a sucker for those."

He pauses, shivering and huddling into himself. Peter takes off his coat and gives it to him. Leo looks at Peter, then wraps the coat around his own shoulders.

"He started doing me favors, protecting me from other inmates, stuff like that. And I started opening up to him a bit. I didn't like talking much, not even to my cellmate, Cliff, but Frank had a way of getting stuff out of you. I realize now that he was just a collector of other people's secrets, anything he might be able to use one day to get something he wanted. And his obsession with Cromley wasn't just about us being 'neighbors.' If it had stopped there, maybe it would've been okay. But then Marianne came to see me . . ."

He stalls again, looking between them all, then down at his boots. His old Doc Martens are almost destroyed, the leather cracked, the toe gaping. His trousers are ripped and Alice can see bruises and wounds underneath. What must he have been through over the last week, while she's been shouting about pub signs and trying to get him barred from the village? She can't regret it, though, not exactly. He killed her son; she lashed out in return. Doesn't she need to forgive herself as well?

She looks at the spot where Georgie fell and her stomach does an even bigger somersault.

"When Marianne told me Peter was my dad, I was shocked, of course. Finding out Ethan wasn't my dad, Ethan who I . . ." He falters, closing his eyes. "And Robbie being my cousin. But . . . worse than that . . ." He opens his eyes, wider than before. "What Robbie said to me that night took on a whole new meaning."

"What did he say?" Chrissy asks, frowning. She glances at Alice and there is a beat of tension. This was what put the final nail in their friendship's coffin, after all. The matter of whether Robbie provoked Leo, whether they should even be asking the question.

Alice swallows. It's still hard to acknowledge that there must've been something. But she was there that night; she saw the friction between them. It doesn't mean Robbie deserved it. And she realizes she's been desperate to know, too. Desperate to understand, but too stubborn and sad to find out.

"He called me 'Daddy's boy,'" Leo says, hanging his head. "In fact, he said, 'I know your *secret*, Daddy's boy.' All day he'd been saying cryptic things, needling away, and I thought it was about Ethan. I thought he knew what I'd done and I got so, so scared. But from what Marianne said, I don't think it was that. I think it was about Peter . . ." He looks over at him; Peter's face is solemn.

Leo releases a heavy sigh. "When I realized I'd gone crazy over something that didn't matter, not in the scheme of things, I couldn't take it. I was already tormented by what I did to Robbie, but . . . to realize he didn't even *mean* that, didn't know what I thought he knew . . . I went back to my cell after Marianne's visit and I was an absolute mess. And Frank was there and I ended up pouring it all out . . ."

"All of it?" Chrissy asks anxiously.

"All of it. Robbie. Ethan. The whole mess."

Chrissy inhales. "I told you never to tell *anyone* about Ethan, Leo." She glances at Alice, then at Peter, warily, as if unsure what they think now that they know the truth.

Alice probes her own feelings. Is she shocked that it was Leo who killed Ethan, not Chrissy? That she has carried the wrong person's secret, all these years? Protected the person who would go on to kill her son?

She doesn't know. It hasn't sunk in. But that knee-jerk reaction, as she listened to Georgie screaming threats at Leo . . . Alice hugs herself, her insides in knots.

"Did Frank use it against you?" Chrissy asks.

Leo winces at the memory. "At first it was just small stuff. Getting me to sign over my canteen money to him, cigarettes, toiletries, that kind of thing. But then . . . then he made the link . . ." He looks over at Peter again.

"He worked out who your real dad is," Peter says grimly, as if he's known where this was going all along.

"I must've said your name, at some point, when I was spilling my guts. Stupid. I was so stupid to tell him *anything*."

Chrissy puts her hand on his arm, but Leo brushes her off, growing angrier with himself. "I mean, I even recognized Frank vaguely, when I first got to the prison! I must've seen him in the news before, or seen a picture of him from back when you arrested him, but I didn't make the connection. I had no idea I'd be setting so much in motion . . ."

"Why would you?" Peter says. "Frank Jordan has hated me since I got him sent down. But you couldn't have known that, Leo."

"But it *all* could've been avoided." He shrinks inside Peter's coat, still draped around his shoulders. "Every single thing I've done . . ."

"Hindsight," Alice speaks up, surprising herself. "Everything is so much clearer, so much easier, in hindsight. But moment to moment, life is hard."

Chrissy gives her a grateful look, then puts her hand back on Leo's arm. This time, he doesn't shake her off. "Tell us what happened, Leo."

He raises his head, wipes his face again. Hearing another siren, much closer now, he seems to gather himself to press on.

"Once he found out about my connection to Peter, he wouldn't drop it. Kept on about how you were scum. I had to pretend to hate you, too, just to stop him from beating me up . . ." He looks pained at this, but Peter shrugs, gesturing for him to keep going. "And when we found out we were being released within a few weeks of each other, things stepped up a gear. He said he was going straight to Cromley when he got out, to find you. I told him you didn't live there anymore, but I don't think he believed me. He said if he couldn't find you himself, it would be up to me to bring you to him . . ." He stops and clears his throat as his voice becomes hoarse. "He— he wanted me to engineer it so you would pick me up from prison. And then . . . I don't even know what they were planning, exactly. Him and his mates were going to intercept us, I think. Were going to . . ."

"Get the revenge they've been wanting for years," Peter says, his words falling heavily.

Alice looks at him. She can see the realization sinking in, that he is at the center of all this. She touches his hand but he's far away, his eyes on Leo, his thoughts clearly racing.

Leo looks back at him. Alice sees the resemblance between them, undoubtedly, for the first time. It hits her in the gut; she doesn't know how she never saw it before.

"I couldn't let them do it," Leo says. "I couldn't let them hurt you."

Peter moves toward him, at last, and wraps his arms around him. Leo hesitates, then hugs him back, burying his face in Peter's shoulder. Alice feels an instinctive twist in her stomach, watching them. It's impossible not to think of Peter enveloping Robbie in his coveted bear hugs.

Chrissy is watching, too, her eyes glassy. But then she sits forward, eager to continue. "Is that why Frank took you?" she asks.

Leo pulls back from Peter. "He was furious. Him and his two mates bundled me into their car, knocked me about, took me to this barn . . ."

"Because of me," Peter mumbles, shaking his head.

"You must've been terrified," Chrissy says, overlapping with him.

"I was so scared they were going to hurt you and Peter," Leo says to her. "They brought me your locket, and some of your hair, to show me they'd been to your house . . . That's when I got desperate . . ."

"They came to the village." Peter shakes his head. "Fuck. They were bold as anything."

"Did they set the barn on fire?" Alice asks, refinding her voice.

Silence falls, and she has the feeling she's asked the wrong question. Leo looks down, shamefaced again. "No. That was me. I told you . . . I'm a killer. Frank Jordan, too." His chin lifts. "That's why I went on the run, knew I couldn't come back. Why I was going to . . ." He looks over at the viaduct's edge.

"What happened?" Chrissy prompts him. "With the fire?"

Leo drags his gaze back to them. He looks exhausted now. Moonlight illuminates the hollows under his eyes and the bruises on his face.

"They had me tied up in the barn. They were coming and going, I had no idea what was going on, how much time was passing, what they were going to do with me. But one day, Frank dropped his lighter on the floor of the barn, and then he went outside and I managed to grab it. I tried to burn through the ropes that were tying me up. But as I was shaking myself free, a piece of rope on fire fell into the hay and the barn went up." He gestures, raising his arms. "It happened so fast. Then Frank came running back in—he mustn't have gone far—and I just . . . I hit him. As hard as I could . . ." He starts to cry again, struggling to get his words out. "And I looked at him, lying there, and the fire was spreading but I . . . I left him. I ran . . ." He folds over, crying harder, and Chrissy rubs his back.

The sirens rise up the hill. Chrissy looks at Alice, fear glowing in her eyes.

"It was self-defense," she says to Leo, but with her eyes

still on Alice. "You had to do that, Leo, to escape. Frank
would've killed you. He might've killed Peter, or me . . ."

Her gaze moves between Alice and Peter, begging them
to agree.

"That's what I was afraid of," Leo says. "Him going after
you, after Peter. But I'm a killer. Three people. I'm a killer."

Suddenly, Peter grips him by the shoulders, looking into
his face. "No. You're not. You're nothing like Frank Jordan.
Nothing like most of the criminals I've seen. And nobody . . ."
Peter hesitates, and his voice gets a little lower, but no less
fierce. "There is nothing in any of the reports that can link
Ethan's death to you. I made sure of that at the time. I'll carry
on making sure of that. Now that Georgie is gone . . ." He
bows his head. "There's nothing."

Alice stares at him. He knew all along? Knew Ethan didn't
take his own life? And guessed, in fact, far more than she did:
that it was Leo, not Chrissy, who needed protection. She has
barely processed it before his last words roll over her: *Now
that Georgie is gone, there's nothing.* Leo is back inside the cush-
ion of his mum and dad's lies and it was her, it was Alice, who
made it happen.

She thinks of Georgie going over the edge. Remembers
retracting her hand, holding it against her body, knowing it
made contact but not quite believing it. Did anybody else realize? Do they think Georgie fell in the scuffle, or are they all
just silently agreeing to another shared version of the truth?

She holds Chrissy's gaze and a new certainty surges
through her, thick and frightening: about what she did, who
she did it for. Not just for Leo, not to prove, in some warped

way, that she forgives him. But for Chrissy, whom she has loved for such a long time. Possessively, sometimes. Perhaps unhealthily. And maybe they're in a new phase of friendship now, for better or worse; maybe the four of them are a new kind of strangely shaped family.

Whatever happens, they will all be bound, forever, by a tangle of secrets.

A police car appears over the crest of the hill and bumps to a stop on the grass. The four of them look intently at each other. For a moment, Alice imagines a wall around them, a circle of defense.

"We all saw Georgie fall," Chrissy whispers, leaning forward.

Alice's head starts to float.

Peter nods. "And we all agree that she seemed . . . incoherent. Any theories about Ethan's death were clearly . . ."

"Nonsense," Alice fills in.

Chrissy nods. Leo nods. Their skin is the same shade of pale. Peter's expression is one Alice has seen before: He's preparing lines in his head. The car doors fly open and two officers rush toward them, the orbs of their flashlights dancing over the earth. Chrissy squeezes Alice's hand. Alice presses her other palm against her own chest, feeling the violent thump-thump of her heart where the locket used to sit.

ACKNOWLEDGMENTS

It's hard to believe I'm on my fourth book! The idea for this one goes back a long way, but it's taken many conversations and collaborations with some brilliant people to turn it into the book you've just read—and that I'm very grateful to you for reading.

As ever, a huge thank you to my agent, Hellie Ogden, for being my cheerleader and sounding board—very proud to have reached book four with you! Thanks to the fantastic team at WME, and especially to Ma'suma Amiri, for all your hard work and support.

It's been exciting and rewarding to have worked with three talented editors on this book. Thank you to Tarini Sipahimalani at Putnam, and to Bethany Wickington and Cara Chimirri at Hodder, for your inspired ideas, insightful editing, and encouragement every step of the way. I've really enjoyed the journey!

Thank you also to all the people behind the scenes at

Hodder and Putnam who do so much for me and my books. This time, in particular, to Helena Newton, Janice Barral, and Madeline Hopkins for the brilliant copyediting, Shina Patel, Kristen Bianco, and Alainna Hadjigeorgiou for marketing and publicity, and everybody else who has done such a brilliant job of the design, production, and promotion of *My Darling Boy*.

I particularly struggled to get the beginning of this book right, so I really want to thank Leicester Writers' Club for so much great feedback on the first few chapters. I also was pretty clueless about how prisons work when I started writing this story, so I am hugely grateful to Holly Webster and Jay Eales for answering my questions. (Any errors are mine!) And as ever, thank you to all my bookish friends and fellow writers for your friendship and support—especially Leicester Writers, Leicester Speculators, and Anna Sun for all the chats.

It's no exaggeration to say I'd be lost without the long-term support of my amazing family—Mum, Dad, Grams, Christine, Yass—plus all my wonderful friends (you know who you are!) who've been there through thick and thin. And more recently, the lovely people who, by the time this book is out, will officially be my in-laws.

I've dedicated this book to my nephews, Idris and Aryn, even though it is a bit of a grim tale at times! In contrast, you are always a joy and an inspiration.

Finally, to the person who, by publication day, will be not only my best friend and beta reader, but also my husband. Phil, you helped me turn this book from an interesting idea into a much more exciting and emotive story. And as always, you kept me sane through the writing of it. For many, many reasons, I'm ever thankful to have you by my side.

DISCUSSION GUIDE

1. Discuss how the title of this novel, *My Darling Boy*, primed your allegiance to certain characters. Did you find you were more inclined to offer your sympathy to Alice or Chrissy?

2. This novel explores friendship, loyalty, and community. Alongside the plot of *My Darling Boy*, discuss whether the village setting fosters and/or tarnishes its sense of community? How does life in a close-knit rural community differ from that in a big city? Which setting would have been better for both Alice and Chrissy following the tragedy?

3. *My Darling Boy* is told through four perspectives: Chrissy's, Alice's, Leo's, and Georgie's. Why do you think author Helen Cooper felt it was important to structure the

story in this way? How would the absence of Georgie's perspective alter the read?

4. Before the tragedy, Chrissy and Alice seem to have an unbreakable bond. Discuss why this seemingly strong foundation wasn't enough for them to consider each other with more sympathy following the tragedy. To what extent would anyone in their situation react the same way?

5. Both Alice and Chrissy are faced with impossible choices, each governed by guilt, grief, and anger. If you were in their positions, how far would you go to stand by your child?

6. Alice, Chrissy, and Peter all hide grave secrets from each other. Discuss which situations warrant secret-keeping, even from those you love. Or should one never keep a secret?

7. This novel explores themes of justice, punishment, and forgiveness. To what extent, regardless of the situation, do you believe everyone should be allowed a second chance? What if the situation were personal? What does it mean to get justice?

8. *My Darling Boy* is filled with surprising twists and turns. Which reveal shocked you the most, and why?

9. Cooper takes us on a raw, intricate journey of both rooting for and being frustrated by Chrissy and Alice. How does Cooper portray motherhood through these characters?

10. Where do you think Chrissy and Alice (and the others) go from here?

ABOUT THE AUTHOR

Helen Cooper is the author of *The Other Guest*, *The Down-stairs Neighbor*, and *The Couple in the Photo*. She is from Derby and has an MA in creative writing and a background in teaching English and academic writing. Her creative writing has been published in *Mslexia*, *Woman*, and *Writers' Forum*; she was shortlisted in the Bath Short Story Award in 2014 and came in third in the Leicester Writes Short Story Prize in 2018.